Finch Books by Lanne Garrett

Single Books
The Cinder City Embers: Singularity

A Cursed Crow
The Seven Year Crow
The Court of Less
The Song of Blood and Bones
A Court of One
A Curse So Dark and Twisted

A Cursed Crow

A CURSE SO DARK AND TWISTED

LANNE GARRETT

A Curse So Dark and Twisted
ISBN # 978-1-80250-591-7
©Copyright Lanne Garrett 2024
Cover Art by Erin Dameron-Hill ©Copyright January 2024
Interior text design by Claire Siemaszkiewicz
Finch Books

Published in 2024 by Finch Books, United Kingdom.

Finch Books is an imprint of Totally Entwined Group Limited.

A CURSE SO DARK AND TWISTED

Dedication

For Dave

Then lions come with glaring eyes,
And tigers growl, a dreadful noise,
And ogres draw their cruel knives,
To shed the blood of girls and boys.

—excerpt from *Queen Mab* by Thomas Hood

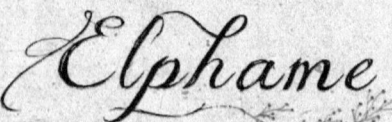

Elphame

~ ALFHEIM ~
THE GOLDEN COURT

SPRING COURT

SEELIE COURTS

SUMMER COURT

THE COURT
OF BLOOD
AND BONES

WILDELANDS

THE GATE

THE COURT OF
SHADOWS

THE COURT OF LESS

UNSEELIE COURTS

THE
HALLOWS

~ TYLWYTH ~
WINTER COURT

AUTUMN
COURT

Chapter One

We are composed of a junk drawer we carry around in our souls. We're made of baggage we can't let go of. Some of us pack light, while others drag around every memory they've ever had or thing they wish they'd said. Some, more than others, hoard every regret, slight, tear or unwilling parting in life like a troll under a bridge with his precious trinkets. We all have odds and ends hanging off our souls. Some of us just pack it differently. The trick is learning to carry that baggage the best we can while figuring out how to unpack it and face what we've towed around from place to place, person to person. That's what healing forces a person to do — dump it out and sit on the floor with all the broken pieces you haven't been willing to face or throw away, deciding what to take and what to leave behind. Sometimes we do the same thing with people or places we once loved. We let them go. We move on. We choose to become better versions of the person who had a death grip on all the junk that kept us in the moments of yesterday.

Unpacking my baggage was what coming to Whitwick was supposed to do for us all. It would let us look into the black hole we all carried on our backs and take pieces out, brick by brick, using them to build the foundation of a new future...a new beginning. Instead, we used those bricks to beat each other bloody. No one was safe from the anger or blame, and everyone was at fault. The Guardians of Whitwick hadn't protected the people, only their own children. The children marked for the Taking didn't leave fast enough and caused the deaths of those who didn't need to die. The Fae tormented more than they needed to. A Crow, in their mind, had broken the Gate, and now Fae could roam as they pleased. It didn't matter that I wasn't the one who had done it. I was still responsible because, somehow, I hadn't stopped it. It was easier to unload the bricks of the past onto someone else than to let go of them. And every time I came to Whitwick to repair the wounds, it felt like new wounds opened, fresh reasons to bleed for Whitwick Gates.

"I'd rather be holding my own guts in with my bare hands while I crawled through the caves of the Winter Court, being ridden like a pony," I muttered to Nix and motioned to the room. "Anything over this."

"There's no place like home," Nix whispered from my shoulder as we watched the arguing unfold before us as though we weren't even present. We were currently back on the topic of recreating a Gate that was no longer there. It always came back to the Gate. "Remember when I told you I wanted to return to our garden after the war? I take it back. I don't like being here any more than you do."

I nodded my agreement. I didn't want our garden this bad, either. I leaned back in my chair and tried to sigh past the anxiety this place brought me, but I could never get a deep breath in the mortal world. Jare, one of Zephyr's men, stood behind my chair. His eyes never stayed still. He scanned the room, his legs apart, arms folded casually but ready to grab any unfortunate soul who reached for me. He looked terribly out of place, towering over us all. But he was pretty relaxed under the Fae threat that was rolling off him. A decade in the bowels of Blood and Bones, tortured and broken daily, made everything else look like a walk in the park to him. Coming to Whitwick was supposed to heal wounds, but neither Zephyr nor Solas felt comfortable with me going anywhere by myself, let alone to a different realm. Jare glanced down once with a smirk that said it all. He saw this for what it was — a game of blame, an endless talk in circles. And by the time we were done each time and I returned home to Elphame, I was weaker, exhausted, drained of magick, and it seemed like we hadn't done anything more than find new wounds.

"I feel like I've been cursed to suffer, first as a mortal and now as Fae," I whispered to Nix. Hearing the words come from my mouth made them feel more real — heavier and sharper.

I rubbed the cramps that had started in my thighs from having sat in one position for too long and watched a dozen red-faced mortals attack each other with venomous words, each meaning more harm than the last. They were no different than Fae around a war table, who haggled over whose threat of bloodshed carried the most weight. Here, they argued over who had suffered the greatest and who held the most blame for it. Mortals could be just as hateful and vengeful as the Fae, if not more.

I had watched for hours and added nothing more than a head shake or nod. Nix hadn't bothered to say a single word. They didn't like him any more than they did me. I was too Fae and Nix was too small for either of us to matter. Why I was there had nothing to do with what I could offer and more about what they could blame me for and demand I do—both of which were ridiculous. It had been like this for weeks and only worsened with each visit. I hadn't expected my homecoming to be celebrated, but I certainly hadn't been expecting the hate my arrival had caused. They had no idea what I had given up and endured for their survival. Nothing I said would change how they saw me. I was Fae. I was one of *them*, part of the problem.

Whenever I tried to speak, to add to the conversation, they accused me of lying to protect *them*, the Fae. I was either too Fae to care about man's plight or too young to understand. Or, as I had been told to my face only moments ago, it was because I was the whore of Elphame. They had conveniently forgotten I had once been dragged through the Gate and that I'd given my life to save Whitwick from the plight they accused me of not understanding. Crows in the mortal realm got about the same level of respect as they did in Elphame...*none*. It had taken the death of a king, escape, wars and the killing of a Royal Seer before anyone in Elphame had looked at me with anything more than contempt in their eyes. I wondered if the same would apply in the mortal world. I didn't want to do here what I'd had to do in Elphame to earn an inch of regard. Mankind wouldn't survive how Fae gained respect.

When I'd signed up to help mend the fence between realms, the scared butterflies in my stomach had told me that coming here would become the war of broken souls. While no one remembered I had taken the same walk of fate that so many before me had, that I'd survived and was living there was all that mattered around this table. No one cared that I suffered whenever I came to Whitwick, only that I chose to stay with the Fae. And after our first meeting weeks before, I would rather be in the middle of a bloody battle on the fields of Elphame than this. Out there, in the trenches, I had a better chance of winning. Here, the four walls around us felt like a prison, where the captives fought each other to the death for scraps of meat. I was the meat, and I didn't like the looks on their faces.

My eye finally started to twitch in frustration when the same question was asked of me. "For, quite literally, the hundredth time, I *can't* bring back the Gate. I can't repair it. I can't bend it back into shape. I can't glue it or tie it. It's *gone*. I tried to fix it, but it's gone." My voice rose over the back and forth arguing. "I don't know how else to say it in a way you'll understand. It. Is. Gone."

"Try something else." The man to my right nudged me. "Maybe we can help?"

"I appreciate that, but it's actually gone. I don't mean that it's so broken I consider it gone and of no use. I mean, when we pass between realms, it's not there. It's an empty patch of grass. It's gone and isn't coming back," I answered. "We only still call it the Gate because there is no other name we use for the point between worlds. But rest assured, there is *no* Gate to speak of. It no longer exists. It rusted and blew away in the wind."

"Can you do a spell to bring it back?"

"No, I can't. I can't call one from thin air or build one from scratch. I don't even know how or if it's possible." I looked to my father, who sat at the end of the table and shrugged. "I'm sorry. I will do what I can to help, but I can't do what you're asking me. I'm not powerful enough. It took three Darkmore witches to build it and an original on the other side, who is dead, to sing a Gate to life with Elphame magic. I am *one* Darkmore witch and can't sing to save my life. Bring me an idea that can work, and I'll be more than happy to help. Until then, we're beating a dead dog."

"I bet you'd do it if Elphame wanted it," another spoke up.

I whipped my head to face the commenter and glanced down the table. "No, I wouldn't, and I couldn't. You're not hearing me. I'm not saying that I don't want to do it. I'm telling you I *can't* do it. I'm not powerful enough. And quite frankly, I don't care who is asking. The answer will remain the same, no matter what."

"You're the reason it's gone. Fix what you did!" he yelled.

I wanted to snap back and tell them it wasn't my fault, but I didn't. The silence was easier. If they knew Solas had played a part in breaking the Gate, this would stop being a conversation and move straight to pickaxes and shovels. Solene, Solas' sister, was given all the blame, and they couldn't ask for her head because she was already dead. Soon, I feared, it wouldn't matter what I said or how hard I tried to keep them from marching into Elphame with war on their minds. They would spill blood eventually. Fear would drive them to stupidity. It did that to all of us, mortal and Fae.

"I'm sorry this has happened," I finally stated. And I was. If I were in their position, I'd be terrified right now.

"It's easy to be sorry when you're not the one at risk. You have no idea what removing that Gate has done. While everyone else fears what will come next, you sit in your castle."

"The Gate didn't save any of us…ever. It didn't do a damn thing to protect mortals. It certainly didn't keep me from suffering. And it didn't save me in Elphame, where I fought every day to keep you all alive. Now, there are oaths to protect you, Fae armies that will protect you," I replied. "Arguing isn't going to solve any of our problems. We need to move forward. It was never the Gate that saved us. It was oaths. Now, there are new ones, and the Taking of mortals, for any reason, is prohibited."

"What about those who are not protected?" he asked. "You can't save everyone."

"Every mortal is protected," my father interrupted. "No one has been left out of the oaths."

Nix groaned and flopped down on my shoulder as the bickering continued. "It doesn't matter what you say, Perdi. People see and hear whatever they want. It's hard to move forward when you're as scared of the future as you are of the past."

The room grumbled. The man who swore up and down that the Fae would forget to protect everyone stood and faced the room. "Maybe we should be calling on a different witch, one that's not Fae?"

I almost screamed at his comment. All that would do was cause more problems for Whitwick than we were currently shoveling. "First, sir, witches are part Fae. It is what gives us the ability to use Elphame magic. There are no other full-blooded witches out there, because the mortal world saw to their execution all those years ago. But call on whoever you'd like. It won't help you do something that can't be done. I am the last Darkmore. There is no witch stronger than my bloodline. And if I can't do it, no one can."

My father lifted his hands to the argument beginning again. "All right, everyone. I hear what you're saying. I feel the fear myself. But we will need to think of a different way. The Gate cannot be rebuilt, and Perdi is not powerful enough, on her own, to build a new one. Think on it over the next week, and when we reconvene, we will discuss alternatives."

The room cleared with bickering, as it had the last time I had come and the time before—mumbles that I wasn't welcome in Whitwick, that I had no right to discuss the fate of *their* people and wishes that I hadn't survived the Taking. Fear and anger were potent fertilizers for hate. I could feel the pressure slowly building and knew it would boil over sooner or later into a mess no one could clean up. Not even I could fix what would be coming. I could feel it like an unspoken promise. Their fear would push them to become creative.

"Six hours of useless arguing over the same thing…the Gate," I griped from the table. "And in those hours, we got nowhere. I don't know how many ways I can say the same thing before they believe me."

"It's hard to see the truth when they want a lie so badly," Nix answered. "They want the Gate back. When you've lived your entire life being told a chunk of metal is what protected you from the monsters, you live and breathe that truth. They think another one will protect them."

"Unlike the hundreds of years before, when it didn't do a damn thing to save anyone. We still died," I countered. I dropped my head to the table and groaned into the wood. My head was pounding from lack of sleep, hunger, irritation and being away from Elphame for too long.

"This is true, but at least they knew when it was coming, Perdi. Right now, they fear it can be any day," Nix answered.

"They don't want Fae coming into the mortal lands." My father lifted me from the table and pulled me standing into a hug. "I appreciate you being here, but I don't think we'll solve this problem unless we return to the way things were."

"They don't want things back to the way they were, either. That wasn't living. That was waiting to die," I replied. "What they want is a reality that isn't possible. It isn't something anyone can give them, not even me. They want Elphame to go away, and it isn't going to. Fae are here to stay, as much as mortals are. And I don't know how to keep the two worlds apart."

"I know, but we had better find a solution soon before meetings won't stop what's coming," he replied.

"Fools." I groaned. I knew what would come. Mortals always reached higher than their grasp, thinking some God would catch them on their way down. God wouldn't, but Fae would — and it would be a bloody mess.

"I agree." He kissed my forehead. "Nix, always a pleasure."

Nix popped out of my hair and shook my father's hand. "Good night, sir."

"Let's go home, Nix, Jare." I turned from my dad, my shoulders slumped and knotted with tension.

"It's okay, Perdi. We'll find a way. *You'll* find a way. It may not be what each side will want, but you'll figure it out." Nix hopped off my shoulder, and Jare and I followed him to the Gate, passing the Elphame guards. Each gave Nix a sly wave and Jare and me a tip of the head.

"You have more faith in me than I do," I replied. I stopped on the other side of the Gate and breathed in Elphame. Each time I went back and forth, it got a little easier, but I always felt better once I came back. "I'll never get used to being there...not really. It feels awful, like I'm sick and spent hours running myself into the ground. Even my muscles hurt."

"Homesick," Nix answered. "That's what you're feeling. We all feel it when we leave Elphame. And that, unfortunately, never goes away."

"Did you feel like this every day you were with me, before I became a Crow?" I asked.

"It got easier, like it will for you. I doubt you'll have to get used to it, though. Their dislike for you grows every time we go. There may come a time when it isn't safe for you to step into the mortal world."

"I can't shake this sinking feeling in my gut. If we don't find a solution, mortals will find it and die because of it."

"I have the same feeling, Perdi. Desperation breeds ingenuity. But mortals will never be as clever or as brutal as Fae...and that scares me more. You're the only Fae here who loves them and can forgive them for their words and hate."

I called the shadows, who wrapped around us and brought us to the front door of my home with Solas. They didn't linger as they usually did. They could feel my defeat and would go report back to Zephyr, who, without a doubt, could already feel it. Whenever I left, they always told Zephyr of my condition upon my return.

'Protective' wasn't the word. Zephyr was terrified something would happen to me but tried hard not to show it. Deep down, I think he was more scared for those around me if they touched me or threatened me. He feared Elphame learning what I was, to the point that he ran me through training on what to do if they called me a Soul-Eater out loud. After I killed them and anyone who heard, I had to go to his island and call on him. He and Solas would set fire to the rest of Elphame. We'd wait it out with those we loved from the safety of our home. When I had laughed at his suggestion, he'd made it clear how serious he was. *No one* could know there were two of us. Solas wasn't any help on the matter. He liked the flames and kept a stock of marshmallows for the day we'd burn the world. We'd toast them on our way out.

"Do you ever get the feeling that no matter what you do, it isn't going to help?" I asked Nix.

"Yes. And it usually means it won't," Nix answered. "What does your gut tell you?"

"That it's going to get worse, and if I keep trying to help, I'm going to be in the middle of it."

"Then perhaps it's time you stop before you're eyeballs deep and choices you don't want to make are forced upon you. Between the mortal and Fae world isn't a good place to be for any reason. Sorry, Perdi, but you're not mortal anymore. Maybe having a Fae help them isn't what they need or want. Unfortunately, I think you're more of a reminder of what could come for their children than you are a support," he continued. "Regardless of the 'maybes', this is a hard place for you. Knowing that it doesn't matter what choices you make, you'll never make everyone happy. I'm sorry, Perdi. I wish they could remember who you are and not see you as what they fear."

I nodded. Nix was right, but I had difficulty convincing my soul that he was. I rubbed the center of my chest, trying to massage out the worry I felt. "Thank you for coming with me. I hate being there."

"Anytime, Perdi. I've got to run. Good night." Nix took his leave. "Are you coming, Jare? You said you'd help if I gave you jam."

I jumped and turned around. "Sorry, Jare. I forgot you were still here. Wear a bell or something. You're too quiet."

"I'll keep that in mind." He smiled. "Good night, Miss Darkmore."

"Perdi," I corrected him, but it was better than his usual 'ma'am' or 'my lady'. "Where are you both off to?"

"We're helping Orrian," Nix answered. "She needs a few small trees moved. She says they're blocking the sun from her window. I'll see you tomorrow for breakfast."

"Send Orrian my love," I called to them both and stepped into the manor.

The moment I closed the door, I felt secure. It felt like the rest of the world could be crumbling around us, but my life would go on without a care. This was the only place in either world where I felt like nothing could pull me in every other direction. I was just Perdi here — nothing more, nothing less. And as I breathed in the scent of home, the pressure in my shoulders lifted away.

"I can feel you, Zeph," I whispered as I walked from the front door. "Why are you skulking in the shadows?"

"I wasn't skulking. I planned to leave you be, but you smell of sadness. I wanted to make sure you were all right." Zephyr stepped out of the darkness along the wall with a soft smile. He could blend into any corner, and you'd never know he was there until he wanted you to. But for me, I could feel him through our shared pearls, our souls. "I heard your meeting went as well as the last one did."

"Your shadows move quickly," I replied.

"From your lips to my ears."

"It didn't go well, but it never does. It feels hopeless." I answered and leaned against the wall opposite him.

"Why do you still go if you lack hope?"

I shrugged. "The situation feels hopeless, but I don't feel that…not yet."

"Always the bleeding heart," he answered and pushed off the wall. "Be careful, little Crow. I do not trust them."

I laughed. "I don't think you trust anyone, Zeph. But why don't you trust mortals?"

"Mortal or not, I don't trust those who believe they have nothing to lose," he replied and stepped around me to the door. "Just be cautious."

"I will," I answered. "Where are you off to?"

"Orrian needs help," he answered. "Since I was already close by, I offered."

I smiled at the simplicity of his answer. For how difficult life could be in Elphame, the smallest things made me smile ear to ear. I was already picturing Zephyr lifting trees out of the ground with Orrian and Nix barking orders, because I knew damn well that Nix would enjoy ordering the Aos Si around. Nix was small but mighty. "I thought you weren't working tonight? Why were you here?"

"I'm never *not* working, Perdi. I just choose where I work," he answered, then paused at the door. "Something feels off. I came to talk to Solas about it."

"Something is always off in Elphame. Can you be more specific?"

He shook his head. "Unfortunately, no. In my gut, it feels like the eve of war. Like something big is coming, and I don't know what it is. It feels like I've overlooked something important."

"That's an uncomfortable thought," I replied. I tilted my head and asked the same question I had asked him every day since the Last War. "Have you found Solene's body yet?"

"No. The Seers didn't take it from the field but have agreed to continue searching for her," he answered. "Rest easy. Solene is not a flavor any of us could forget, and she is *not* who I feel."

"Damn. I was hoping it would be a simple solution for once." I cringed. I knew that feeling well. "Are we heading into some war I don't know about?"

He grinned. "We're always inches from war, little Crow. Stay close to home, for now. Training for tomorrow and the next few days is canceled until I figure this out. I don't have a good feeling."

"Has your gut ever been wrong?"

"No," he replied.

"I trust your gut more than my own. It's going to hurt like hell, isn't it?" A shiver ran down my spine.

Zephyr leaned into me and breathed me in like he was trying to find his way home in my smell. "This unease... You feel it too, don't you? I feel the beginnings of it on your pearl. I can feel your anxiety and panic like you're ready to run but don't know which direction to head in."

"I don't know. I thought it was just Whitwick, but it's more than that. I feel worried but can't put my finger on the exact reason I feel that way. It feels like when I have to make a decision I don't want to make, and I'm searching blindly for a different answer," I answered. "I have to meet with my father tomorrow afternoon. Do you want me to cancel? It's just lunch, but I could ask him to come here if you'd like?"

"Not yet, but don't go alone," he answered. "First sign of trouble..."

"Burn them to the ground," I answered.

"You sound like Solas." He frowned. "Run, Perdi."

"Or run." I smiled.

"Speaking of, I had better run as well. Orrian has trees to move, and my being late is not something the little queen would tolerate. She would take it as an insult," he said. He turned his icy stare to mine. "Perdi, if your gut tells you to burn them to the ground, do it. Don't hesitate. Always save yourself, no matter the cost. There will never be a cost greater than losing you, so do what you must. We'll clean up the mess later, when you're safe."

"Good night, Zeph," I called out as he left.

I moved through the halls to the dining room, which was finally repaired and had all its windows, no thanks to mine and Solas' tempers—though, I hadn't minded the breeze. One window had been fixed with smashed shards. Tiny veins of silver held the glass together like a scar. It reminded us of what we could lose at a moment's notice. Each time the sun shone through the scarred glass and cast rainbows on the table, it told the story of what we could endure for our family. It didn't matter what came for us. We'd always find a way back home.

I stopped at the entry to the dining room and watched Solas at the table, rifling through his paperwork. He looked calm, but I could feel the waves of frustration pouring from him, as he could likely feel mine. He smiled without looking up. I smiled in return.

"Are you spying on me, little Crow?" he asked.

I walked to the table. "Perhaps. I'm sure your secrets would fetch a pretty penny on the open market."

"I have ways to keep you quiet." He pulled me into his lap with a laugh and kissed me.

"Please tell me it's a prison, and you're locking me away for the next year." I tucked myself into his chest and breathed him in. "You smell like pine needles and moss and...sugar?"

"I took the long way home. I needed to clear my head," he answered. "I ran into Zephyr's pixies, and they attacked. Did you know there was a clan living behind the house? They said Zephyr gave them permission to live here."

"Yeah." I laughed. "Zeph built them a house when they were displaced during the war to close the Gate."

"They're worse than fairies," he grumbled, but I saw through it, and he grinned. "They were a nice distraction until they shot arrows at me and chased me into your morose garden in the back."

"Do you want to talk about what sent you walking from Blood and Bones in order to face off against the angry butterflies?" I asked.

"Angry butterflies?" He laughed and tickled my knees until I screamed.

"I surrender! You're a dirty fighter." I squirmed. "What has you all wound up?"

"I heard you and Zephyr speaking in the hall. That's pretty much it. He's stressed about something but doesn't know what it is. It makes me uncomfortable when he senses something off. When he worries, it's worth paying attention to. And you are as wound up as Zephyr is," he continued. "Do you want to talk about your day?"

I shrugged. "There isn't much to say. It was the same as every other time, only with more anger. Whitwick wants what can't be done, and it makes me nervous for what they'll try to do in place of that Gate."

"I'm sorry. Going home shouldn't be so stressful."

"I'm home now," I answered. "Whitwick isn't my home anymore."

"Just the same, little Crow, I had hoped it would be healing to see the mortal realm again. I'm sorry it's been so difficult for you."

He kissed my neck, sat me in the chair beside him, and served me dinner. He always waited for us both to be home before eating. And every time, he put potatoes on my plate. It was a tribute to Aoife and a long-standing joke between us. He talked about his day, and I pushed my food around on my plate and missed everything he said. My mind, a million miles away, couldn't follow the conversation at hand. Rather than needling or pushing me to talk, he scooped me into his arms and carried me to bed.

He helped me out of my clothes and curled in behind me. He tucked an arm under my head and the other around me. "Close your eyes."

"I love you," I mumbled around a yawn. "I'm exhausted, but my mind is racing, and I can't stop thinking."

"Just close your eyes," he whispered and kissed my neck. "I can help you fall asleep."

"No spelling me to —" I didn't finish my sentence.

"Shh," he whispered.

He ran his hand up and down my side, grazing my skin lightly, just enough to send shivers across my flesh. It was somewhere between a tickle and a rub and calmed me to my soul. His touch was soft in some places and rubbed deeply in others. He held me close and hugged me until the world went quiet. My consuming thoughts went to places I couldn't reach. It was only with him that I could be free from it all. I could die at that very moment and be happy.

"Close your eyes, little Crow." His whispers were all I needed to pull me from the chaos of our world. "*Sleep. I'm right here. I'm not going anywhere.*"

With a gentle push of his magick, I drifted off peacefully. It felt like I had only closed my eyes when Solas stirred beside me. But it wasn't him I woke to. It was Zephyr. His pearl gently nudged against my Malice to tell me it was okay. I didn't need to run from the monster who entered my room in the middle of the night, because this particular one was on my side. I lifted my head to see Zephyr and Solas talking at the foot of the bed.

"Either talk loud enough for me to hear or go into the hall so I can go back to sleep." My voice was gravelly.

Zephyr came around the bed and knelt on the floor. "Good night, little Crow."

"What's going on, Zeph?" I asked. "You didn't come here to say good night."

He smiled. "I come every night."

"You send your shadows," I answered. "That's not the same thing."

"Sometimes the shadows are exactly what you need," he replied. "But even when it is just them, I always say good night."

I reached for his hand and squeezed it. "What's wrong? I can feel your unease. It feels like I ate something bad and it wants to come back up."

"I don't know," he answered. "I don't know if what I'm feeling is about me, you, Solas, Elphame or all the above. There's word of people missing in the villages. I don't know if they've earned their fates or if they've been taken."

"How did we not know that our people are missing?" I asked.

"People go missing all the time, little Crow," Zephyr replied. "It is the way of Elphame. Either way, I asked Nix to stay in the manor tonight. I only ever feel this way before war."

"Do we need to prepare?" I asked.

Solas sat beside me and stroked my hair. "We're ready, Perdi. It's what Zephyr has been doing all night. The Aos Si, Royal Guard and Sluagh are all prepared. We've sent word to Faolan to ready his men, just in case."

I nodded. "Is there anything I can do?"

"No, not yet. Go back to sleep for now," Zephyr answered and stood.

"How do I sleep now?" I asked.

Solas leaned over and kissed my temple. "*Sleep*, little Crow."

"I hate when you do that," I mumbled and drifted off to sleep under the power of his magick, listening to the two of them talking in the background.

I was safe and would wake instantly if something were to happen. My Malice wouldn't sleep, even if I was out like a light. I drifted in and out, restless, fighting the urge to be awake and knowing I needed to rest. Each time I came to the edge of wakefulness, Solas tucked himself tighter around me and whispered in my ear until I settled. As the night faded, I finally felt him get up for the day. Without knowing the time, I knew he was getting up for meetings. He always woke before the sun and wrestled his day into submission before dinner. This was our life, fighting to get home, and I didn't have the nerve to curse the Gods for it. Anything other than this was war here in Elphame.

"Stay the day with me," I whispered, barely cracking my sandpaper eyelids. "The sun isn't even up yet."

"I have a meeting at Blood and Bones this morning. I'll never be home for dinner if I don't leave now. I'd rather start early and come home to you than risk missing dinner," Solas answered. He leaned over the bed and kissed my cheek. "Go back to sleep, lazy bones. You have the day off from training. Enjoy the break."

"I wish I could order you to stay," I answered.

"As do I," he answered. "Zephyr told me things are getting tense over in Whitwick. How bad is it?"

"When was Zephyr here?" I asked.

"He came while you were asleep. Don't you remember talking to him?" he answered.

I dug around in my tired brain and finally remembered. "Vaguely."

"He told me of your meeting yesterday, who heard it from the shadows and replayed by Nix, who needed Zephyr's help to pull out a tree because of a sunlight issue Orrian had. She's scared her berry bushes won't get enough sun and won't blossom."

"She's going to rip out the damn forest for her garden." I laughed softly at him, recounting the trail of information ending in Orrian and her tree problems. From tension and possible war to something as innocent as a fairy wishing her berries could have more sun. "Do you think I should still meet my dad for lunch today? If Zephyr feels something is off, shouldn't I stay home?"

"I won't tell you where you can and can't go. But I know Zephyr, and I would feel better if you stayed close to home," he answered. "If things are as tense as Zephyr believes, going to Whitwick could be the unease he feels."

"Unease… Zephyr doesn't feel uneasy. He's scared. I felt it."

"As did I. Perhaps, remain home? The last time Zephyr was scared, you almost died. I'd feel better if you stayed close, if you don't mind?" He made it a question, which I appreciated. "Zephyr will be close by today, helping Nix. He said he'd let you sleep in and drop Nix off for brunch. And tonight, we can talk about what's going on in Whitwick and come up with some possible solutions to take to them. I can discuss the tension with the Seers. Perhaps they have some ideas?"

"Thank you. I'll take all the help I can get." I smiled, which turned into a groan. "Whitwick... They'll never be happy. They weren't happy when the Gates were open, not happy when they closed and aren't happy now that they're gone. There's no winning. I don't know how to help. I can't change what's happened, and they keep demanding I create a new Gate and close Elphame off to the mortal lands for good. They don't believe that I can't do what they want. They think I'm lying. It really isn't a matter of not wanting to help. I simply don't know how to do it. And because I don't know how, I think they'll find some witch to try."

"Can you blame them, Perdi? Truly? That Gate symbolized a lifetime of losses, but it also was a symbol of protection, however false it was. It's only been months since the Gate was destroyed. Imagine the fear of knowing we can step through whenever we want? If I were them, I would want a new Gate, as well. As to whether they believe you or not, pain makes us believe what we want, not what is true. Pain makes us blame others. It's easier to deal with it when we can point our fingers at someone else. We, the Fae, are not faultless in this and have earned that fear. And unfortunately, now, the fingers land on you, as much as the rest of us."

I nodded. "I'm not blaming them, nor am I even angry about it. I understand the 'why' behind their emotions. I'm just frustrated that I don't know how to fix it."

"You can't fix it. All you can do is listen and act to ensure their fears are addressed. We can't expect others to overcome generations of trauma, just because we said it would stop. Trauma doesn't just go away because you will it so. You know this, little Crow," he answered and sighed. "We knew this would be a fallout to the Gate, that not everyone would be as pleased about it. We see it as a way to start anew, to bridge our relations. They see it as a way for us to go unchecked. Both are hard truths to be faced."

"I love you. I'll try to remember that while they scream for my head later."

"And I love you, little Crow. Don't worry about Whitwick. They burn witches, not cut off their heads."

I rolled my eyes. "Because that's so much better."

"I'll let Zephyr know you're staying home today. That will calm his nerves." He was gone before his last word hit my ears, his calm wind pushing the covers back over me. It didn't take long for the warmth of the bed to pull me back under. There were a million things to deal with, but all I could think of was how much I wanted to go back to sleep.

Chapter Two

I sensed the shadows before they wrapped around me and tugged me from my warm bed. I growled Zephyr's name as they dropped me on my back in the forest, knocking the wind out of me from the force. Before my eyes even opened, I moved to protect my vital organs until I could breathe again. Even in shock, I remembered what Zephyr had taught me. Protect myself at all costs. Use every tool at my disposal. Make the situation I stood in into a weapon. I grabbed the first thing I could reach, a branch, and jumped to my feet, makeshift dagger in hand, and scanned my surroundings.

The sun felt like acid to my half-asleep eyes. It made my vision splotchy. I snapped the branch in half with my naked knee, leaving each hand with a sharp, homemade knife. I twirled them in my grip and glanced over the empty forest for a hidden attack. This wouldn't be the first time he had done this, and it wouldn't be the last. But this had not been on my agenda today. I guessed this was the why behind the blitz attack in my sleep. We never could plan for every inevitability, which would be my lesson for the day. Even on days I wasn't prepared to fight, the fight didn't care what I had planned. I loved Zephyr to pieces, but I hated him this morning.

"What the hell, Zeph? You said today would be a day off. Get out here, you worm!" I screamed into the surrounding trees. "I'm going to beat the crap out of you. For crying out loud, I'm in my goddamn underwear!"

I spun around again and shivered. I cursed Zephyr loudly for bringing me into the forest in underwear and a shirt again. He never grabbed me when I was wearing shoes. My feet weren't quite used to stomping around on rocks and sharper bits like his were. He could full-out run, on glass, without so much as flinching. I was made of delicate things and couldn't walk ten feet on gravel without begging to be carried. If ever I was in a barefoot race where the winner lived and the loser died, I'd have given up and died, just to save myself the pain of walking.

The shadows rolled out of the forest to my front. They twisted and turned in panic. Their terror prickled along my arms in warning. I could feel them, actually feel their fear. I could almost taste it on the back of my tongue, a dread so thick that I gagged. I hadn't felt them like this before. And unless I was wrapped inside them, I usually sensed no emotions. Even then, they didn't touch my soul as they did that morning. The shadows hadn't stirred my Malice ever. Now, it took my breath away, and I staggered. Too many souls, too many emotions, all of it slamming into me at once, and I couldn't make sense of it. I felt like I stood in the middle of hundreds of people, each screaming something different, each pulling at my arms for attention. I shook my head and tried to fight against their force. My equilibrium teetered as I struggled to make sense of the shadows. The world tilted with their despair.

I covered my ears. The constant ringing was too much to handle. "Stop it! Stop screaming at me!"

"Perdi, Zephyr is missing," they said through jumbled words. They were too scared to form one voice, so hundreds shrieked at once, and it felt like a hot slap. "He bound us to you, and now he's gone."

"Wait! What? Bound you to me? What are you talking about?" I asked and searched the link he and I shared.

Zephyr had taught me to tune him out since I started to pick up his every thought and dream after taking his pearl, a piece of his soul. I had walked into many of his nightmares that had terrified me and some that left us both uncomfortable for days. This morning, there was nothing at the end of his pearl. My heart started to beat wildly in my chest, and I held my hand over it for fear it would leap from my bones and smash into pieces onto the dirty ground.

"Why the hell would you bring me here if he is missing?" I asked.

"Because this is where he brings you when he has to tell you bad news. He said this was the only place where you could safely burn your rage, far away from flammable people," they answered, and I staggered again from the force of their alarm. "If we told you in bed and you started a fire, how would we put it out?"

I shook my head at their comment. I supposed they couldn't do much without hands. "Bring me some clothes, at least. You should also know I don't like standing around half-dressed."

"Out here, there are no witnesses you'd need to track down if you burned with anger. Were we wrong?" they asked as they pushed clothes from their inky center, and I pulled them on, still trying to whisper through the link to Zephyr. There was nothing on the other end of that link. It wasn't gone. It was empty, like knocking on the door of a home no one lived in.

I closed my eyes and calmed myself. I focused on one thought, Zephyr, and pulled on his pearl like a string, but received not even a tug back. When he didn't want to be disturbed, he'd slam the door in my face or simply push me back to show that he was busy. Today, there wasn't even a whisper. There was a black hole at the end. It was as if no one owned the pearl. No one claimed the pull on the other end.

"No, you weren't wrong," I answered. "Bring me home, to the island. Sometimes when he's there, I have a hard time feeling him. When he's in deep meditation, sometimes he simply doesn't hear me, and I can't feel him."

They wrapped around me as I pulled my hair into a bun. The loose strands twisted in the wind around me like escaped flames from a fire. Inside, the shadows felt uncomfortable and tight. I could feel everything around us and smell the forest, the leaves and the ocean nearby. Nothing blocked out the world around us. And once we were on the island, I stepped away quickly and rubbed the remnants from my arms. It felt like they were stuck to me. It was a feeling I hadn't had with them before. My arms felt wet.

"You're crying all over me," I finally said and leaned over with the urge to vomit. "Oh, God, I can taste the salt from your tears."

"We can't help it. We are…scared," the shadows answered, and I flinched at their voices. "We have never been without Zephyr."

"Why can I hear all of you at once? Pick one voice, or one soul, to speak, like before. It's too much. It's disorientating, not to mention confusing. I can't focus like this. All I can hear and feel is you."

"Is this better?" they asked with one voice.

"Yes," I answered. It was the voice I was used to, with all of them together. "You need control. I can't concentrate when I can feel you this deeply. You're pushing your emotions down my throat, and I can't think past them."

"We cannot control what you feel from us, Perdi. We are bound to your soul. It is *you* who must control *us*. Before, it was Zephyr. Now, it is you," they answered. "We will try, but so must you. You are the one who is in control here, not us."

I nodded and tried to do as Zephyr had taught me. I pushed my Malice to the surface, not enough to release her, but enough for her to eat away at the energy around me and give me back my control and focus. Zephyr had said this was how he could walk through a battlefield without flinching. He ate the hate and horror around him rather than let it coat his confidence and drag him down. It had sounded easy at the time, but now I realized it was a constant effort.

"Can you feel him here?" I asked.

"We're no longer bound to him and can't feel him as we once did. But we feel no one here but you," they replied.

"Let's spread out. Zeph has to be somewhere. Maybe he's hurt?"

I searched Zephyr's home. The shadows covered the rest of the island in the time I took to explore the house. Nothing was out of place from the last time I had come. There was one addition to his artwork, though. He had moved a painting of a field in Elphame and replaced it with a small black frame housing a note I had once left him.

Zeph,
There may not be room for greatness in Elphame, but you are as close to it as they will allow. I am a better person for having known you.
You have all my love, now and forever.
Little Crow

I ran my finger over the top and found not a speck of dust. It had been cared for and loved, just like I was. I stepped into Zephyr's dining room and found the table filled with maps of Elphame. Red and black symbols marked the map throughout all of Elphame. Seeing his maps and reports on the table wasn't unusual, but they were usually more organized and rarely left scattered for me to pick through. He never hid them from me, but also never liked pushing the awfulness of Elphame into my face.

"What is this?" I asked the shadows.

"Zephyr tracks everything in Elphame, he and the Aos Si. The map on your right, with the red markings? They were tracking Parrish and skirmishes throughout the territories. The red are instances of Parrish sightings, and black is where they found Parrish's people."

"What happened when they found Parrish's people?"

"They did not see another day," the shadows answered.

"Why is Zephyr spending his time hunting down Parrish?"

The shadows swirled and danced back and forth. I could feel their nervousness. "He's been tracking him since the Last War when Parrish escaped. He doesn't trust him. He believes Parrish will try to harm you."

On the map was Faolan's territory with black markings that marred his land, and I wondered why Parrish's people would be found there. "Why would Parrish try to go to Faolan's territory?"

"Faolan once had a treaty with him. Their territories border each other."

I pointed to small red crosses on the map. There were dozens of them. "What are these for?"

"Zephyr marked those last night for those who have gone missing," they replied.

"Did he find out what happened to them?" I asked.

"No. He mentioned to Solas that some were found dead for obvious reasons, and the rest were gone without a trace. Zephyr sent a few of his men to investigate. So far, they have had nothing to report. Perdi, it's not uncommon for our people to go missing."

"So, I've been told. It's uncomfortable how calm everyone is at the prospect of people disappearing without a trace," I replied and took one more glance at the maps. "Bring me to Zeno. He's his second in command. He might know if Zephyr is out hunting down Parrish or our people."

The shadows pulled me from the island and through Elphame into the caves of the Sluagh. I landed on the lip of Zeno's cave and stepped forward, calling out to him. The back of the cave was lit with candles. It was nicer than the trainees' dump of pillows and old wine bottles. Zeno's one-room cave was one massive bedroom with handmade bookshelves lining the room.

Zeno jumped out of his bed, surprised, holding a pillow over his hips. "Perdi?"

The blankets behind him jerked and laughed, and I grinned. "Can you get dressed and meet me outside?"

"Of course," he turned, flashing me his naked rear.

I walked to the mouth of the cave and waited for Zeno. I was curious about who was in his bed, but only because I was nosy. I wouldn't ask. It wasn't my business what anyone did in their free time. Zeno came to the lip of his cave, dressed in leather, ready for a fight.

"Are you okay?" he asked. "You smell sad. What has happened?"

I shook my head. "Have you seen Zephyr? I can't find him."

"Not since early this morning, before the sun rose."

"Do you know where he'd be?" I asked.

"You'd have a better idea than any of us. Have you tried to call him?"

"There's no answer," I replied. "I may be overreacting, but can you get a few others and start looking for him?"

"If you feel we should, I'll get a group together. Better safe than not," Zeno replied. "Soul-Eaters can always find each other. That you're here, looking for one, is cause enough for me to get dressed."

"Sorry to interrupt your…date." I smiled.

He glanced back. "She'll understand."

"If you find him before me, tell him I'm looking for him. His pearl isn't answering my calls."

"I'll let you know what turns up." He jogged back into his room.

I motioned to the shadows, thinking of Zephyr's maps. "Bring me to the Winter Court. If anyone is stupid enough to take Zeph, it would be Faolan."

In a blast of cool air, my feet touched down next to the caverns of the Unseelie court. Dread instantly settled into my bones, and I groaned. It wouldn't matter if I unleashed all of my Malice here. She'd never be able to drink enough of the terror in the air for me to feel the slightest bit comfortable. I had almost forgotten how horrible it felt to be on this side of the border. I closed my eyes and could feel Oberon coming, along with the full force of his power. The fear in the pit of my stomach grew as the bodach got closer.

"Perdita!" He popped out of the earth. Although he held a friendly smile, I still stepped back. *Oberon isn't my enemy*, I told myself. If anything, he was a friend. That knowledge was the only thing that kept me from wanting to run. "I got your last package, thank you. The blanket was lovely, as were the sweets from the mortal realm."

"You're welcome," I answered.

He smiled as he pulled himself from the crevasse. He held out a wrapped candy, and I shook my head. I didn't like sweets as I once had as a child. "You don't need to keep sending me gifts, Perdi, although they are treasured. I helped you during the Last War because you asked and it was the right thing to do, not for there to be a debt between us."

I shrugged. "I appreciate and value what you've done for my family, and I want to show it."

"You could always come caving again." He grinned, and I shook my head but laughed. "But to hear you say you value me is the greatest of payments."

"If you ever need help, call on me, and I will always come," I replied, and he nodded.

Oisin was next to climb out. His face was scratched and his knuckles were bleeding. "Hi, Perdi, what's up? If it's war, I'm going back into the caves and not coming back out."

"Even I know you're lying. There has never been a frontline you've not been on. I swear you were born in the middle of a war and fought your first fight from your mother's arms. You live and breathe war, just as Zephyr does," I answered, and Oisin grinned.

"You say the sweetest things to me." Oisin laughed.

"Speaking of war, have you seen Zephyr?"

"No," Oberon answered first. "I have not seen him in many moons since I last saw you. I have felt him, though. But it has been many days since he's been through here." He frowned, looking from me to the shadows. "You look scared, Perdi. And Zephyr's shadows are jumping all over the place. They're usually more relaxed than this."

I nodded and looked at the shadows, who twisted around my legs like a scared animal. "They don't know where Zephyr is, either."

"I saw him a few times after the Last War," Oisin added. "He was watching Faolan — debating whether to kill him or not, I imagine. But it's been days since he's come here."

"He's been here a lot more than you think," I answered. "You only saw him because he wanted you to know he was watching you. Take it as his way of warning you."

"Figured as much," Oisin replied, motioning to the forest behind him. Both he and Oberon slinked back down into the caves. "Faolan is coming. Want to hide down here with us?"

"Tempting," I answered with a smile. I didn't dislike Oisin. I respected the hell out of him. He reminded me of Zephyr. It wasn't his fault that his king had lied and used me. "But not today."

Faolan stepped through the trees. He kept a fair distance between us. "Hello, Perdi."

"I'm sorry to come without permission, Faolan. I know I should have come to you first." I winced at the protocol between courts I had skipped over.

"You have safe passage here. I never took it back. I only come to see why you're here and if you need aid. But if it is to speak to the Oberon or Oisin, I'll take my leave." He stopped and breathed in the air. It irritated me that he could still do that, smell my emotions. "What's happened?"

"I hate when you guys do that," I answered. "Have you seen Zephyr?"

"I'm sorry. It's hard not to notice," Faolan answered. "No, I haven't seen him. We got word from Solas last night that Zephyr sensed something was off, but it was by messenger, not Zephyr or Solas themselves. You're welcome to check all of Tylwyth if you'd like. The Winter Court has nothing to hide from you," he answered and stepped to the side. He stretched his arms open with an invitation. "I swear to you, he is not here. I would not be in such good condition if he were."

I nodded. He was telling the truth. He was in one piece, after all. "Why did the Autumn Court come here?"

"They came weeks ago and asked for sanctuary," Faolan answered. "I didn't grant it."

"What happened to them?" I asked.

"As soon as they arrived, I held them and sent a messenger to Solas. I reported their arrival immediately, and the Aos Si took them," Faolan replied. "They were considered war criminals. They're likely dead. The Aos Si do not take prisoners."

"Sounds about right," I mumbled. If Zephyr hadn't been here for weeks, where the hell was he?

"You're welcome to come and check all of my lands," Faolan offered again.

"No, I believe you. But thank you," I replied. "One more thing... Have any of your people gone missing lately?"

"One wandered off a few days ago and was found dead in the mountains. He went into the wrong cave and didn't make it out in one piece," Faolan answered. "Why? Have your people gone missing?"

"I'm not sure if they're missing or dead or why," I replied. "If they turn up in your court, can you send them home? Rather than wage war?"

Faolan smiled. "I'll have Oisin bring them home. I'll keep an ear out for any talk of taking from your court."

"Thank you," I answered. "Good luck down there, Oisin." I turned from them with a wave. I pulled the shadows back up and went home. "Bring Solas home immediately."

Solas was spat out onto the dining room floor and rolled to a stop in less time than it took for me to take a seat. "Zephyr! You piece of shit. If you ever send your fucking shadows to fetch me like that again, I'll rip your spine out through your asshole, you gutless prick."

Solas rarely swore around me, and he didn't like it when others did, either. To hear it was amusing. But today, I didn't feel like laughing about it. "It wasn't Zeph. It was me," I said, my voice shaking. I stood and hugged myself. I was cold and hot at once.

"Perdi?" Solas blinked for a moment, confused at being spat out on the floor. I had only ever asked the shadows to bring me to Solas, never to have them bring him to me.

"I'm sorry. I should have told them to ask you to come. I told them to bring you home immediately. I didn't think this was how they'd bring you back."

Solas jumped to his feet and ran to me. His irritated look was replaced with worry once he realized it had been me who brought him. "No, it's okay. I'm sorry. Always send for me when you need me. I don't care what I'm doing. Are you okay? What has happened?"

He breathed in deeply, and the beast within him growled. He could smell the Winter Court on me. Even I could smell the lingering scent of Christmas. His face went a darker shade of rage. "Faolan. What's he done this time?"

"No, it's not him. It's Zephyr. He's missing."

"No. He's probably at home," Solas answered. "Why do I smell the Winter Court on you?"

I shook my head. "No, I went to the island first. Then I checked with Zeno, who hadn't seen him since before the sun rose. After, I went to Faolan's, thinking he would be the only one stupid enough to take him. But Zeph isn't there either. Oberon hasn't seen him, and neither has Oisin. Faolan might lie to me, but they wouldn't." I rubbed the center of my chest with the palm of my hand. My chest felt too tight to breathe fully. "Something is wrong. I feel it in my soul. That unease, it's grown into something that's eating at me."

"It's okay, just breathe. There has to be a good reason you can't find him."

"It's not that, Solas. There are plenty of times I can't find him, and it takes me all day to track him. Hell, he and I have trained for this—me tracking him, him tracking me. But I can't *feel* him. I can't sense him. I can always feel him, even when he doesn't want to be bothered or found." I struggled to explain it. "I have his pearl. I'm always connected to him. But it's like he's not at the other end of it. He'd never just do this. He'd never leave me. He swore he'd never leave me. I'm telling you something is wrong, and I need you to believe that."

"I believe you." Solas hugged me and kissed the top of my head. "He's left many times before, but never like this. We'll find him. I promise."

"Can you feel him?" I asked. "Couldn't you find him if you wanted to?"

"Zephyr and you are hard for me to track. It takes a lot of concentration for me to find you because your energy is too wild. Sometimes you feel like you, other times like Zephyr, and sometimes you feel like all of Elphame wrapped into one tiny body. I have to pick through it all to find you. But Zeph? I can't find him unless he's close by. He is Aos Si. They are difficult to track, even for kings," he replied. "It doesn't help that he's Soul-Eater. They're impossible to find when they don't want to be found."

"Can you call him? He's told me before when he's heard you calling for him. Could you try, please?"

Solas nodded. "I have been, Perdi, since I got home. But that requires him to listen in on me. I don't feel him lingering. Wherever he is, I don't think he can hear me."

"Would I know if he were dead? Would I feel it?" I asked, and my voice cracked at the painful thought.

"Yes, you would. Zephyr felt it when you died to close the Gate. He told me it felt like his soul was being burned alive. He said that up until the moment of your death, it was like skinning an animal before you've killed it. I think it would feel very much like you were dying, yourself."

I shuddered at the thought. "And if, for some reason, the link between us was broken? Would I still feel it?"

"We'd all feel it if he were gone, with or without a pearl. The world would tremble at his passing," he replied. From his arms, I felt the tension in his body begin to climb. His muscles tightened, and a slight vibration began. "Zephyr told me the bond you share is unbreakable, so I'd think you'd know if it were truly gone."

That wasn't much of an answer, but it was all he had. Solas wasn't a Soul-Eater. He was only guessing. The person I would ask such things was the person that was missing.

I paused for a moment and thought of Solas' words. "Does it bother you that Zephyr and I are linked like this?"

"At first, but not anymore. Neither of you can help it. You're Finis. You're drawn to each other."

"You know I have no desires for him, right?" I asked.

"I should hope not, given he sees you as his little sister," Solas smiled. "Finis are territorial, protective of their kind to the death. No power, dead or alive, could keep you two apart. Not even the realms kept you two apart. That's what brings me so much worry about the situation. If he were to just to up and leave willingly, you'd be gone too. He'd never leave you behind unless he had no other choice."

I nodded but didn't feel as confident with his answer as he was. "When I was on the island, I saw Zephyr's maps. Did you know so many people were missing?"

"Not until Zephyr told me. He thinks Parrish is connected to it and has them," he replied. "Zephyr was going to send a few Aos Si to check it out. Nothing has come of it yet, but I've also updated Lily and asked her to check Whitwick."

"And if they're somewhere in Elphame, being held against their will?" I asked. "We're going to go bring them home, right? We wouldn't just leave them, would we?"

"Never would we leave them, Perdi. The Dark Courts don't leave their people behind, ever. We would war for the return of just one person. Holding several would be the complete annihilation of their court and any who knew about it or helped in any way," he replied. He squeezed my arm in comfort. "We'll find them. They'll know we won't leave them."

I nodded and settled a little at his comment. "Whoever is responsible for taking our people will burn for this. If it's Parrish, I volunteer to kill another king."

Solas smiled. "I'll hold him down for you."

"Always the gentleman," I replied.

The shadows slinked across the floor like beaten dogs. "Perdi, we haven't told you why we brought you to the forest."

"Oh, there's more?" I asked sarcastically. "What more could you possibly tell me?"

"We fear you will burn when we tell you," they replied.

"Spit it out," I barked at them, instantly feeling bad when they jerked and pushed themselves flat against the floor. I saw myself in those actions, flinching from anger and wanting to be smaller and go unnoticed. "I'm sorry. Damn it. Please, I'm sorry. I shouldn't have done that. Tell me."

"When Zephyr bound us to you..." the shadows began.

Solas gasped. "He *what*?"

"When Zephyr bound us to Perdi, he wasn't alone," they answered.

"Who was with him? Who took him?" I asked.

The shadows inched back as if scared of how I'd react to what they said next. "Zephyr had Nix with him."

My mouth dropped, and my breath swooshed from my lungs as if I had been punched in the chest. I shook my head. "No, but...no. Not Nix. He can't...wait... Jesus, I can't breathe." The world sparkled. Little flashes of light began to dance in my vision. My chest tightened. Each time I tried to gulp air, it wasn't enough. My breathing began to speed up, quick and shallow.

"Calm," Solas whispered. "Slow down before you pass out."

I nodded but still struggled. Fear coursed through my veins. "What do we do?"

Solas steadied me against his body and bent me forward. "Nothing until you can think clearly. Cup your mouth and nose. Deep breaths, Perdi."

I closed my eyes and let out a long, shaking wheeze. I breathed in through my nose, into my stomach, held it for the count of ten then back out through pursed lips. The room finally stopped spinning, and the sparkles disappeared. When I stood, I nodded, but Solas kept his body close in case I finally stopped breathing and passed out. The marble floor would not be forgiving if I landed on my face.

"Okay, I'm okay. I need to hear the rest. Zephyr and Nix were together?" I asked.

The shadows rolled around in front of me. I thought they, like Solas, were waiting for me to faceplant. "We weren't with them, but Zephyr and Nix were alone. He bound us and told us to stay with you. He was no longer our master. You were. We felt nothing after that. We went to where we last felt them. We knew you would have wanted us to do so, even without your order, but we found no one."

"Where were they?" I asked.

"They were in the Wildelands," they answered. "Last night, Zephyr was here. Nix slept in his bedroom all night after returning from Orrian's court. They both remained within the Dark Courts until this morning when Zephyr met Nix, and together they walked to the Court of Less and into the Wildlands. Yesterday, Zephyr was at Blood and Bones with Solas, the day before, his island to train with you. In between, he has been to every court in search of possible war or issues within the courts. He always came back, until this morning, when he didn't."

"He's not at Blood and Bones. I was just there," Solas added. "Blood and Bones is not how it once was. It's still tense, but they wouldn't have done this to Zephyr. They hail him a hero for his actions during the Last War. He has always had the respect of the Seers. Solene was the one who didn't like him. The rest didn't have any problems with him. As for Nix, they'd never do something like that to a gnome, especially not to Nix."

"Zeph isn't on his island. I was just there. It's exactly how we left it, right down to the broken windows and the burned deck."

"What kind of training are you guys doing? Making explosives?" Solas asked.

"No, it's hard to win against Zephyr. Sometimes I have to smoke him out." I smiled at the memory of Zephyr jumping out of his front window to escape my flames. I turned my attention back to the shadows. "Why weren't you with him?"

"We are not always with him. When we are home or in the Dark Courts, we have freedom. If we are not with him, we must remain close to you. It is the bargain we have with him for freedom. You were at home at the time, so we were in the back garden with your shadows. We like to speak to them. They are so new, and they are scared."

"You have shadows?" Solas asked.

I swallowed hard and felt my face flush. I was instantly embarrassed. "Yes, and before you scold me, I didn't mean to trap them."

"Does Zephyr know?"

"He's teaching me how to release them since I don't want my own collection. I've ordered they stay in the garden so they're not trailing behind me." I fidgeted with the hem of my shirt, not wanting to make eye contact. I still felt the shame of binding souls. "So far, I've released a dozen. It's not as easy to release them as it is to trap them. But there's a couple of hundred back there, from the night the Golden Court attacked after I escaped and they invaded."

"*You* did that?" Solas asked.

"Yes. Zephyr took the blame because I was still hiding who I was," I answered, then started to squirm. "At the time, I didn't think I was lying to you. I was protecting myself and Zephyr. Neither of us wanted the world to know that there were two of us. But now, looking back, it was a lie. And once I realized shadows that weren't Zephyr's were following me around, I was ashamed and didn't want you to know what I had done. I thought that if I got rid of them, I could pretend I didn't do it at all. In my head, it made perfect sense. Saying it out loud to you now, I just feel like a liar."

Solas hugged me into his chest and kissed the top of my head. "You do not need to feel ashamed for that. You did what you did to protect all of us. Do not judge yourself so harshly. To know you tried to fix it, to free them, that should tell you a lot about who you are inside."

"There's no room in my wounds for me to sit anymore. But thank you for saying that." I pulled back and returned my attention to the shadows. "The last time you felt Zephyr, where exactly was he? What was he doing? Did you feel anyone else? Tell me exactly what happened."

"He met with Nix this morning before they were to come here to meet you for brunch. They meet once a week, usually. Nix is a strong warrior, but his heart hurts for his deeds, and Zephyr is helping to guide him. Nix wanted to give you one of his pearls to keep you both bonded. But he must face his memories before he can share them with you without shame—which is what Zephyr is helping him do. A Soul-Eater does not just eat souls. They eat the pain held within them. They help guide them to a place of peace. But that is all we will say on their conversations."

"You're right. That's Nix's story to tell, not yours," I replied and smiled softly, thinking of Nix trying to heal his wounds and face who he had been.

"Today, they were picking flowers for you. They were sampling the scents to find something not found in Seelie courts," the shadows added and answered a lingering question about why they were found together so far from home. "Zephyr wanted to give you something to take away a bad memory. He wanted flowers to mean something different to you. They had selected several and were about to go to the Golden Courts to ensure those flowers didn't grow there."

I nodded. Of course, it would be flowers. I hated the very smell of most of them after being in the Golden Court. Some scents triggered memories I still struggled with, such as anything remotely similar to my time in that cursed court.

"They were alone, Perdi. We sensed no one nearby," they answered. "One minute, we could feel Zephyr and hear Nix's laughter, and the next, they were just gone, similar to when you're at the Gate. One minute we feel you, and once you step into the Gate, we feel nothing until you come out the other side. It's static in between. Our connection is just suddenly gone."

"Solas, why did you react that way when you found out they were bound to me?" I asked.

"A Soul-Eater without his souls... I've never heard of it. He has never released his shadows," he answered. "Your shadows, the ones you're releasing, you didn't mean to bind them. I understand the reason why you're setting them free. But Zephyr? Never. Every pearl he has, he collected for a reason."

"Respectfully, Zephyr has released those who have served out their sentence. He has released hundreds over his lifetime," the shadows corrected Solas. "But yes, you are correct in that he's never done it all at once."

I rubbed the center of my chest. "He's in trouble. I can feel it, even though I can't feel him like I used to. Both of them. Nix, this horror isn't his world anymore. I promised him the wars and fighting would be over for him. I swore I'd keep this hell from him, and he'd have peace again, that he could sit in a garden, and we'd go back to arguing over where to plant flowers and how to poison the grubs eating his vegetables. I gave him my word."

"Perdi." The shadows called my attention away from my impending panic. "Of all the people to be taken with Zephyr, Nix is a wise choice. He may be small, but he is fierce and can survive much better than you. We are sorry he is taken, but we do not fear for his life as we would if it were you or another Fae. Nix can take almost as much torture as Zephyr or Solas. He will live longer, in unimaginable conditions, than almost all others who could have been taken."

Solas nodded in agreement. "I'd agree with that. Nix is pretty hard to hurt."

"That doesn't make me feel better about it," I replied. "I know Nix is tough, but he shouldn't have to show it every bloody time something happens in this goddamn place."

"I know. We'll find them. Elphame isn't big enough to hide Zephyr. No world could hide a force like him. And Nix? Nothing has ever held a gnome before—not for any length of time—and survived it. They're too small for our magick to hold them. It's how they walked in and out of the mortal world without consequence. They're too vicious for anyone to risk trying to take them."

Though Solas' voice was confident, I didn't feel it. "Zeph would only leave me if he couldn't protect me. And Nix? He'd never leave me unless he had absolutely no choice."

"I was thinking the same thing. But Perdi, what if they left to draw whomever away? What if they don't want us to come looking?" Solas asked.

I stared at him and wondered if he were joking. He wasn't. "Then why bind his shadows to me? He would have kept them for himself if he didn't plan on me coming to find him. And I will find them, Solas. I hope whoever has them understands what they've done, the fate they've welcomed."

"I will begin my search here, in Elphame. I'll meet with Zeno and see what the Aos Si have turned up. You go to your father and see if Zephyr has been seen entering the mortal realm." Solas didn't bother telling me I had to stay put, that I couldn't risk my safety. He knew I wouldn't and would resent him for even hinting at it. "Be careful."

"Solas, I gave Zeph my word. I would always come find him. I oathed myself to both him and Nix. I swore I would come for them, no matter the cost. I can't not go. I can feel a tug deep inside, and it won't let me stand by. My body physically can't sit still. I'm as antsy as a fish in a hot pan."

"That, little Crow, is the oath. It binds your soul to the receiver of that oath. It's how Zephyr came when you were in the Gate. It's how I always find you when you're in trouble. My very soul wouldn't let me stand by, even if I had wanted to."

I nodded. "What happens if I fail?"

"You'll feel it, and it'll be the most pain you've ever felt. You will wish for death, Perdi. It hurts that bad. You've felt a world of pain since you've come here. Imagine it all coming down on you at once. That, little Crow, is what your soul will feel."

"Have you ever broken an oath?" I asked.

"Yes. I've failed before and wished for death," he replied.

Chapter Three

"We do not like coming here, Perdi." The shadows worried around me as we walked through the Gate. It wasn't often they came into Whitwick with me.

"Why not?"

"We fear their intentions toward you," they answered. "Their emotions linger in the air, and we do not like what we're feeling."

"They hate me?" I asked. "Tell me something I don't already know."

"Worse, they fear you. Hate makes you do cruel things. Fear makes you do stupid things." Their logic couldn't be argued. It was basically the same thing Nix and I had just talked about.

The Gate pulled the Elphame air from my chest as I passed through, leaving me with a lungful of smells my stomach no longer liked. My feet dragged as though my shoes were lined with lead. Everything was a little duller here, empty of the brilliance I was used to seeing. I didn't know if it was because I didn't consider it home anymore or because the mortal world simply lacked the magick and beauty that I had grown used to in Elphame. On either side of the Gate, between realms, stood two Seers and two Aos Si soldiers, who rotated to guard the Gate. It was never left unattended. We weren't a trustful lot on either side. We schemed and plotted and reached for power any place we could. They let me pass as they always had, but I didn't doubt they'd drag me back to Elphame by my hair if I stepped out of line. No one was allowed to scare the mortals, not even a retired one like myself.

The bells over Whitwick chimed once to signal someone had stepped through. It wasn't a call to arms as it once had been, but it still stung. It was a reminder that I wasn't one of them anymore. I watched my father coming down the street to meet me. He motioned with a wave, and I met him a block away from the crowd who had come to see who was visiting. Every time I came, I felt like they were inches away from poking me with a stick, like some sort of sideshow animal.

"I missed you at lunch today. Are you okay?" His eyes scanned me for any sign I was injured. "What's wrong, Perdi?"

"Zephyr and Nix are missing." I didn't bother trying to hide the anguish in my voice. Anyone who looked at me could see I was sad, and I was okay with it. Pain wasn't new to Whitwick. "Has anyone come through the Gate? Have you seen them?"

"No, I haven't. No one has come from Elphame. They changed guards last night and again this morning. You were the last to come into Whitwick, you and Nix. But he left with you, didn't he?"

"Yes, they went missing together this morning," I replied. Each word felt like it was caught, having to squeeze past a rock of unshed tears in my throat.

"Nix has never come to Whitwick without coming to see me first. He asks permission to enter into the garden to bring back fruit and vegetables for you in Elphame. And Zephyr? He's not come here at all. But I'll have the Guardians search and ask the Seers to help."

"Don't bother with the Seers. They won't tell you anything. They never do." I glanced back at the Gate. The Seers didn't say much—and never about the future. They were entrusted with the knowledge for reasons I didn't know. If they had the answers, why not share them? It would save the rest of us a lot of hurt. They thought that if they told us, our fates would change and never in our favor.

"They may not tell us a thing, but they'll be able to help us look. They're better at finding Fae than I am," he answered. He stepped back from me and pointed at my hip. "Perdi, why is your shoulder bag moving like you have two feral cats stuffed in there?"

I opened my bag, and the shadows spilled out. They quickly found darkness to hide in, around trees and flowers. "They're Zephyr's. I don't know how to hide them as he did. I couldn't just march in here with these trailing wildly behind me. Things are already testy. Imagine what everyone would think."

"So, you put them in a bag rather than ask them how to hide them?" my dad asked, and I frowned.

"Of course I asked them, dad. They don't know either," I snapped and squeezed my eyes shut. I groaned my frustration. "I asked them, but they didn't know any more than I did. It has to do with wrapping them in my soul and releasing them as needed. I don't know how to do that. Zephyr always controlled them, and I never thought I'd need a reason to learn. I only know how to call them, not hide them."

"I did not mean to insult you, Perdi. I meant to say...I don't know. I was trying to help and feel lost in helping you in any matter that is Fae."

"I'm sorry, too. I know you're trying to help. I'm just scared." I leaned into him. "I tried to stuff them into a jar, but they wouldn't get in. They say they are insulted."

"Wouldn't you be? I understand you panicked, but you will need to find a better solution than trapping them in a bag." He pulled back and kissed my forehead. "Perdi, tell me how I can help."

"Make sure that if this doesn't end well, I don't burn everything to the ground."

"I have seen you with the shadows, as well as Zephyr. When you come here, they're always behind you. I watch them slither about, as does everyone else. They duck in and out, and you don't even notice them. You've grown so accustomed to them that you only notice when they are gone, not when they're with you."

I looked at the shadows. "You follow me in here?"

"We follow you everywhere, Perdi. Zephyr doesn't like you out of his sight," they replied.

I nodded, then smiled. "That little spy."

My dad pulled back from our hug. "If anyone could stop you from burning the world, it would be them. They are always there, never too far from you."

I glanced back to the lawn at my side. If I didn't know the shadows were there, I'd have missed them. They blended as well as Zephyr when they were trying to hide. "Let's go look around."

They groaned in hundreds of voices and rolled back to my side, up my legs and back into the bag. "We do not like this feeling of being trapped."

"Neither do I," I responded and cringed at the thought. "I'm sorry. It won't be for long. I'll figure out how to hide you, so I don't have to do this again."

"We will think about how Zephyr does it. Perhaps there is a way, and we are uncertain of the words," they answered.

My father nudged me. "Ask them for help, Perdi. Do not assume they'll just know what you want. They've spent lifetimes with Zephyr. They've not had nearly as long to get to know you and your needs."

I nodded and opened the bag to them rolling over each other in a small storm for only my eyes. "Whatever happens, do not let me kill everyone. If my rage takes over and I command you to let it burn, don't listen to me. Take me somewhere safe and keep me there until I am no longer a threat."

"If this doesn't end well, Perdi, we fear we'll keep you away forever."

"So be it," I answered.

"It will be difficult since we'll want to watch it burn with you."

My father stepped back. "Let us search and pray you don't start any fires. I will ask around."

My father went one way, and I went the other. When we were free from prying eyes, I opened my bag and let the shadows pull me from place to place. They tracked Fae magick throughout Whitwick. Wherever Elphame energy rolled, we stopped to check it out. We found every other creature — wee folk who were always around — but not a Soul-Eater and no gnome that was Nix. Each time we stopped, I told them to return to Elphame. They left without needing to be asked. They, like me, feared anything that could take a Soul-Eater and a gnome in one grab.

My reasons for sending them home had little to do with whoever was foolish enough to touch my family and everything to do with a fresh coat of dread painted on my soul. My nerves were frayed at the ends, and the thought of leaving Fae in the mortal world tugged at a part of me that screamed a warning for only my ears. I couldn't put my finger on it, but in the hills of Whitwick, I felt it best to bring Elphame home. We searched every inch of land and surrounding forests. We went farther than any other soul could be felt. I didn't find Zephyr or Nix, nor could I find the source of my panic.

"Do you feel that?" I asked the shadows.

"The dread?" they asked. "We feel it."

"Where is it coming from?"

"We don't know. It's everywhere. It's pouring off you but is also a lingering smell as if dread was here before us."

"I don't have a good feeling," I replied.

"Nor do we," they answered.

My father met me back at the Gate after spending three hours searching. "No one has seen Zephyr or Nix. There is talk, however."

"Talk of what?" I asked.

"War, retribution, hate," he answered. "I'm sorry, but not all wounds are healed or ever will be. They are glad for two less Fae walking the earth."

I nodded. "I don't blame them. I want to, but I understand their grief."

"It's rage, Perdi, not just grief. They mourn lives that'll never be returned to them. And they blame Elphame for that pain. They cannot see beyond it, to peace, to who helped save us all from the fates we once lived. Not having a Gate, some sort of wall between us, feeds their worry. I fear, if Zephyr or Nix were found on these lands, injured, they would not leave here alive."

"Has there been any fighting or killing of Fae?"

He shook his head. "Not that I know of. But eventually, once the fear is gone, it'll be replaced with foolish bravery and fury. It'll need to go somewhere."

"Elphame," I muttered. "Fools. They will never win against Fae—not even if all of Whitwick were halflings and could walk the fields of Elphame."

"Indeed. But they see you that survived and think they have a chance."

"I died, Dad. I didn't survive. I was killed and brought back," I answered. "If I have to fight every day for my next one, they stand no chance of surviving a single minute there."

"The neighboring villages have joined in on that anger. Although they've tasted nothing of the Fae, they are mad simply because they are mortal and feel any slight against Whitwick is a slight against themselves. They speak of war."

I sighed. "There will always be war."

"As long as there are men to hold swords, men will fall on them."

"Dad, if any mortal crosses that Gate with a sword, there will be war," I answered. "And I won't be fighting for the mortal world. I'll be fighting for my home."

"I know," he answered. "It doesn't help that Elphame has guards stationed here. I know why they're here, as do you, but the others do not see that they are here to keep Elphame back. All they see are guards at the Gate, and the town fears them. Fear is an ugly creature that only grows and matures over time."

"One problem at a time, Dad. I'll come back when I can, and we can sort this out. I hear what you're saying, and I understand the urgency of it. I just can't do anything about it right now. But I'll come back and work to see how Fae can make amends, how to lessen the fear. I'll tell the guards at the Gate, make sure they know there could be an uprising at any minute."

"I'll do what I can here, Perdi, to buy you time to find your friends," he answered.

"I love you, Dad." I hugged him again and left him on the street with the others. They were happy to see me go. My dad wasn't ever happy about it.

"My lady." The Aos Si guard dipped his head when I approached him.

"No one from the mortal world steps foot in Elphame and no Fae can enter Whitwick until I return. Those returning home can cross, but that is it." I finally spat out the words I didn't want to say. I didn't want to police both realms. I didn't want to be anyone's caretaker. "Keep a close watch. They're getting restless, and I wouldn't doubt there will be a revolt soon."

He looked hard at me. "Are you certain? What about your father?"

I sighed. If I showed my dad favoritism, it would only make things worse. "Unless his life is at risk, no one crosses. If they ask, tell them I said I would return, then we can discuss the talk of an uprising. And until then, the Gate is closed by me."

"As you wish. And those who force the matter?" Aos Si liked clear-cut rules. They lived and breathed a code of exactness. Although they could outperform anyone on the battlefield, even in the gray areas, they were black-and-white thinkers. There was a right way and a wrong way of doing things.

"Kill no one, but they don't cross. Remember, they do not heal like Fae. The smallest of injuries can kill them," I answered, then realized I hadn't included myself as a mortal. I didn't say *we*. I'd said *them*. I had already decided I wasn't one of them anymore. I was Fae. "Call me if someone tries. I'll return."

He dropped his head in a quick nod. "I wish you success in finding our Commander and Nix. If I may be of any service, please let me know. I, of course, will send word if I see or hear anything that can be of any assistance."

"Does it bother you to be stuck guarding the Gate rather than searching?" I asked. It would bother me, but I always had my nose in places it never should be, hence all the running for my life since the first time I stepped through the Gate.

"I would like to say no. It is an honor to have been selected by Zephyr for this duty. He has shown considerable trust in me to believe I am ready for this. To be chosen by my Commander to stand as the first line of defense is an honor I cannot begin to put into words."

"But what do you really want to say? If no one ever knew what came out of your mouth next, what would you say?" I asked and dragged my finger across my heart. "My lips are sealed."

"I'd say I feel useless, my lady. I owe a great debt to him," he answered. "Before Zephyr, only one in ten Aos Si children lived to become full-ranking Aos Si. Had it not been for him, I would have perished those first few years. Standing here feels like I am not honoring who he helped me become."

"And now, how many children survive with Zephyr as Commander?"

"We all do. Even though not all become fully ranked members, he doesn't allow a single one of us to perish under his watch."

"What happens to those who do not become ranked?" I asked.

"Zephyr doesn't give up. Some have been in training their entire lives. Those who he believes will never become more, he grants them positions within the Dark Court guard. But honestly, Zephyr just doesn't give up. He saved my life."

"I think he's saved all of our lives a time or two." I smiled at the memory of his pep talks.

"For many years, others thought I was his favorite. But the truth is, he kept me by his side, day and night because I was going to kill myself the moment he wasn't looking. I wasn't his favorite. He was just there to keep me alive," he answered. "Once, the only way of out Aos Si was death. I wanted out bad enough that I was going to do it. After longer than you've graced this world, I wanted death. But soon, my will to live grew bigger than my wish for death."

"Is it still that way, having to die to leave?" I asked.

"No. Zephyr outlawed forced service once he became our Commander, but old habits die hard. I thought that would be my only way out. And once Solas became our king, he allowed those who became his guard to leave when they no longer wished to serve. Because of them, death is not our only option."

"I'm happy you're alive." The smile I gave him was genuine.

"Although I will treasure those words, you do not know me. How could you be happy one way or the other?"

"Zephyr fought for you to live. If he saw something in you, I trust what he saw, and I am grateful for whatever purpose he sees in you," I answered and leaned forward. Some words were so heavy that they could only be spoken in a whisper. "You're not the only one who wanted it to end, who wanted the mercy only found in death. He saved me many times. I owe him my life."

He nodded his head and sighed. He understood what I meant in ways many others wouldn't. "Now you see my predicament."

Beside him, Lily — the Seer who guarded the Gate — stepped forward with a tip of her head. "Perdi, it is lovely to see you once again." She smiled. I had seen her at Blood and Bones. She had sent me home once, saved my life and gifted me the very blade that killed her sister-in-arms, Solene.

"Lily, I'd like to say it's always a pleasure, but Seers don't seem to talk unless they're the bringers of bad news," I replied.

She rolled her eyes. The gesture made me grin. She wasn't like the others. She was cockier and built of better things. I had yet to see her step back when Zephyr or Solas walked into the room. I liked her more for that.

"That is not true. You just don't seem to want to talk to us unless it is bad news you are seeking. When that is the only topic you wish to discuss, you're bound to think that is the only conversation we have," Lily replied.

"Sorry. That wasn't fair of me to say." I winced a little at her truth. I had only ever spoken to them when I needed something. "How are you, Lily?"

"I come with bad news," she answered and when I felt myself pale and my stomach flop, she laughed. "You deserved that, Perdi. I don't have bad news. I offer you guidance, if you're willing to accept it."

"Yeah, I deserved that." I smiled, but it came out on the spicy side of happy. I took a step back, then grimaced. Standing this close to someone who knew my fate made me feel like I stood too close to death.

Putting distance between myself and death was instinctual.

She raised her brows at the new space between us. "Your fear is misplaced. I have no ill feelings toward you."

"It's not that, Lily. It is intimidating, standing with you. It feels like you can see my death and won't give me a courtesy call."

"If it helps, I usually see your death dozens of times a day, each in different ways. You have been a walking disaster since you stepped through that Gate. But you've always managed just fine without my warnings," she answered, and I scrunched my face. No one wants to know when they'll die, yet everyone wants to see if they can change that date to something further down the line. "Every choice you make opens a new path. On that path, hundreds of choices lead to various other paths. It is not as simple as saying you will die at a specific time, on a particular day, in a certain way. Trust that when you do, nothing can be done about it because you, Perdi, will choose that ending yourself. And with your death, you will shake both worlds."

"That's not very comforting." I balked.

She shrugged. "I could tell you it will be painless, but I'd be lying, and you'd know it."

"Death isn't painless. It'll hurt. It always does. Maybe not for me because I'll be dead and won't care, but it'll hurt others," I answered. "So no, don't bother lying."

"It'll be for love," she answered and closed her eyes. I watched a slight smile curl and a sigh escape. "It will mean everything you want it to mean and nothing less, and it will be magnificent. The Gods and Goddesses will come to watch, and history will remember your name."

"Worth it then, I say," I replied and felt fine with what she saw. There was no better reason to die than for love. "So, what guidance do you have for me today? How to keep the mortal world from setting a fire they can't put out? How to keep them from using my body to smother the flames? How to save my friends? How to build a bloody Gate out of thin air? Or how to keep Orrian from ripping down the entire forest because she wants light from every direction? Jesus, how many fruit trees can a fairy need?"

She blinked at me for a moment before she started to laugh. "That's what you all have been arguing about here? Building a Gate?" She laughed again until her eyes glittered with tears. She bent at the waist and laughed until she needed to prop her hands on her knees to keep herself standing. She stood and dabbed her cheeks, shaking her head. The look on her surprised face made me laugh with her. "Oh, that's rich. Perdi, there is no Gate to rebuild. The magick to build one, I've not heard of."

"What about the first Gate?" I asked. "The magick had to be here for us to make the first one."

"This is true, and I mean no disrespect, but the first Gate took three Darkmore witches, who, respectfully, were ten times the witch you are. It also took the will of Elphame, the very songs of my people, to allow it. You are one witch, without a song or a realm who wills it so," she answered. "Honestly, without all the rest, do you believe you can wield the kind of magick it would take to do it? The power you'd have to hold within your soul would be astronomical. The amount of magick needed almost killed the three Darkmore witches."

"No," I answered. "I honestly don't think I could do it. I think it would fry my brain, and I'd burst into a million Crow feathers."

"Then that is not a question you need to have answered. You already know that it cannot be done, at least not by you and not by any other power alive." She told me what I already knew. "As to saving the mortal realm, you can't stop them from burning down their own community any more than you can stop Fae from torching their own backyards. You can try to put out the flames, one at a time, but soon, the blaze will be too great, and your home will burn with theirs. Or you can protect your home and land and watch the rest burn around you. Those are your choices and the only ones you have. Let them burn or burn with them."

"It doesn't sound like I have many options." I groaned.

"No, you don't, but that is the life you've chosen. As for Orrian, let her tear the forest apart until she's happy. She deserves the light, and the trees can grow elsewhere. She is Fairy and has called her people home. It is her duty to ensure they all have food. Let her fill her land and feed her people. Let her be happy. It's what we're all looking for."

"It certainly is, thank you," I replied. Orrian was worth clear-cutting swaths of land and more.

Lily looked out over the crowd, always watching, always ready to pounce. "But if I may, the guidance I've come with may help you with your other matter. It may or may not solve a thing, but it is still valuable information to have." She motioned her head to the Aos Si guard. "The trainees, those who are not full rank? That is where you'll find the help you need. When you first met them in the caves of the Sluagh, they risked death and dishonor to help you at Blood and Bones. To go against Zephyr's order is a death sentence, and they still showed up for you. They'll do it again."

I smiled, recalling the night I showed up in their cave, asking them to help me do the impossible — get in and out of the Court of Blood and Bones, steal a blade made of blood and bones, and kill the Caller of Crows. I huffed a laugh at the memories. "They're good men."

"They are Zephyr's and Solas' most utterly loyal men. They're not oathed and will still not flinch in the face of death. They are the men who have not been given up on, and they, in turn, will not give up on you or your call. If anyone can help you find those who you seek, they are the men you want guiding your way. I do not know your Nix well, but the trainees do. Nix has delivered them fresh fruit, vegetables, food and flowers from home. He comes almost every day, with pieces of home, on his way to collect from your garden to do the same for you. He stops and asks us all to smell flowers, to see if they smell of the Golden Court, since Zephyr refuses to come here himself to ask. The trainees feel very protective of him. The moment Nix comes, they drop everything they're doing to offer him aid, joke with him, laugh with him and share meals with him. They see Nix as someone worth protecting, and that is a hard thing to do with Aos Si. To have their protection because they want to do it and not because it is their duty. Or perhaps it is nothing, and I'm simply worried for Zephyr and my friend, Nix."

"It isn't nothing. You wouldn't waste your time talking any more than I would," I replied. I would take what Lily said as seriously as the situation. Seers didn't offer mere guidance. There was power in their words, meaning in every sentence. They didn't waste their breath on idle chitchat. It was who they were, even when we only came for bad news.

"And that is where you'll find the most loyal to you. The Aos Si see you as someone worth following. That is nearly impossible with them. You freed their Commander. You came into Blood and Bones and wouldn't leave without three of their strongest while bleeding from a stab wound. You damn near died to kill Solene. They see you as someone worth honor, worth standing beside in war."

I smiled and felt my face flush. "I didn't do it for the honor of it."

"That's exactly why they'll follow you. You looked death in the eyes because it was the right thing to do. And now they'll gaze into the same abyss for you."

"Can you bring other Seers to the Gate? The Aos Si are needed at home," I finally announced.

"Of course," she answered and smiled that I would heed her word. "We will guard the Gate as you've instructed. There shall be only minor issues once the men of this village learn that women from Elphame cannot be slapped aside as easily as their own. They've not enjoyed our interventions so far."

"What interventions?" I asked.

She grinned, and I instantly felt uncomfortable. I fought the urge to shrink away. "Those who step too far outside what you or I would consider moral or righteous behavior."

"This is likely the reason the mortals are railing against the Fae," I added.

"Most certainly. We've interrupted their ways. But if they wish to war over their need to beat their wives and children, I am very much ready for the fight. I will not allow the weak to be kicked as dogs, not for anyone's people, and not to stave off a war. No order given would force me to allow it," Lily answered and went back to her post. I agreed with her. I'd sooner war than allow the weak to be beaten upon. She looked back to the Gate. "Another has come to take the place of the Aos Si."

"Send for me if things continue to heat up," I said as I moved to leave, then turned back and risked asking a question. "Lily, do you know where they are? I know you can't tell me the fates of others, but can you just tell me if they're still alive?

"When your father asked me, I was truthful. I haven't seen them. I can't see their fates beyond this morning. The last I see of Zephyr's fate is him sending his shadows to you, but I can't see the reason for it. I saw them grab you and you being dropped into a forest. I fear, Perdi, I do not see anything more of you beyond when you broke the branch in half and held it in your hands as two daggers. I can't see you anymore."

"That can't be good," I groaned.

"I do not know what it means. It could simply mean that my fate is tied to yours. But it is the same for all Seers. For the first time, we are blind to Fae and Elphame. All of our fates are linked to outcomes not yet unfolded. Whatever is coming will affect us all."

"Thank you." I touched her hand and squeezed. "For now and before. I never had the chance to say thank you for how you helped me in Blood and Bones."

"I wish I could have helped you sooner. It was a careful dance we were all forced into. I never thanked you, either. Solene was cruel and did many things I wish I didn't know and didn't dream of."

"You're welcome."

"Perdi, you have hard decisions coming. I can feel it in my bones," she added. "I do not envy you for what is coming with your name on it. Trust your gut. Trust that Solas will surround you with only the strongest.

There's a dread hanging in the air, and it's following you around."

"I feel it, too," I replied.

"I wish you luck, Perdi." There was nothing more we could say about the unknown fate following me. "Trust Zephyr's men, but remember, they are his men and not yours."

I frowned. "What does that mean?"

"Exactly what I said. The Aos Si will follow you, but they are utterly loyal to Zephyr, his calling, training and his word. They will not go against him and survive twice. They got one free pass for helping you in Blood and Bones, but Zephyr will not allow them to have two. Do not get them killed because you pushed them to abandon their duty."

I nodded. I wanted to say I wouldn't do that...but I would. As selfish as it was to admit it, to save Zephyr and Nix, I'd have risked them all. "Thanks, Lily."

"Don't thank me yet. This shitshow has only just begun, and I feel it will boil over and burn us all."

"Your mind must be a dark place to be. As always, it's been a delight." I grinned and walked away.

The shadows wrapped around me when I stepped back onto Elphame soil. Commanded to take me to Solas, they brought me to my front door. When I opened my mouth to blast them for not listening to me, as I couldn't feel Solas anywhere near me, they swirled at the front door. A small white box wrapped in a red silk ribbon sat on the steps.

"When you ask to be brought to a person, we stop at the places where we feel their energy. Sometimes we have to scour Elphame until we find them. We do not have a link to Solas, not as Zephyr did. And since we find it difficult to read the link you share with Solas, we are left with searching. We do not have access to your pearls, as we did with Zephyr," they said. "We saw this on the doorstep and knew you would want to see it more than go to Solas. Were we wrong in this? We are still learning, and you are a difficult learning curve for us. You're too much emotion for us to read a single thought. You want many things, but we can only give one thing at a time."

"What is it?" I asked. "And yes, you were right in stopping here."

"We do not know what it is." They twisted around it and pulled back. "Whatever is in there is not poisonous, so long as you don't eat it. We do not believe it will physically harm you, either."

"What about emotionally? Some pains in the heart are worse than losing a limb."

"We don't know. You measure your pain and hurt on scales that kill most people."

I shrugged. That was true. "Carry it to the dining table for me? I'm not opening it without Solas."

They scooped it up, and I followed them into the dining room. I leaned toward the small white box but pulled back. I wasn't brave enough to open it. Curiosity would not kill this Crow.

"Go get Solas," I said, then called them back. "Wait. Go find him and tell him I need him home. Don't snatch him. *Ask* him."

I paced in front of the table. A box no bigger than a fist sat innocuously on the table, yet I was terrified of what was inside. It wouldn't physically harm me, but it could destroy my soul. I trusted nothing in Elphame to be harmless. Not even love was free in the land of tricks and riddles. When most people here died at the hands of their loved ones, caution was a wise choice.

"Perdi." Solas stepped into the room. "Thank you for not sending them to pluck me mid-sentence."

I pointed at the table. "It was on the doorstep when we got back."

"I know, the shadows told me. I asked the guards. They didn't see anyone come or go, and I couldn't sense who had come. There's no energy lingering in the air outside that shouldn't be here."

He stepped up to the table and picked up the box like it was nothing. When he opened it, I stepped back and gasped at his audacity. He was bold where I was not. He was brave where I was prudent.

"What is it? Is it an ear? Please tell me it's not Nix's little ear." My words were twisted around the sob stuck in my throat. "Is it a finger?"

"What? No, Perdi. I would have smelled the blood or flesh…as would you have. You're not so mortal to have missed that smell," Solas answered and lifted out a small purple flower. "Wolf's Bane."

"Why would someone send us that, a single flower?"

"It's not just a flower. It's what it represents. Hatred," Solas answered. "This is a warning. Whatever they send or do next won't be just a warning."

"Shouldn't they have sent that *before* they took Zeph and Nix?" I asked.

He shrugged. "They probably sent a warning that we overlooked. I don't know what the warning is now, but I'm also not going to listen."

"Neither am I," I answered. "I'm going to save that flower for their funeral."

Solas barked a laugh. "As if there will be bodies left to bury."

"Then I'll toss it into the fire we set."

He put the flower back into the box and pushed it across the table. "I can smell your father. How was the search in Whitwick?"

"It's unsettling you can do that, just breathe me in and know what I've been doing," I answered.

"I can only do that with you," he answered. "With others, I can smell familiar smells and usually guess it right, such as what territory they've been in, who they've been with, that sort of thing. But with you, I know your smell better than anything else. It's the same with your emotions. I've smelled your tears a thousand times. I know how they taste, how they feel between my fingers. I know what each smell represents because I feel the emotions with you."

I nodded as if I understood what he meant. I didn't. Not really. It was a weird answer, but nothing about Fae behavior was normal. "I met with my dad and searched Whitwick, the forests, and beyond. They're not there and haven't been seen. But he did say something interesting. The mortal realm is angry with the Fae, but it's way more than I had thought."

"Can you blame them?"

"No, I can't. But sooner rather than later, there will be an uprising," I said, and cringed at the thought of man against Fae.

"That risk has always been there."

"Not like this, Solas. They are free now. The Gate is open, and I don't think they're as scared as they should be. I think their anger is clouding their judgment. They don't remember just how bloody terrifying the Fae are."

He nodded. "We'll burn that bridge when we cross it."

"I told my dad I'd go back, when I could, to help him sort it out."

"*We* will go back, Perdi. I will do what I can to help. I think this is something we should do together to show them that things can be different," he answered and touched my arm. "If you're okay with that?"

"I give you an hour before you start looking for a new Gate to hammer into the ground yourself." I rubbed my temples. The tension in my shoulders had wormed its way up and had a stranglehold on my head. "I spoke to Lily at the Gate. She said those in Whitwick who have an issue are those the Seers have had to stop from beating their wives and children. She also mentioned that the trainees should be brought back to help with the search. I've called them home and replaced the guards with more Seers. I hope that's all right."

"If Lily mentioned it, it was wise to listen. I'd have done the same thing. Whitwick isn't going to enjoy more Seers there. I'd rather deal with a pissed-off Aos Si than Lily or her people."

"Same here," I replied. "No news from Zeno?"

"No, they're looking in the usual hiding places of the Aos Si."

I stared out of the windows over our little slice of Elphame and prayed I wouldn't burn the beauty of it to the ground to find my family. The scarred window made my eyes water at the memories of each fight we'd had and survived. Solas hugged me from behind. As his hot breath rolled down my neck and nipped at my skin, I knew he was thinking the same thing as I was. We were war and death, and we were pissed off. If I cared at all, I'd pity those who had my people. But I didn't care about them or that they'd never be able to cover the cost of the rage mounting in my stomach.

He picked me up, and I thought about fighting against him. I didn't want to sleep. I didn't want to close my eyes. But he sat me on the kitchen counter and opened a bag of cookies rather than tucking me into bed as I thought he would.

"The last time we stood here, eating cookies, the world was crumbling around us." Solas passed me a cookie. "But even then, in the face of both of our deaths, the deaths of our people, we found a way out. And that was against the most powerful in all Elphame. Now, we are the strongest. We'll find Zephyr and Nix."

"You're always so sure about everything. Don't you ever have any doubts?" I asked.

"I'm most sure when I'm with you. But I wasn't always this way. Long before you and before Zephyr, it was a battle. And it wasn't all Solene and her grip. It was hard to see my life as anything more than death on two legs and the constant fighting and grabs for more territory. Then I met Zephyr, and it became about our people. I learned a lot from Zephyr, and he was a harsh taskmaster. He never let me falter. He has this way, you know? To build you up, even when everyone else worked to break you down. I'm certain in all I do because I know that he would be just as certain. He gives strength when you want to give up."

"He's irritating with his pep talks, and you're not the first to mention them," I replied. "But they oddly help, even when you don't want them to."

"Nix is worse. Holy hell, is he worse." Solas laughed. "I remember once when I left the Golden Court and came home. I was well and truly done. I couldn't stomach it. They call me the nightmare, but not even I could watch what they did. I sent word to Nix to return from Whitwick. I couldn't do it anymore. And he did. Nix returned and marched into my home in the middle of the night. I woke up to him standing on my chest with a knife to my throat. I never even felt him coming, the sneaky bugger. He demanded I suck it up and return. If you were Taken and no one was there to protect you, he'd find me and leave me splayed for the vultures to pick at my liver over and over."

I laughed. "That must have been a year before I was Taken."

"Yes, about ten months before. Did Nix tell you?"

I shook my head. "No. But he was reading about the Gods the year before I came here. He loved the story of the Titan Prometheus, who stole fire from Zeus and gave it to man. As a punishment, Zeus sentenced Prometheus to eternal torment. Prometheus was tied to a rock, and an eagle was sent to eat Prometheus' liver every day. Prometheus' liver regrew overnight, only for the cycle to continue to the next day."

"And our Gods and Goddesses are tough on us?" Solas smiled.

"Look around, Solas. Doesn't it feel like we gave fire to man when we destroyed the Gate?"

"*We* didn't destroy it, Perdi. I did," he corrected. "You shouldn't take the blame for something you didn't do."

"And you need to stop taking all the blame when you weren't the only one responsible. You didn't destroy the Gate. Solene did," I countered. "Solas, I could have stopped you at any time. I chose not to."

"You would have had to kill me to stop me."

"Ending your life had nothing to do with it. I didn't stop you because I don't think I wanted to. I didn't want the Gate. Deep down, I think I searched for other ways because I wanted the Gate gone. Had I wanted you to stop, if it was the right thing to do to protect our people, I would have taken your life. It would have killed me to do it, but I would have," I answered and squeezed his hand. "We both had a part in what happened to the Gate, both for different reasons. You were forced. I gave up on it willingly."

"This is the first time you've said that out loud," he replied. "I didn't know you felt that way. That must be some weight you've been carrying around."

I nodded. "No different than you."

"If I'm not being crushed under the weight of my decisions, can I even call myself a king?" He sighed. I didn't envy his position any more than he envied mine. "And now, we're both tied to the rock and having our livers eaten for stealing back freedom for mortals."

"We shouldn't have given fire to those who were not ready to have it. Now we'll burn for it. I can feel the vultures circling."

"Was Prometheus ever saved?" Solas asked.

"After eons of torture, yes." I rubbed the center of my chest. Nothing I did could relieve the pressure that was building. "But I don't think anyone is coming to save any of us."

"You can feel it coming, can't you?" Solas groaned. "Soul-Eaters always know when other souls are going to die."

"I felt it the last time I was in Whitwick. I can't tell you who or what it is, but I can feel it in my gut. In the hills behind my dad's house, dread hangs in the air and coats the trees like fresh raindrops. Something is coming, and I think we'll find out sooner rather than later."

"Let's focus on one thing at a time. We will deal with tomorrow, tomorrow. Today, we go to war to save our friends, our family. Tomorrow, we will war against what's coming that day. Keep your gear on, little Crow. I don't think we'll need to take it back off for a while." Solas hopped off the counter and positioned himself between my knees.

"We opened the Gate and invited this madness in. Now we bloody well better figure out how to send it back, or we might as well call the next war, The Never-Ending Battle." I scowled at the thought.

"We've had two of those already. Combined, they lasted almost a century."

I rolled my eyes. "Of course you have. Don't you guys know what peace is?"

"I don't even know what the word means," he joked.

"How does Elphame not run out of people?"

"We breed like rabbits." He grinned and wiggled his eyebrows.

"Not happening."

He pulled back. "Never?"

"Not at the moment, no," I replied. "A few months ago, I thought I was pregnant. It didn't feel like good news, Solas."

"I know. Zephyr told me. The thought was both happy and frightening."

I nodded. "I see children in my future, but I also see war. I don't want both. I don't think I'd live through that. I don't think my sanity could survive the constant threat to our children."

"Looks like Elphame will learn peace if it kills them," he whispered into my mouth as he kissed me.

"Cookies and war, then peace," I countered. "Priorities."

"You always say the sweetest things to me."

Chapter Four

I never thought I'd see the day when Faolan stood in Solas' home not surrounded by guards. The fact that he still had all his blood inside his body was even more surprising. But there he was, with Oisin, and both were in good health, not even a limp between them. Unfortunately, I knew many firsts were on the horizon, each as unique and uncomfortable as an enemy smiling to your face while commenting on the artwork on your walls.

Oisin leaned into my ear. "I'm as shocked as you are."

I shook my head. "Sorry?"

"We're standing here, and it isn't because we're captive and chained in your jails."

"Captive? The Dark Court has no prisons," I answered.

"Where do you put your enemies?" he asked.

"We kill them," Solas answered from the other side of the room. "We don't house and feed them like pets."

I stepped away from Oisin and reached for Solas, who stood at my side to face Faolan and Oisin. "I don't mean to be rude, but I'm not here for small talk. Do you have any news?" I asked, hopeful.

Faolan shook his head. "I'm sorry, Perdi. Nothing. We've searched the Unseelie territories and questioned everyone who would be foolish enough to try something like this. But there isn't a soul in my territory who could take Zephyr. And if Nix was with him, nothing short of death would take Nix from him. And to be honest, no one would take Nix."

"Why, because you don't see him as a threat?" I asked, defensive.

"Just the opposite," Oisin answered before Faolan could. "We all know Nix is a greater threat than he gets credit for, all on his own. But no... It's simply because no one dislikes him. And even if they did, no one would be stupid enough to take him. If it wasn't the entire Dark Court coming for him, Orrian and her people would savage any man dumb enough to try it. Even I would come for whoever harmed him. He is a friend to me...to all of us."

"Neither of them would just up and leave," I snapped, feeling the grip on my calm slipping. "Search again. They're here somewhere. Look harder. Search better, damn it. You're a king, Faolan. Don't tell me you have searched all your lands and have come back empty-handed. They didn't just vanish."

He put up his hands in surrender. "I know that. But they are not in my territory. I'm not hiding their whereabouts from you, Perdi. You're free to poke around in my head if you'd like. I'm not hiding anything from you."

"Zephyr has been in your territory over twenty times in the last month alone. There's a reason for that," Solas countered, and even that number was a surprise to me.

"You know the reason he comes," Faolan answered. "He comes because he doesn't trust me. He comes because Parrish's people thought they'd find refuge with me. And as you see, I'm still standing, so Zephyr has found no reason to kill me."

"There are plenty of reasons to kill you, Faolan," I answered.

"Perdi." Solas lifted my hand to his mouth. It was a simple kiss, but behind it was the power to soothe the fear twisting in my stomach. "This is not the way. We're both feeling desperate and lashing out at those around us. Faolan is right. If he's still standing, Zephyr found nothing there."

"I have nothing to hide," Faolan added again.

I stepped forward, propelled by anger and unhealed wounds. "You have a great deal to hide, Faolan."

"Not about this. And if you need to dig around my head to know, then so be it." Faolan opened his arms. "Not all secrets are worth keeping...not anymore. I swore I'd never stand against you again, and I haven't. Do what you must, so we may move on and find your people."

"My *family*. They are my *family*," I corrected him. I was reaching forward to grab his hand when Oisin stepped in between us. Solas tensed and stilled the air behind me, but he didn't say a word. He knew I would say enough for the both of us. I looked Oisin dead in the eyes. "Do we have a problem?"

"I give you my word, Perdi. Faolan may be right. Not all secrets are worth keeping, but he is my king, and not all secrets are yours to have. I swear on any oath you want, your people are not in the Winter Court territory, nor are we withholding information as to their whereabouts or who would have taken them."

"It's not enough. I'm sorry, Oisin," I answered.

"You don't accept my word?" He looked hurt. "I've never lied to you...not once."

"And you've also never loved another as I love them. I'd peel your mind like an onion if I had to," I answered and grabbed Faolan's hand. "And if Faolan hadn't offered this freely, I would do the same to him."

"Do it," Faolan finally said. "I'd rather you do it than have you always wonder. Wonder is a scary place to live. It drives wars and hate. And I would sooner do this simple task than have my people suffer for my fear again. There truly are no secrets worth the suffering of my people."

"If you do this, Perdi, I'll never look at you the same." Oisin stepped away.

"And if I don't, I'll never look at you the same," I answered. "I can live without your friendship and trust, but I can't live without my family."

With his hand in mine, I let my Malice rove through Faolan's soul. I didn't shred his memories as my Malice wanted, but I did read him like an open book. With ease, I roamed. I could see his hurt, his shame, tasted regret but saw no deed that should be punished. Like Zephyr, I found no fault to hang him with. Acts done long ago—he was already punishing himself enough for them. He had told me the truth and held nothing back. I pulled back and looked at Faolan.

"Thank you," I whispered. "Your soul is a dark place to be."

He nodded. "Didn't like what you saw either, did you?"

"Some of it, no," I answered. I wouldn't throw stones. It looked eerily like my own baggage.

"That makes two of us," he replied. "Now what? How can we be of help? Just say the word."

"Are you doing this to repair the relationship between our courts?" I asked. Before I'd ask for his help, I had to hear him say the words out loud, the 'why' behind his offer. There were dozens of reasons floating around in his mind, but I needed him to say it, and he needed to hear my words in return.

"Not our courts, no. But between us, as people. Our courts are fine, but we are not, and there is a long road between us that feels like hell each time I walk it. We are neighbors, and I'd like it if we could begin to mend what has been done. I would like to try. I am not so foolish as to think we will be friends, but I would like the hate to fade into something less scary. I'd like to not fear for my people each time I feel you near my border."

"I don't know if we can mend things, Faolan. I want to say yes because I want your help finding Zeph and Nix, but I won't lie to your face," I answered him with the same level of truth. "I don't trust you."

"Fair enough." He nodded.

"But I know what you're saying is true. I felt it when I was in your head. I'm willing to give you a sliver of benefit. And we can work on the rest as it comes. As for your people, I wouldn't harm them because you ticked me off. They're safe," I answered, and he nodded, looking slightly more at ease than when he first walked through the door. I turned to Oisin. "You, I trust completely. I know where I stand with you. I'm sorry I put you in a bad place between your king and me."

"I appreciate that." He spoke, but appreciation was not what I heard. "It wouldn't be the first time you put me in a position I didn't like, and I'm certain it won't be the last."

I nodded. I did not envy where he stood. "Why are you here, Oisin?"

"Faolan requested I assist him," he answered. His words dropped to the floor like stones. He wasn't happy with what I had done. "Do you actually care, though? My King has commanded I help. So here I am."

"This is uncomfortable. Usually, Zeph would break the awkwardness with some witty comment." Solas laughed. "I think we're going to need more wine."

Solas went for wine, and I stood between a man who needed to prove he was worthy once again and a man who wanted to prove I couldn't touch his king again.

"I'm sorry, Oisin. I truly am," I finally said. "I put you in an unwinnable position."

"It wasn't that, Perdi. Faolan can fight his own fights when it comes to you. You didn't take *my* word. I've never stood against you. I've always been upfront and honest with you. I've defended your name, your honor. When you came to our lands, I protected you. When you went to Blood and Bones to face Solene, I came. I ordered my men to die for you should you need our help. I've stood at your side, so you wouldn't feel like you were standing alone. I didn't want you to be afraid. I wanted you to know I was there and had your back, just as I said I would. I was willing to kill for you and die for you. And this is how you repay my kindness."

I dropped my gaze from his and felt a pang of guilt. "You're right."

"I understand your pain. I would kill anyone who stood between Faolan and me. He is my family," Oisin added. "I have always shown you respect, much more than you've just shown me. You have my loyalty and friendship and...love. It hurts that you cannot show it in return. I've done nothing to deserve that."

"It's okay," Faolan interrupted. *Always the peacemaker*. It took so much to get him riled up.

"No, it's not." I lifted my eyes and met them both. I felt small and cruel, like I had abused my magick. My eyes watered with shame. "I'm embarrassed for what I just did. I'm sorry. Fear makes us do stupid things. I'm scared, and I'm feeling desperate. Oisin, I'm sorry I disrespected you and didn't care how it would make you feel as a person. And I appreciate how hurtful that could feel. You don't deserve that from me. You've always been kind to me, and what I just did wasn't showing you the same in return. Faolan, I'm sorry for digging around in your head. I shouldn't have done that to you."

"Thank you," Oisin said. "That's all I wanted, a sincere apology. It's done, forgotten and now let's move on. Fill us in on what you know so far."

"Thank you." I blinked away my tears. "I've searched Whitwick. They're not there. No one has seen him or Nix. The Aos Si said they'd have felt if Zephyr came through, but they haven't. Nix hasn't been seen since he was last there with me, which is odd since he's there every day in the garden."

"His strawberry and rhubarb pie is worth killing for. I traded him a tree for some jam just yesterday." Oisin smiled and licked his lips. When he saw us all stare, he flushed red. "I haven't crossed your territory, but I've met Nix on the border."

"Why?" I asked. "You could have just asked to meet with him. You'd have been welcomed here."

"Old habits die hard." He shrugged. "I've been trading with him. He gives me pie, and I give him frost grapes from the Royal Orchard for jam. Sorry. Anyway, you were saying."

"That's where he's getting those grapes. I thought he was sneaking into the Winter Court and stealing them." I shook my head but smiled. "I spoke with the Seers, and they say they haven't seen them. They also said they could see no fate of either of them since this morning. The last thing they told me they saw was me being dumped in the forest by the shadows. They say they cannot even see me anymore. They cannot see the path for many Fae, now."

"That's not good." Faolan shivered. "It's never good when your fate is hidden."

"No, it isn't." Solas returned and passed us each a wine glass. "And that explains why they called for a meeting with me this morning."

"What did they say?" I asked.

"Nothing. Your shadows grabbed me."

"They're not mine. They are Zephyr's, and when I find him, he can have them back." My stomach boiled at the hint that Zephyr would be lost forever.

"Perdi..." The shadows rolled down the walls and slinked around my legs. "We feel the full force of your anger. It is something we are not accustomed to at this volume. It is loud and screams at us. We don't know what to do. Are you going to set the room on fire? You feel as Zephyr did before he killed on the battlefield. Are you going to kill? Tell us what to do. Do you need us to trap your enemies for you? Faolan and Oisin won't get far before we grab them. We can dump their bodies where they will not be found. No one would ever know."

"Now, it's uncomfortable," Oisin whispered and took a step back from me.

"No, and they're not my enemies," I replied. "This is just how I am when I'm angry and scared. I'm going to kill, but not anyone in this room. If you see flames shooting out of my hands, help me. If not, just stay close."

Solas grinned. "Now you know what the rest of us are feeling right now. They're figuring it out as we had to. They'll learn that there are many layers to your anger."

I closed my eyes and breathed until the shaking stopped. They was the kind of jitters that couldn't be seen, only felt on the inside, like I had drunk far too much coffee. I calmed myself into something that wouldn't terrify small children and shadows.

"Much better." Solas patted my hand in his. "Go easy on the shadows. It'll take time for them to learn. They can only learn what you teach them. Even Zephyr spoke to them, motioned to them, explained anything they didn't understand."

"How did you get shadows from a Soul-Eater?" Oisin asked. "They can only be commanded by another... Fuck me."

"Stop your mouth from finishing what your brain is thinking...*now*," Faolan interrupted Oisin. "It's none of our business. And we don't ever want it to be our business. Trust when I tell you, we don't want to know. Some things are better left unsaid. To know is death for all who hear."

"Got it," Oisin answered but stared at me knowingly. I trusted him not to say it out loud but didn't trust that his curiosity wouldn't get the better of him. I hoped that day didn't come. It would hurt me to kill him. Oisin sat between that place of knowing he could be a good friend and ally and the darker side of knowing he'd kill me because he killed those he didn't trust fully. He and I had more in common than I was willing to admit.

"Smart man." Solas grinned. "The truth won't set you free — not with this information and definitely not where Perdi is concerned."

I raised my hand to stop the conversation from going in a direction that would end in death. "Solas, can you take me to Elda? She once said Zephyr was bound to me. We were each other's fates. I need to know why. I need to know if I can use that bond, in some way, to find him."

"Of course," he answered. "I'll send word. With Zephyr gone, the Aos Si will sit with her for guidance and comfort. We'll go when they are done."

"What would you have of us?" Faolan asked Solas.

"Can you search the other courts?" Solas asked. "You have treaties with them. They'll let you in without a war. Speak to those who are too scared to talk to me, which is pretty much every court outside of ours. We'll meet back here at nightfall tomorrow."

"We'll see you then, hopefully with encouraging news," Faolan answered.

I watched them walk from the room. I fought against the restless and helpless feeling in my gut, like I was standing around while my friends were in trouble and had no control over it. It was a powerful feeling, edged with fear I hadn't tasted before. My rage bubbled and rolled in my gut. It wanted out to seek that which troubled me. And for a moment, I wanted to let it out, to let it hunt the world for Nix and Zeph. Solas grabbed me and pulled me into his chest before the shadows had the chance. His cool touch ate the burning wind that reached out from my stomach. And as the first bit of fire rolled across my flesh, Solas was there to catch it. My fire had never hurt him. Even as it burned others, he danced in flames. Monsters loved fire, and he was my very own monster.

"You must take a break, Perdi, before you lose control. You're tired, and you're struggling to control your temper. Just a nap, that's all. It's not saying that you're giving up on them. It's saying that you're saving energy for the coming fight. Even Zephyr naps before war. And Nix? Well, he's always sleeping."

"No, there's still so much to do." I pulled from him.

"You need *sleep*." His magick rolled over my hand and up my arm. The moment he said the word, I grew drowsy.

"Not fair. No magick." I yawned.

"Yes. You need to sleep, or you'll burn all of Elphame. How do we rescue our friends if you burn them to a crisp before we get to them?"

"I fucking hate when you do that," I grumbled as he picked me up.

"Such a saucy mouth you have." His laughter pushed me into my much-needed slumber. I didn't remember anything after he stepped into the hall.

Chapter Five

I stepped foot onto the island. Reality slipped away as I moved into the dream. I could feel the blankets tucked under my chin as I slept, a world away. I could hear Solas faintly in the background, reassuring me.

I breathed in the smells that had grown as familiar as Elphame and my home with Solas. Even the flowers here, I loved. They grew nowhere but on Zephyr's island, and I appreciated that fact. When I had started coming here and stayed clear of the lilies, Zephyr had torn them out. He was uncomfortable with the thought that I didn't like certain parts of my home with him. Here, our home was a place out of reach from everywhere else — untainted. The birds I had fed and watched and drawn pulled my attention to the house, to Zephyr, who leaned against the white post of the steps and faced me. It looked as it always did, but different in some new way. Everything gleamed with a freshness you could only have when someone tended to it daily. Not a flake of paint, not a smear of dirt. The windows gleamed from daily cleaning. Something neither Zephyr nor I did.

"Why here?" I asked as I stepped up to the house on the island. "Of all places to bring me, you choose here? Why not show me where you are?"

"This is where it all began. You need the history, Perdi, if you are going to be its future."

"We, Zeph, are its future," I countered.

From behind him, a scream filled the house, and a young man raced past us to the yard. "It's a boy!"

Behind me, misty memories of people clapped and cheered. The yard was filled with Aos Si in their black leather and various men and women I had never met and never would. With a smile, I stepped inside the house and watched the birth of Zephyr. His mother cried as she held him. I could see both happiness and grief on her flushed and tired face. She would have known who her son would become. Even as a newly born child of the world, I could feel his magick crackle in the air, power that rolled off him with his first breath. She held him tighter as if her very love would keep him from a destiny none of them had the power to bend. Zephyr's eyes roamed the room from face to face. He was curious in his first few moments. I knew that look. It reminded me of when Zephyr took in a room as we walked into it. He always knew who was there, where they were, their abilities, intentions and how many exits there were. From the moment he was placed into his mother's waiting arms, he was a man of war. And when his eyes met mine, I could feel everything he would become in my soul. It hurt like only a broken heart could.

The room tilted, and the baby boy was replaced with a grown version. Zephyr, as a young child, sat with a dead bird in his hands. He rocked gently, back and forth. His small face was wet with tears and sadness. His blue eyes were brilliant and held more pain than a child of his age's ever should. It was the pain of seeing death for the first time. He gripped the lifeless creature and looked at his mother, who stood at the side of the room with a hand at her throat and one over her *heart. I knew that pose. I had done it many times, worried my heart would leap from my chest, scared a scream would tear out of my mouth and gripping it in hopes of controlling it. I wanted to tell his mother that there was no point. Cries from the soul always found a way out.*

"It's okay, Zeph." His mother smiled from the side of the room. Hearing her call him that made me smile. It was why he'd reacted so strongly when I had used that name the first time and why he always melted just a little, no matter his anger, when I called him 'Zeph.'

He breathed life back into the bird as only a Soul-Eater could. And with that simple act of kindness, he sealed his fate. His mother and father both wept. At the front of the room, the Aos Si stood. They had come to test him, to see if he would become more than what his parents had wanted for him. At my side, Zephyr watched his memory play out. He, like his parents, would have given anything for this moment to have never happened. I understood then that not every child born to Finis parents would become a full Soul-Eater. Only the strongest developed those abilities. And once a power this great was found, the Aos Si would take them.

The Commander knelt before him and placed his hand on Zephyr's little shoulder. "It's okay, son."

Zephyr, whose face was still wet with tears, pulled back. "I am not your son."

"One day, you will be."

As small as he was, Zephyr leaned forward, and pure confidence poured off him. "No, before that day comes, you'll be dead at my hands."

The Commander stood with a grin that said Zephyr would learn the hard way. Zephyr and I had so much more in common than I thought. The soldier moved back to his men. "He's fiery, but they all are when they first come."

"You'll burn under that fire," I mumbled.

They left Zephyr in the living room and took his parents outside. After a moment, he looked up from the bird, perched on his finger, and looked at me. I could have sworn he looked right into my eyes. I had watched a child turn into a soldier in an instant, and I hated it. I wanted to return to him as a child, before the moment he was fated with the life I knew he hadn't wanted. His life was now no longer his own. He would leave his home and would return a full Aos Si. In a sense, he'd been taken, just as I had — a fate he hadn't earned and one designed to kill him.

"You'll make it," I whispered to him. *"The world will tremble at your feet. You'll be their biggest regret, just like I was. Hold on, Zeph. It'll hurt, but I promise you, it'll be worth it."*

The room faded, and Zephyr stood at my side. "I felt that, Perdi. I always have."

"What's that?"

"Our similar fates, both decided for us. You were dragged into a world that wanted you dead. I was dragged into a world that tried to kill me every day. And, like your parents, mine never wanted this for me. I remember them praying every night to any God who would listen that I would be spared a life as a Soul-Eater, an Aos Si. It is a hard existence to be fated, and they feared for my life long before I had grown in her belly. Both our worlds, mortal and Fae, call for sacrifice. And we both have had to pay with our very souls. Every day is a new sacrifice we make."

The room tilted, and it was Zephyr returned from battle. His memory breezed through me as he stepped into the house and cried. He was crusted in blood and dirt. His leather was slashed and torn. But it was his eyes — ice-blue, brilliant, but hollow and filled to the lashes with agony. His misery broke my heart. The tension and sadness were thick in the air and hard to breathe through. Every breath felt like hot soup. It coated my mouth and throat and tasted of every time I'd sat on the brink of grief so vast that I was content with my own death.

"This was the first time I had taken a pearl by accident. I released it later that night after hours of trying and cursing the Gods," Zephyr said. "When you cried for the souls you trapped in the garden, and I told you my heart hurt for you, it is because I remembered the pain of it. I remembered the pain you felt, the horror of it all. I was careful after that. I was so bloody careful. I'm sure if there had been any other Soul-Eater alive, they would have considered me an awful one. Killing got easier, as it does after decades of stepping over bodies, but the taking of a soul never does. When the choice is not yours, the pain of what you do stains your soul in ways you never truly heal from. When you are forced to do it, to burn the world, the cost is greater than you or I can pay."

"It's worth it, though, isn't it?" I asked.

"You tell me, little Crow. Was it worth trapping those souls? Did it feel worth it when they cried out to you each night or when you can't go into the yard anymore because they haunt you? How does it feel when you look in the mirror and meet your own eyes?"

"No. It wasn't worth it," I whispered. "I don't regret killing those who came for my life, but binding them forever, I do regret. They didn't deserve that."

"That part never gets easier, Perdi. It gets worse. Every soul you take, you take away a chance to be more than this." He pointed at his memory, screaming into the heavens. "I don't want this for you. Trust me when I tell you that the pain doesn't ever go away. Still, to this day, I feel this. I feel every soul and the fear I've caused. When I walk into a room and everyone steps back, it's never a good feeling. But this is the cost of winning. This is the cost of being a Soul-Eater. Nothing is worth doing this to yourself. Nothing is worth *becoming the terror of Elphame. You will never find peace. You will never rest."*

Zephyr's living room morphed into flash after flash of him breaking windows and walls, to him laughing and reading. Every shade of emotion one could feel played out over and over. But what had always remained was his loneliness. He had spent his life alone. He was always on his own. He never had another to share his happiness or sadness with.

"Who would I drag with me?" Zephyr asked, as if sensing what I felt. "Who would I curse to follow me into hell?"

"Are you saying I should be alone like you were?" I asked.

"No. But it does make it easier," he answered. "Having those you love makes the world easier to handle. But having those you love gives the world ideas on how to bend you to their will. You've already felt that cost many times over. Soul-Eaters have always lived in solitude, only connecting with other Finis who understood our sacrifices. It is easier on everyone else not to be the pawn in a game they don't even know they're playing."

"You have me." I smiled.

"I have another Soul-Eater, little Crow. I surround myself with those too powerful to become pawns. But you don't see many around me who can't set fire to the world, do you? How many do you see in my life who can't wage war and stand their ground on their own?"

"None," I answered. "Neither do I."

"We surround ourselves with death because those are the only people who can survive us."

I followed Zephyr into his bedroom, where he motioned to himself, sleeping in bed, tossing and burning the blankets that covered his body. Zephyr stepped back and watched a moment that made him close his eyes. He didn't want to relive this moment with me.

"Perdi!" Zephyr sat straight up in bed. "Perdi!"

I tilted my head and stepped to the side, away from the door. His eyes tracked me. I moved again, and he watched me as if I were standing before him.

"Hello?" I asked.

Zephyr jumped out of bed and stood as if he was about to fist-fight me. I watched his body as I had so many other times. He was both tense and relaxed, ready for whatever was dumb enough to fight him. It made me smile and relax my own body in preparation for what could come.

"Who the hell are you?"

"Perdi," I answered. "How can you see me?"

"Because you're standing in my fucking bedroom," he answered.

"Polite, as always." I snorted a laugh. "No, Zeph, I'm not here. I'm in your dream hundreds of years from now."

"Zeph? No one calls me that anymore." He eyed me suspiciously.

I smiled. "Yeah, I know. But I do, and it used to irritate the hell out of you. I never knew why it bothered you until now. Your mom used to call you Zeph."

He smelled the air. "Soul-Eater?"

"Yes, among other things."

"Crow. I can smell the Gate lingering on your skin, but it's different. The smell is off," he whispered. "You're a little Crow, aren't you?"

"Yes, and you call me that, even though it used to irritate me."

"I've dreamed of you. But this is the first time you've fully come to me like this." He reached for the blanket, only to realize he had burned it in his sleep. He finally pulled on some pants. "Sorry."

"It's all right. I've seen you naked a hundred times now. You don't even wear clothes when you go to the kitchen for a snack. Not even a housecoat." I grinned. "You're not very shy. At least, not around me."

"No, I'm not. You get over it, when you grow up surrounded by thousands of others who don't have time for things that don't matter." He glanced around the room. "You're not alone."

"No, you're here," I answered.

"Of course, I'm here."

I laughed. "No, I mean, I'm in your dream of this memory, your dream-you is here. I don't know how to explain it. He, your future you, is showing me your history as I walk through his dreams. And somehow, you can see me, even though no other version of you has seen me."

"That's not true. I've always seen you, out of the corner of my eye, a thousand times. It's how I know your name. I've heard it as many times. You've been there, watching every moment of my life where change has been difficult. I once thought you were fate because you always smelled of home. Your smell… I remember it most. Like lavender and tears and the smell of war before it's begun."

I smiled. "You smell exactly how you've always smelled…like home – if home was a little slice of hell with flower beds and fruit trees."

"I've never had my smell be described so pleasantly." He smirked, only to soften into a smile. "Why am I showing you my history? We only share our darkest parts with those we love, those we share pearls with. Do we love each other?"

"In a manner of speaking. We share pearls with each other. I love you more than life, more than freedom, more than my own soul. And you love me. But we're not together, not as me and Solas are. You are family," I answered and smiled at the very mention of Solas' name.

"Solas? The Darkness?" he asked with a look of doubt on his face. "Little Crow, one should not meddle with powers that'll swallow you whole."

"Yes, but that is a story you'll have to learn on your own," I answered. "Sometimes the darkness is the only safe place to hide."

"It's also a great place to die," he countered.

I huffed a laugh. "Been there, done that."

"We love each other but are not lovers. I smell the winter on you, yet you are with Solas, the nightmare of the realm. And you're in Elphame. I feel pity for you, little Crow. You've aligned yourself with those who carry hell on their backs and eat the souls of those who fall off. You are powerful. I can feel it pour off you like rain. But I do not believe it is enough to withstand the pain only we bring to our lives and those within them."

"Don't pity me, Zeph. It's a life I died to have, and I would have stayed dead if it weren't for you coming to my rescue. It's a constant with us, me not listening to your warnings then needing you to save my life. But I've saved you once, myself, after I became a Crow. You were locked away, and I freed you. If it weren't for you, I'd be a dead Crow a few times over. So, I feel like we're even," I answered, then stopped and scolded myself. "I can't say more. I don't want to screw things up and wake up back in those cursed Golden Court dungeons because I twisted fate. I don't think I could survive it twice. I barely made it out the first time."

He nodded and didn't push for more answers. "Why are you here? What's happened? You have stirred my dream, and we only do that for two reasons — love and war. We only dreamwalk like this when we are at our most desperate."

"You're missing, and I can't find you. You won't tell me where you are. I came to you, dreaming, to find you. Instead, I've been given the grand tour of your memory lane. As much as I love peeking into the life of my version of Zephyr, I'm not here for that."

"I must have a good reason to keep this information from you if I won't tell the person I love."

"Is there a way I can force you to tell me?" I asked.

He laughed. "You're either a fool or you don't know me as well as you think. If I'm refusing to tell you, it is for a reason. You cannot force a Soul-Eater to do a damn thing."

"Isn't that God's honest truth?" I groaned in frustration. "It was worth a try."

"As a Soul-Eater, when was the last time someone could force you to do something you didn't want to do?"

"True enough," I answered, dropped my eyes and felt the first tear fall. "I don't know what to do. I can't lose you, Zeph. I won't make it without you. It'll kill me, after everything we did to stay together. You've dragged me from hell twice, only to leave me? You promised you'd never leave me, and now, you're gone. Just tell me, please, how do I save you? Please help me. I will give you anything you want, anything. Name it, and it is yours. I don't know how to do this without you. You're breaking my heart, Zeph. Please. Don't make me burn the world to find you."

"I'm...later me, he's not going to like this." He moved quickly and pulled me into his arms. His shadows sealed around us. "You smell like you've danced between fire and ice for far too long, little Crow. Two great powers in a world that kills for less, with a Crow flapping in the wind between them."

"I'm not flapping in the wind. I've always had you to help me brave the storms."

"Pay attention, not with your eyes. Not even I can block all your senses. You're Finis. Use your soul. It's the strongest part of who we are. Breathe me in, hear with your soul, feel me. If you love me, nothing will stop you from getting to me. But be willing to pay the cost of finding a Soul-Eater who doesn't want to be found before you look. I fear it will not go well for you. If you're going to burn the world, be willing to pay that price. If I'm hiding the truth from you, it is to save you. It is because I love you as much as you love me. You will pay, little Crow. We always fucking pay. Fate makes everything hurt for us."

"I will always find you, Zeph," I answered. "I'd pay with my life."

"I fear it'll cost more than your life. You will not like the payment in the end."

The dream within a dream smashed, and Zephyr stood with me in his empty bedroom, his hand on my shoulder. He smiled. "I remember all of that, Perdi. The night you showed up in my bedroom was the reason I sought answers. I also remember you trying to find ways to outsmart me. But, if you hadn't come and told me what you had, I would have never met you at the Golden Court. I had dreamed about you and seen you throughout my life, but that night pushed me to find you, to find Solas, to lock myself away and wait for you. I didn't know when you'd come, but I was willing to wait out all eternity for you. That night changed the course of history. Knowing I'd find love, that I'd find someone who would love me back without wanting anything from me, pushed me to become so much more than I was because I wanted to be someone you could love and would be worthy of that love."

"That actually happened?" I asked.

He nodded. "Soul-Eaters walk among souls, Perdi. Time doesn't move in one direction for souls. They don't care about such things. We were always destined to find each other. And now, it's come full circle. You were the first face I saw in life and will be my last."

"No, it's not the end. Not yet," I replied.

I closed my eyes and listened. I pushed away what surrounded me – the sounds of the birds I knew weren't real, the feel of Zephyr's body heat as he stood close enough for me to hear his heartbeat. I breathed past the scents of his life and smelled the salty ocean and roots. The sun-kissed warmth was replaced by wetness and cold. A light wind shivered down my back. I focused on his heartbeat. It was real. He was alive. Beyond him, I could feel the rapid flutters of a gnome. Nix was alive.

"You're a quick study, little Crow." Zephyr felt me pushing into his dream and shoved me back to his side, on the island, at his cottage. "You're getting stronger, but not strong enough for my mind."

"Why, Zeph? If you tell me where you are, I can come get you."

"I don't think you'll live, that's why. I believe you'll do many bad things to find me and won't be able to stomach what you've done. It'll tear your soul in half. I don't want my life so badly as to force you to live a life of pain afterward. Neither Nix nor I want you to suffer for us. You've given enough. Why can't you see that? You've given everything to me. Everything I've ever dreamed of has come from you. You've given me purpose and love, and I can die in utter happiness, knowing you will live and not suffer for me. And that, little Crow, is enough for me. It is more than I could have ever hoped for."

"I think you're wrong," I countered, my face streaming with hot tears. Each breath came out in a force. "I'm not done. It's not enough. Zeph, I'm not that weak. I can help you. Let me try."

"I have loved you every moment of my life, Perdi. There was no moment when I didn't feel your love, and I can't thank you enough."

"But you haven't given me a chance to love you for all of my life!" I screamed my sadness into his soul as my own broke under the pain. He was leaving me, and I couldn't stop him. He was saying goodbye. I cried as if he were already dead.

"Once, I told you I'd give anything to have someone love me as fiercely as Nix loved you. But I see now, you've loved us all with that ferocity from the moment I opened my eyes *in a world that wished me dead. You have been there, always, giving me hope."*

"I'll find you," I whispered, barely able to form a sentence. Every inch of me hurt in ways that were all too familiar. The pain reminded me of the day my mother was taken from me, and I had been powerless to stop it. It brought me back to childhood, standing on the street, waiting for her to come home, unwilling to believe she was gone. Each day, I did that. And every time she didn't return, I felt her death anew.

"I know you'll search all of Elphame for me. But you won't find me. Before I go, I need you to know you can do this without me. You have it in you to be more than I ever was. Trust in yourself. Trust in your gut. Trust in your heart. It will never steer you in the wrong direction."

"Zeph, this isn't goodbye," I cried.

"I love you."

He shoved me out of his dream, and I knew he felt me claw at his soul to remain with him.

I woke up screaming his name, with Solas putting out fires around the room. He didn't tell me to stop. He just stood there, ready for the flames with the scent of ash and Zephyr hanging over us.

Chapter Six

"I think you'd survive the fall," Solas said as I looked over the edge of the cliff to the caves of the Sluagh.

I pulled back. "I have my doubts about the landing."

"Shall we, or are you still contemplating jumping?" Solas asked. "The first time we were here to speak with Elda, you *did* jump."

"The first time I was here, I was fine with dying. Not so much anymore," I replied.

"I'd call that progress, little Crow," he replied and winked. "No one really likes coming here. It takes a lot of courage to walk into the caves. Between the uncertainty of what you'll learn and the hesitation of finally knowing, it's uncomfortable. We all want answers, but only when they align with our hopes."

"Do you come here?" I asked. "For answers?"

"I used to, a lot. Not because I needed the answers but because I hoped they would change, that I could do something to keep destiny from unfolding. Now I come simply because the Sluagh and Elda are family."

"What destiny were you trying to change?"

"My own, yours, our people. I never wanted to be king. I never wanted to take Crows. But I did want to protect my people. If I didn't become king, someone else would have, and I couldn't risk what they would do to our people. If I didn't collect Crows, someone else would have gone in my place, and the risk was too great that I would miss the one Crow I needed, the one I was fated to love. So, even though I came wishing for a life none of us could ever have, I was also praying that I'd stay on my path and get to you. It was both complicated and simple. I didn't want this but couldn't risk not having it."

"I understand that perfectly. I never wanted to be a Crow, but I'd never wish someone else to become one in my place. And now that I'm here, it was worth it. But at the time, I didn't feel it was. I'm glad for where I am, but I also wish it never had to happen the way it did. Does that make sense?"

"To me, yes," he answered and hugged me. "This is where we're supposed to be, and for a bigger reason than we know, but it's still difficult to be in this position."

"Did you know Zephyr's path would lead here?"

"No. What is said with Elda stays there. After events have passed, he's told me about knowing it would come, but we don't interfere in the fates of others."

"I'd have tried to stop it," I answered.

"After lifetimes of this, we've learned that nothing we can do will stop fate. But damn it, if I don't keep trying." His small laugh echoed against the rock, and I shivered. It didn't sound friendly when standing at the caves of the Sluagh. "We may not be able to keep fate from our door, but we can make it harder for her to get in."

"No matter how many times I come here, I don't like it."

Solas raised his eyebrow. "And how often are you here, without me?"

"I've been to the caves a few times without you. When I was hunting those in the Dark Courts who had come during the Taking, I had them dropped here, and a few times, I came to collect their bodies. Once, drinking wine and mapping out Blood and Bones with the trainees. But the last time I saw Elda was when I was stabbed."

"I don't feel it when you come here without me," he replied.

"Why would you feel it?"

"I can feel the Sluagh like a faint hum in the back of my mind. I know each time someone who doesn't belong steps foot here. The Sluagh send out a call whenever someone comes here. If I don't want them here or don't know them, they don't stay for long. With you, they see you as belonging here, as an extension of me, and they don't mind that you're here poking around."

"Should I be happy about that?"

"I would be. If you weren't, you'd have been splattered at the bottom the first time you crawled up the cliff without me."

"Small favors." I smiled and turned to face the mouth of the cave.

At the end of the passageways, Elda, Claviger of Dreams, Master of Mirrors, the grandmother of Solas, sat waiting for me. I had only come to speak to her once before, but I still remembered the fear, how the rocks pressed against me, trapping me with every turn and dip. I remembered it as if I had come every day, and not one of those days had I enjoyed the journey. I hadn't gotten over my fear of small, dark spaces, a fear I had only developed because of Elphame. I'd have to navigate chains of long, narrow tunnels that linked the lunar caverns. One wrong turn, and I'd end up in places I'd prefer not to go to alone. Solas wouldn't tell me the way. If this was where I was supposed to be, I'd find Elda on my own. If not, I'd find another reason I didn't like small, dark places.

The opening in the rocks that led deeper into the world of the Sluagh could not be seen by just anyone. The entrance, tucked behind layers of shadows and magick, carved by teeth and claws, was hidden from those who shouldn't come. And like the first time, standing at the opening, my skin crawled like someone dancing on my grave. Everything about stepping inside the rock told my body to run in the other direction. Even though I knew it was magick, to send away those who were foolish enough to come, it still clung to my skin like spiderwebs.

"Are you coming in with me?" I asked Solas.

He shook his head. "You know I can't. Elda's words are for your ears only. Plus, don't you want me to make sure no stray Sluagh comes in behind you?"

"No," I answered and smiled. "They don't care. My brain tells me I should fear them, but my soul doesn't see them as a threat...not anymore. Plus, there's a wee one who keeps following me around. I think he'd help me."

"They're not pets, little Crow. How many times do you need to be bitten by Sluagh before you realize they aren't dogs to be leashed?" He nudged me forward. "Run along. Stop stalling."

"I got bitten once, and now you bring it up every chance you get," I replied, thinking back to trying to coax a small creature and having his mother try to swallow me whole. I rubbed the scar on my thigh, trying to get rid of the tingles that always flared to life whenever they were near.

"Once is usually enough for most people to grow a healthy fear of them."

"I'm not most people," I answered and turned to the entrance.

I ran my sweaty hands over my pants and groaned. For something I didn't want to do again, I sure made it a priority to come. With one foot in front of the other, I moved away from Solas and into the tunnels. It smelled warm, wet, earthy—with the faintest hint of Solas and home and underneath, the Sluagh and their leathery flesh. I breathed in through my mouth and out my nose and tried to calm the urge to run. I'd have brained myself on the rocks had I tried to do anything more than walk.

As my eyes adjusted to the darkness, the caves came alive. The first time I was here, I was terrified. The second time, I was still scared but calm enough to see beauty where I hadn't before. White moss grew in the cracks of the stone, and tiny flowers no bigger than a teardrop crawled on vines that were no thicker than a hair. I inched my way forward until the fear peeled away, and I could walk at a pace that wouldn't draw my day into the night.

"Elda?" I called out when I got to the end. I glanced around the torch-lit room. She wasn't where I thought she'd be, in the middle of the room, surrounded by pillows.

"Over here, Finis," she called from the side. She had called me that before, saying it was a term of endearment. When really, she had called me a Soul-Eater, and I hadn't known it at the time.

"Thank you for seeing me." I entered the room and could finally breathe deeply. The sticky webs on my skin had fallen off at the door.

Elda motioned for me to join her. She had two chairs at the side of the round room. Between the chairs, our steaming tea was already prepared and sat on a small wooden table. I took a seat and accepted the tea nervously. I'd come with questions and now felt uneasy about asking them, scared of her answers.

"You smell of dreams, Perdi." She broke the silence as if she felt my hesitation. But I supposed many didn't know where to start when sitting with someone who saw futures and was more willing to talk than the Seers. "Dreams you walked through. That's a rare gift, even for your kind."

"Zeph," I answered. "I was with him — all the versions of him."

"Oh, so it has come full circle, then?" she asked, as though she already knew that moment would come and go.

"That's the same thing he said," I answered and felt a twinge of pain in my heart. "It's not the end."

"Nor did I say that. As before, you have a curious way of hearing what you wish, rather than listening to the words spoken," she answered and passed me a gold bracelet from her wrist. "Show me where the end is."

I held the band and turned it in my hand. "I can't even see where it starts."

"And that is my point. A circle has no real start or end. Coming full circle simply means that after a long series of happenings, the same situation you started with still exists. There is no end to it. You've simply gone back to the original source. In this case, you've returned to the instance that caused Zephyr to find you. I believe, Perdi, he's shown you the why behind his choices."

"I don't know what he's shown me. I don't understand." I set my tea down and shook my head. Anxious frustration swarmed in my stomach. My heart beat too fast. My breathing was too rapid. My head pounded from a headache that wouldn't go away. "He said goodbye. He said it started with me and would now end with me. I was the first person he saw and would be the last. I don't know what any of it means."

"Many times, he has sat with me, and many times, I've called him a fool. Zephyr has the need to protect. It is in his very blood. It is who all Aos Si are, including you. But for him, a lone Finis in a world that hunts those who stray too far away from the herd, he feels the need to protect you over most. I believe he is trying to stop you from a fate that is not his to fight. He's trying to keep you from a life he has lived himself. He, the foolish man, thinks he can protect another Soul-Eater from a fate of their choosing."

"Why does he need to shelter me from everything at the risk of his own life in the process?" I asked.

She smiled. "Because you are Zephyr's only family. He has only one other like him. Why do you feel the need to protect him? Why would you leave your safety to hunt those who were able to take a Soul-Eater? It is certain death, no?"

"Because..." I groaned. "He is my family. Solas considers him family as well, but Solas hasn't tried to stop him."

"This is true, but Zephyr knows Solas will not risk you for him. Solas would never even entertain trading you to save Zephyr or Nix. He would let them both die to save you. For this, Zephyr trusts Solas will make the choices Zephyr feels are right," she answered and shook her head as if both men were fools. "But more than all the answers I could give you, it boils down to who Solas is not. He is *not* a Soul-Eater. Zephyr fiercely loves his king and your gnome. He would die for them as quickly as he'd die for you. But Zephyr wouldn't kill you for them. He'd kill them for you. Because you, Perdi, are the only other Finis. So, you are who he chooses to protect. He would rather die than have you risk your life for his."

"I'd never ask him to do that," I answered.

"That's what you're not understanding, Perdi. You'd never have to ask him. He would do it, without a second thought, to save you. He would slay his lifelong friend for you. You know this. Even after all the wars ever fought in your name, he was willing to kill every soul that walked this earth to ensure you made it to this very moment alive. Or, as Solas has said, without so much as a hangnail," she answered, and I smiled at the memory of Zephyr's frustration during the Last War, uncertain how he'd keep me in pristine condition during a war.

"The bond between Soul-Eaters is unlike any other in Elphame or the mortal world. Your souls are intertwined. It is why the Finis are feared. It is why so many of your kind were drowned at birth. Finis are deathly loyal. They stand against all, no matter who they are or what throne they sit upon. No one is safe from a Soul-Eater. Standing between two Finis is death, only death. There is room for nothing else. And Zephyr is choosing his own death rather than risking you making the same decision for him. One cannot be surprised by that outcome. But he forgets, nothing, not even his own wishes, can stand between two Soul-Eaters. He should know this."

"It's eating me inside. I can't feel him. Even before he gave me his pearl, I always felt him lingering. And Nix? I can't even bring myself to think of what is happening to him." My sob broke free and came out in one long whimper. "I won't leave them. I can't. It burns to sit here and do nothing. I feel like every breath I take doesn't fill me, and I'm starved for more. It hurts, unlike anything I've ever felt before. I can't feel anything else."

She reached across the small table and squeezed my hand. "Your pain, my dear, is thick enough that even I grieve with you. It is the pull you feel to act. It is the pain you feel to not act. It is foolish of Zephyr to think they can stop you and silly of you to think you know better than Zephyr. You both are fools in your own way. Two Finis fighting against the other's will. The world will tremble with the outcome."

"Can you feel him or see him?" I asked.

"Zephyr is not one I can feel easily. Once, I could. But now, he is far too strong for me to poke around in his aura without him sitting beside me and giving me permission. I stopped seeing the fate of Nix once he was with Zephyr. It is difficult to read any who are near him," she answered. "It is the same for you. When you're near him, I can't see you. And now that you carry his pearl, I see nothing. As you grow in power, I also lose sight of any who stand too close to you."

"Can you feel Nix at all?"

"I'm sorry, Perdi. He is tied to Zephyr's fate. I cannot see him."

"He's so small. I promised him…" My words caught in my throat on a rock of heartache I couldn't swallow. "I told him when the Last War was over, he could be done with this. He could heal and become more than all of this. He was trying to heal his soul, to give me a pearl."

Elda sighed as she waded through the anguish I filled the room with. "Your Nix is brave, Perdi. He knew, the moment he met you, he'd be tied to war. Nix, before Solas, knew you were Finis. He would have felt it the moment he met you. He is too small for your power to not have washed over him in an instant. And he stayed with you, even knowing the risks of walking a path with a Soul-Eater, out of love. It is the reason he left with Zephyr, out of that same love. But unlike Zephyr, Nix knows better than to fight against your destiny. He will try to do what he feels is right out of love, but he's wiser than Zephyr and Solas. He knows you unlike anyone else."

I groaned my frustration and leaned forward. I grew hotter by the second. I could feel the sweat starting to bead on my lip and brow. The scream that tore from my gut felt as if a deep wound could speak. I dug my nails into my thighs and screamed until my throat was raw and my head pounded from the pressure. The walls echoed my voice and slapped my hot cheeks on the way out of the room. Elda didn't flinch or move or duck for cover. She had probably seen many fall apart at the news of their paths not being what they had hoped. I'd never survive the loss of both Zephyr and Nix. I'd never recover.

"I'm sorry, but I thought coming here would help." I sagged in my chair. "That somehow you would have answers that I couldn't see."

"I do not hold the answers for Soul-Eaters. You are a fate all your own." Her face was creased with pity. "Zephyr knew this day would come. He told me of your walking in his dreams, those many years ago when he came to me."

"What did he say?" I asked.

"That he, his future self, would save you," she answered. "I saw his fate until the day he showed you his darkest days, his history held within his pearl. I told him he would give his freedom for a Crow. And in return, a Crow would rescue him from his pain, and he would help her end the Taking. Together, they would set the world straight, in blood and death. But he would also never get his freedom back once he was tied to her. If he chose to help her, he'd also risk losing his life. To bind yourself so tightly to the fate of another would mean he would never be free again. And in turn, you're bound to him and face the same destiny as he. You'd both burn for the other and never taste freedom again."

"I'm a bloody curse. I am the harbinger of death."

"You both are. Then you are surprised when death comes for you in return." She pursed her lips, like any grandmother would when telling you the obvious. "Zephyr warned you the life of Finis was a hard road to travel. It would be rife with pain and suffering. You have had but a taste of what his life has been from a young child, decades upon decades of this. That is what you look forward to. You cannot balk now. You asked for this life."

"I know that is what I signed up for." My voice was harsh, but it was true. I accepted it but didn't have to enjoy it. "But Nix didn't ask for this. He doesn't deserve this."

"This is exactly what he signed up for. He chose this just as much as everyone else has. He knew walking with Finis could mean his death, and he chose willingly. He also knew what it would mean to align himself with the three most powerful in Elphame. Nix has lived a life of both trial and error, dark and light. He has fought hard to be honorable enough to stand by your side. He has lived a righteous life there. Do not feel sorry for him. You remove all he has done to be a man of honor with your pity."

"I don't pity him. I'm scared for him and Zephyr," I answered.

"Those who know what you are, have chosen to remain with you out of love, just as Solas has. He knew, inviting a Soul-Eater into his kingdom, let alone two of them, could mean the doom of his people. And falling in love with one could mean his very death. But he chose wisely. He chose love instead of fear and is a better man and king for it."

I closed my eyes as reality set in. "This is why Soul-Eaters are always alone."

"This is exactly why," Elda answered. "Linking yourself to the fate of one who eats worlds means your world can be swallowed, along with the rest."

"Why didn't you warn me before, when I was here the last time?" I asked. "I could have saved them."

"No, Perdi, you could not have. The fates have decided their path, and nothing you could have said or done would have changed that. The ending always comes, no matter the route taken to get there."

"What do you see in my future, my paths?" I asked. "Before I faded from your sight, what did you see?"

"Zephyr once told you, to live is to suffer. You chose to live, and now you suffer for it. You will not always suffer, but it will take splitting your soul in half and bleeding over the world for it to end. But that end will be short-lived before it starts over again and again. That is merely the way in Elphame. The cycle doesn't stop. It doesn't matter how many you bury. You will keep digging holes until one day it is your own grave."

"When I dreamed of Zephyr, he said I'd tear my soul in half to save him," I answered.

"He sees the path you're willing to take, and it scares him, as it would anyone."

"He'd do the same," I answered.

"And therein lies the problem. In the end, neither of you will win. You both will suffer and suffer alone. It is the Finis way." She sipped her tea and blew away the swirls of steam as though we weren't having a pivotal conversation. Reading my face, she smiled. "Everything in Elphame is life or death, Perdi. Since I cannot control it, I'll drink my tea before it chills. That, Finis, I can control. I'll leave the problems of tomorrow to deal with tomorrow."

"You sound like Solas." I smiled. "What do I do about my problems of today? I can't get back to Zephyr, to his dreams. He pushed me out, and I can't get back. And when I was there, he wouldn't let me see where they were. If I knew that part, I could deal with tomorrow's problems right now before there isn't another tomorrow left."

"Perhaps your answers rest in someone else's dreams and not those of a Soul-Eater who is training you? He has survived centuries of being hunted and has killed every soul who has come against him. You are trying to best a Soul-Eater who has always been the first on the battlefield and last to leave. He closes his eyes and snatches souls before men know they're even dead. You must see the humor in that. You, a fledgling Finis, are trying to win against the one training you to become half as good as the teacher? Perhaps you are walking through the wrong dream, Perdi. Your little Nix? His mind is not as strong as Zephyr's, and he wouldn't dare fight you too hard for fear of harming you." She smiled and offered me hope. "Sometimes it is not desperate measures you need, but to slow down, let go of the desperation and remember the training Zephyr has instilled in you. You are Finis. *You* are the very tool you need. He has taught you better than this. You need to stop and ask yourself, what would Zephyr do? How would he get around the obstacles in his path that he can't break down?"

"Zephyr, come up against obstacles he can't break down? I can't see that happening, ever."

"You are his obstacle. Your stubbornness has hindered his sanity since the day he met you. Both you and Solas are an obstacle course with deadly consequences at every corner. But he gets around them with ease. If you stopped long enough to think of the problem, rather than overly focusing on the chunks you can't get by, you'd get around them as well."

"Will I find them?" I asked.

"I cannot see that. But, if you wished me to guess, I do not doubt you will. You have proven to always do what you set your soul to do. In the face of certain failures, you've always found a way. There have been many times I've stood on the cliff and waited for the news that you have perished, only to be told you've managed to survive a fire that should have killed us all."

"Will they be alive?" I asked, even though she had no answers. But hope is one of the last things to die before it's just rage driving you forward.

"I'm sorry, Perdi, but I don't know." Her face filled with sadness. "But I do fear what you will do."

"What do you mean, what I'll do?"

"You'll eat the world," she answered. "Whether they are dead or alive, you'll do as Zephyr fears and will rip yourself in half to try to save them. And if you can't, I fear for all of us and what must be done to contain you and your broken soul."

* * * *

After Elda, I curled into the smell of Zephyr on the island and cried. The ground shook under the house, and I did nothing to calm myself. I knew this house could take the rage of a Soul-Eater. It still stood after centuries of Zephyr's anger. It would stand long after mine. From the first moment I had felt Zephyr behind the wall at the Golden Court, imprisoned, I knew I'd save him. And when I released him, I had never envisioned a day without him. I couldn't think of a day on this earth without Nix. The very thought made me sick. I pushed the thoughts from my mind.

"Perdi." The shadows rested over me. "It will be okay. You will find a way. You always do."

"I was just remembering the first time we met." I smiled. "Thank you for helping me, for always coming."

"We do not believe you remember as we do," they answered. "The first time you met us was not the first time we met you."

"What do you mean?" I asked.

"As Zephyr has said, it has come full circle. We met when you walked through Zephyr's dreams. We felt you long before we met at the Golden Court. It is why we came to you. You felt like home. When we wrapped around you, we remembered you and knew you were the Crow who'd come, who'd stood in his bedroom and begged for him to help you. We could taste your tears, and so could he. And because of you, for the first time, Zephyr had a purpose other than death." They twisted around me as they always had. They felt like standing close to Zephyr.

"I remembered you but didn't know why. I wasn't scared of you, as the others were. You felt like home, like freedom and familiar memories that weren't mine. Up until Zephyr's dream, I didn't know why. Eventually, I assumed it was because I was Finis. But touching you was always like seeing a friend from years gone by."

"Will you help him if it means you'll break your soul?" they asked.

"Yes," I answered.

"He would not want that, Perdi."

"He isn't here to stop me, is he?" I felt my mouth twist into a grin. "He would come for me. Nix would come for me."

"Yes, they would. But they will still not like what you will do to get to them."

"*Foolish little Crow.*" I mimicked Zephyr. "He doesn't like anything I do. I'm used to him being ticked off. But

Nix? He'll know I'm coming. He'll have already told Zephyr that I'm on my way."

"And when you're broken into pieces, will you not regret it?"

"Then I hope, if it's really terrible, I break myself to the point I won't really care one way or the other," I answered. "Zephyr will put me back together, as will Nix, Solas and you. You've all done it before, and you'll do it again and again until I learn how to do it myself. And one day, I'll be strong enough that my enemies just stop coming for me. But if they don't stop, I'll be callused enough that I won't break."

"You are a curious creature. We can feel the fight inside of you. One voice is telling you to burn the world. The other tells you to wait until you find the perfect place to light the fire."

I nodded. "I can't rescue crispy friends."

"We wanted to make sure of your intent before we suggested our help. We have an idea, but it's one Zephyr would be angry about if we suggested it. He once told us to stop giving you so many ideas that we'd be the cause of you eating his people. But he gave us freedom with you, so we didn't care how many souls you ate."

"He doesn't control you right now. I'm all ears," I answered.

"The next time you're asleep, sleep within us. We will follow you. We will help you when you are dreaming. We can see more than you and will remember it perfectly."

"I've slept inside you dozens of times. You've never been able to do that before."

"It's very personal, Perdi. We've only ever slept around you, never fully settling into your soul. If we stay and hold on to your soul when you're asleep, we will know a great many things you keep us blocked out of when you're awake. We will see all of your memories, your fears and your weaknesses. If you were older, more powerful like Zephyr, you'd still be able to block that out even in your sleep. But we do not feel you can do that currently," they answered and hesitated a little as if they were suggesting something intimate. Their emotions rolled over me, but I felt no threat or reason not to allow them to stroll around inside my soul. I was surprised they didn't know more than they did. I had never blocked them from feeling all of who I was. They had been the ones to respect those boundaries.

"Now, we're bound to your soul. We can go wherever your soul goes. If you allow us to come to your dreams with you, we can track with you." They paused and rolled around me. "Zephyr will not like it, and he will be angry. He will sense us there and will not be pleased we are rolling around in your soul. Only he and Solas know your soul like that, Perdi. He will be displeased."

"If he didn't want me to use you, he shouldn't have bound you to me, then."

"I doubt this was the purpose he had in mind," they replied.

"What he intended me to do or not is moot. I do what I want, and he's already aware of that irritating fact."

"We thought you'd agree with our idea but still wished to ask. We wouldn't assume it would be okay."

"When I'm dreaming, even if you're not there, would you be able to hear me if I were to call out to you?" I asked.

"We don't know. You've never tried. Before, Zephyr would sense that you were having a nightmare and would send us to you. But it would be interesting to try when we aren't trying to save lives and keep you from eating this world." They stirred around me and lifted me from the couch. "You should go home. Dinner is ready."

"I'm not hungry," I answered.

"And you do not meet Solas for dinner because you're hungry. It is because you love him, and he is your home. He is missing his friends as much as you are. He's just better at hiding it." They pulled me from the island into the arms of Solas.

* * * *

"Little Crow, don't cry alone." Solas carried me to bed after dinner and breathed in my sadness. "I'm here."

"I'm scared if I let it out, I won't be able to stop."

Solas curled around me and pulled his darkness tight. "Burn it all, Perdi. I won't let go. I promise."

"I'm sorry, your friends...your people." I couldn't say the rest. The words got caught and came out as a sob.

"I know. We'll find them."

"Is there any news?" I asked.

"Not yet," he answered. "Rest for a bit, Perdi. Faolan should be here later tonight, hopefully with better news. The Aos Si are out, questioning everyone they can catch. The Sluagh are patrolling every inch of our territory, and our guards are all on duty. There's nothing more we can do for now."

I cracked like an egg, and he held on like he'd promised. I bowed on the bed as my Malice crawled out of my throat and screamed for revenge. The flames wrapped around us both, but neither of us burned. He ate my fire as it poured from my soul until I had nothing left but tears. And even those, he ate.

Chapter Seven

I opened my eyes to the thought of Nix and knew I was with him before I saw him. It smelled of him — herbs, fruit, earth and buttercups. The very smell of him calmed me in ways I had forgotten. It reminded me of every hug he had given me, every kind word said, every noble act done. I remembered how his hands felt on my cheeks or how his stomach growled when he was angry and sounded like boulders crashing together when he was hungry. Every detail I hadn't thought of in years played back like a favored song. I could almost picture him walking beside me, arguing, laughing or comfortable in our silence. He always picked flowers as we walked, as though he was in a constant state of finding beauty wherever we were. In our darkest hours, he always found a way to make me smile or draw out my frustration so I could focus. He brought me the best of life in the palms of his hands.

"Turn around, Perdi," the shadows whispered for only my ears to hear. They were with me, inside of me. They swarmed in my stomach, just as my Malice rolled around when excited. This must be what Zephyr experienced, because he always knew what was around every corner without fail. I turned from the view of a valley to a rock-bricked prison.

"You can panic later." They calmed me the moment my heart skipped a beat. "You're here for answers, nothing more. You won't save them in a dream. Don't waste your time trying. We must do what we came here for before you wake."

I let go of the instant panic and scanned the room. I breathed it in as if to memorize the taste in the air. The room was wet, and I could hear drips in the background. A constant flow of water came from somewhere. The room smelled of salty air and mold. In front of me was a room of bricks... No, stones. They were the same shape and size as bricks, but these were older, hand carved from rock. Against the wall, Zephyr leaned with Nix cradled in his arms. They were both bloodied, but Zephyr bore the worst of it as if he had instigated the fight to land on him rather than Nix. He looked like he had taken on army after army on his own. They were alive, but I knew they wouldn't live through endless abuse. I could see it in Zephyr's shoulders, slumped and tired. They were both chained, and at their wrists, their skin had burned and scabbed from the iron.

I stared at Zephyr and shook my head. He was more than this. He could stand against an army, literally by himself, and walk away. Now, he sat chained to a wall for the same reason he'd allowed himself to be imprisoned in the Golden Court...for a Crow.

The shadows leaked from my body and swirled in the air around me. Although they were with me, they couldn't get through to wherever Zephyr and Nix were. They struggled against wards I couldn't see and they couldn't break. Whatever held a Soul-Eater crept down my spine. A wall I couldn't see also blocked a Soul-Eater's passage into the room.

"Perdi, we can't move through the magick." The shadows twisted against the wards.

"Neither can I," I answered and tried, in vain, to move forward. A glass wall stood in my way.

"Whatever is holding them, it is stronger than Zephyr. Whoever has them, he fears them. We see it on his face," the shadows said.

"As do I," I answered. "But what the hell scares a Soul-Eater?"

"Nothing scares him outside of losing you."

I closed my eyes and followed Nix's mind. I tried, as gently as I could to pick through his mind and find the information I needed. I felt his fear for my life and his willingness to die to protect me. It was not a new feeling. It was who he had become. The day he'd walked through the Gate into Whitwick, he'd known he would face a hard life. But what he found was a young girl with two braids and sweets, trying to lure him out of hiding with a bag of candy. He found a girl who would soon become a Crow, who oathed herself to help him, hide him and save him from any who stood against him. He found love in her home and garden. After years, the thought of leaving this young girl, even for the chance of returning to Elphame, scared him. He oathed himself to her for the rest of her days, however long or short either of their lives would be. And from that moment on, there wasn't a force that could keep them apart until now. But that oath still stood, and he took it seriously.

I wanted to linger in his memories of us together. The happiness of them, the love and laughter and every bit he chose to hold dear and think back on in fondness. Even now, as he slept, he thought back to berry picking and teaching me what would cause death and what I could survive on. Instead, I pulled back and kept looking for memories I knew he didn't want – his taking, his imprisonment in the stone hell he now slumbered in.

I found him and Zephyr standing in a field. Nix had just lifted a flower to his nose when hands gripped him. He squirmed and screamed for Zephyr. There were too many hands, too much screaming and so much pain that I couldn't breathe. Unfamiliar magick crackled around him and blocked out the rest of the world. No one would hear them scream. Nix was thrown into an iron mesh bag, and Zephyr was on the ground, bound with iron and symbols. Zephyr could have killed them all, but Nix would have died. Nix screamed for Zephyr to sacrifice him, to let him die and to help me. He begged Zephyr to save me at all costs. But Zephyr didn't have the energy to save anyone. It was being taken from him like pulling the plug on a drain. He knew they would have come for me next. And he knew they'd kill me. Zephyr used the energy he had left to bind the shadows to me. Nix and Zephyr gave themselves to buy time for me to know that those who took them would be coming for me. They craved my death for reasons unknown. The memory went dark, and I was pushed out.

"Foolish little Crow. You don't listen." Zephyr looked up from the wall, and I pulled from Nix's mind. "You should not be here. They will know you were here. Do you wish for them to take you as well?"

"Perdi?" Nix moved from under the safety of Zephyr's arm. "I told you, Zephyr, she'd come no matter what you said or did. She is too stubborn to listen. She's more persistent than garden slugs."

"Nix, hold on." I tried to swallow the pain, to blink away my urge to cry. "Please, just hold on."

"Perdi, you need to stay away. They'll kill you. They are a power I don't know. I've never felt their magick before." Nix curled deeper into Zephyr's arms. He was too tired, too injured. His body pulled for him to sleep, to heal. It was the worst defense mechanism gnomes had. They'd hibernate until they recovered. It didn't serve them well in situations *like this. Though I supposed, when you're hibernating, it was harder to get information out of you.*

"Where are you?" I asked Zephyr.

"I don't know," he answered. It was the first truth he had given me. "Honestly, Perdi, I don't know where we are. I know, by now, you've searched heaven and hell for us."

"I can't find you," I answered.

I reached forward to touch him but couldn't move past the wall of power that kept them in and me out. The urge to try to smash the wall to pieces filled my stomach. But if they knew I was coming, stomping around would only bring more harm to Nix and Zephyr.

"Do not come and find us. We did this to keep you safe." Zephyr spoke over my frustrated groan. "Please, Perdi. Don't do this. I've never asked you for anything, but I'm asking you now, don't do this for us."

"I can't do that, Zeph. You know I can't. You knew I'd look for you and try to find you. It's why you left me your shadows."

"No, little Crow. I left them so you'd always remember me," he answered. "I left them so you'd always be safe. They will protect you as they've protected me. I am giving you a chance to live a life I never had. Take it and guard it, don't throw it away like this."

"I can't just leave you both here."

"Yes, you can. We both came free of will. This, little Crow, is where our paths split. I've known of this day my entire life. The day I'd give my life for a Crow."

"No!" I screamed as he pushed me away. I clawed at the dream. "This is not how it ends."

Nix stirred in pain. It was his mind I was walking in and trying to claw my way through. He lifted his head and smiled weakly. "I want to come home, Perdi, but I won't do it at the expense of your soul. Know I love you and that this is the fate

I have chosen, and I'd do it again and again until you are finally safe. Don't give them a reason to come for you."

"Wait!" I held on to the dream. "Why did they take you? Just tell me why."

"It's simple, Perdi, so you will find us," Nix answered.

"But why?" I asked.

"They believe you will come if they take who you love most," Nix replied.

"Then why didn't they take Solas?" I asked, confused.

Zephyr's face dropped. "They already have, little Crow. They warned you, and you didn't listen." Zephyr sighed. "Stop looking, and you may just live to see another day. It's time to wake up."

I shook my head. "But he's...he's at home."

"Protect our people. At all costs, protect yourself," he answered. "You must defend the Dark Courts. Promise me our people will be safe."

"I won't leave you!" I screamed.

"Wake up!" Zephyr screamed and shoved me back as a door creaked open.

As I fell backward from the glass wall, the shadows pulled me from the dream to an empty bed. My heart pounded in my chest, the feeling of falling still fresh in my bones. Instinctively, I ran my hand over the bed beside me. It was empty. I jumped from the blankets and ran through the house, calling out to Solas. The shadows rolled through the halls and out the windows. I checked every room, screaming his name.

"He's not here." The shadows returned without him by the time I finished checking the house.

"Okay, wait. Check the yard," I shook my head again, "No, wait, he would have heard me screaming. Go to Blood and Bones."

"We did. Solas is not there. Perdi, he's not anywhere," they replied. "We felt him, Solas, as Zephyr pushed you out. We felt his energy come into the dream."

"Where?" I asked. "Where were they?"

"In a place we've never been. It smelled familiar, in the way that all of Elphame smells different, yet the same. It looked like every other basement we've been in and felt like every other dungeon that's spilled blood before. It was familiar and different. We don't know where it is. It is a kingdom we've never journeyed to."

I leaned against the wall, slid to a crouch and tried to control a panic attack that threatened to take control. I couldn't breathe. I wanted to be sick. I wanted to curl into a ball. I couldn't think. I was scattered in every direction. I shook my head and tried to settle all the thoughts to the bottom. My pulse sped in a race that would cost my heart its life at the finish line. I breathed deeply and released the tension in a long, ragged breath that turned into a groan. I couldn't burn, not right now. I needed control, or I would be as lost as they were. I had to focus. There was no one left who would do it for me. There was no one left who could put out my fires. The shadows didn't have hands, and I almost started to laugh at the thought.

"A kingdom you've never been to," I wondered out loud. "There are no kingdoms Zephyr has not either invaded or has been in and out of. There is no place in Elphame that Solas hasn't waged war on. Together, there isn't a stone they haven't looked under."

"This is true," the shadows replied. "This is why we said where they're being held is unfamiliar and concerning. There is no place hidden from Zephyr or Solas."

"Okay, all right." I stood and swallowed my panic. I nodded my head over and over and began to pace in a small line, back and forth, grounding myself with each step. "I just have to think. There's an answer somewhere. I just need to stop and think it through...let go of the desperation and focus."

"What answer?" the shadows asked.

"What the hell I do next," I replied. "What would Solas do? Whatever he would do is what I should do." I groaned. "I don't know what he would do. He always has a dozen balls in the air, juggling and planning ten steps ahead of everyone else. I didn't pay enough attention. It was always too much to wrap my head around. And he rarely did any work at home. He didn't want court matters in our home anymore. This place was supposed to be our sanctuary where the outside world couldn't hurt us. When he and Zephyr would talk about the happenings of Elphame, they already had the problem solved before it needed a solution."

"That, what Solas would do, we are unsure of. We could not hear his thoughts, only his confirmed plans. But we can tell you what Zephyr would do, if that would assist you?"

I nodded. "Yes, okay, if Zephyr would do it, Solas would probably do it as well—or argue until it was some version they could agree on."

"If Zephyr were here and Solas were missing, he would call the Aos Si to protect the territory. That was always his first move, shielding his people from whatever came next. Then, Zephyr would inform the Sluagh that Solas was missing, and they would fill the lands and guard the territory and the Dark Court's subjects. We believe they would both protect their people before anything else. Solas never went to war without ensuring war could not touch his land. Zephyr did the same. War has never touched the Court of

Shadows or the Dark Court, because they've never left it unguarded."

I nodded. "Right, okay. How do I call them?"

"There's Aos Si right outside. You just need to call out to them."

"Where?" I asked and looked around. "Outside, in the yard?"

"And inside. It's their job not to be seen or heard, Perdi. They only come when you call."

"If they're inside, how the hell did someone get in here and take Solas?" I asked.

"Solas was likely not here," they answered. "We didn't feel him while you were asleep. When you're wrapped in us, Solas goes about his work. He trusts you're safe with us."

"Guard!" I yelled out and watched as three Aos Si bled from the hall, window and from behind me, from the kitchen. "Bloody hell, how many of you are in the manor?"

A young Aos Si stepped forward and bowed. "There are eight inside the manor, my lady. One dozen in the yard. Should you wish to know how many are on the property, I can find out."

"No, that's fine. You've heard, then, what has happened?" I asked.

"Indeed. When you woke, we called those on the guards to return to the house and start a search. Two hours ago, Solas left the manner to continue his search for Zephyr. He went alone. When we heard your screams, we came inside and waited on you to call for us. What would you have me do?"

"Ahh." I paced. I didn't have the words. "Umm...we need to protect our people first. However I go about doing that, that's what I want you to do."

"My lady, if I may be so bold as to suggest you declare a Royal Call, have all Aos Si and Royal Guard come and maintain guard within your lands. I will see that the Sluagh and Blood and Bones are notified of the call and come to your aid."

"Umm…is that what Solas would do?" I asked.

"Truthfully, Solas and Zephyr are what hell unleashed when someone threatens the Dark Courts. They've never had the need to decree a Royal Call. But, in their absence, I believe they would approve of this declaration if it meant you and our people would be protected."

"Okay, yes, please do that," I answered.

"As you command," he said and backed out of the room.

"Shadows," I called out. "What now? What step would Zephyr or Solas take next?"

"You do not need to call us by name. Just do as you did before. Either motion with your hand and we will see it or call us with your soul. How you call us hasn't changed. Call as you always have, think of us as usual and we will hear you," they replied, and I nodded. "You are to meet Faolan at nightfall. It is nightfall."

"I think I have bigger problems than meeting Faolan," I replied.

"This is true, but Solas felt Faolan could help. You should believe the same thing until proven otherwise. Keep on the path. He chooses his paths for a reason. Follow Solas. He will lead you to Zephyr and Nix. Solas is not a man of idle actions. He is a master of tools, and if he's selected Faolan as a tool worthy of use, so should you. Faolan, as much as we dislike him, can guide you to what comes next. If anything, he's crafty and knows how to protect his people. You may learn something more from him than from us," they answered, and I grumbled. "As to what Zephyr would do, he would wage war on whoever stood in his way and kill everyone who stood against him to get Solas back. I doubt waging wars will help at this very minute, but it may come to that. Are you willing to war for them?"

"Yes," I answered.

"Then you must follow the path at your feet, like it or not."

"I don't know if I can trust Faolan."

"You have friends here. You just have to find them."

I groaned. "Go, ask Faolan to come. Don't steal him. Ask him and Oisin to come. Tell them I need their help."

Chapter Eight

Oisin and Faolan found me pacing when they stepped into the dining room. I looked up and knew I looked like hell had crawled out of my soul. My eyes were puffy from crying. My skin felt sunburned, and every move I made peeled a layer off. It felt like my hand was on a lightning bolt and wouldn't let go.

"What's happened now?" Oisin teased at first until he met my eyes. He rushed over. "Perdi, what happened?"

"Solas is gone," I answered. My words felt strangled in my tight throat.

"He left?" Oisin asked, surprise on his face. "Whatever has happened, he'll come back. He'd never leave you. He loves you more than his own beating heart."

I shook my head. "No, not like that. He didn't leave me. He was taken while I slept."

"Who would be that brave?" Faolan asked. "Of anyone to take, Solas would not be a choice I'd willingly make. I would take Zephyr before touching Solas."

"I dreamed of Nix and Zephyr but couldn't find them." I groaned at the thought of explaining how I got into their dreams. Instead, I stopped talking and stared blankly.

"It's okay, Perdi. We already know," Faolan responded to my dread. "I've known for some time. Your secret will never leave my lips. I oath myself to your secret. May the wild hunt track me to my death for spilling it."

"Another Finis, right under my nose." Oisin sighed. "You have my word of honor and oath. I will not tell your secrets."

"Thank you," I replied, but the unease didn't pass. "I'm glad I won't have to kill you both to keep that secret. I've enough on my plate at the moment."

"Two of you... This is not good, Perdi. If someone other than your friends were to know?" Oisin spoke the truth, just as Zephyr would have. "Could this be why this is happening? Finis are hunted to their deaths. I'm not saying you or Zephyr deserve death, but I think it's worth pointing out a potential reason for this."

"I never thought I'd see the day where you said Zephyr didn't deserve to die," I replied. "Honestly, if they were doing this because they knew who I was, they'd simply come to kill me. They wouldn't risk pissing Zeph or me off. They'd kill us as soon as they could. They wouldn't keep either of us alive. Whatever the hell this is about has nothing to do with what I am. They wouldn't dare do it this way."

"But everyone knows what Zephyr is. Why would they risk taking him and keeping him alive?" Faolan added.

"They took them so I'd come. Whatever their endgame is, it involves luring me willingly. I think they knew that if they had just taken me, Solas and Zephyr would hunt them down before they could kill me," I answered. "Me and the shadows went looking for them. I can't get into Zephyr's dreams unless he allows it. But Nix? I got into his. Neither me nor the shadows could tell where they are being held. There's magick holding them in that I can't get around. They're being held in some sort of warded stone room. They're in rough condition."

"Rough condition. That's saying a lot, given Zephyr eats war for breakfast, and Nix can take just as much as any of us." Faolan winced at the thoughts that crossed his mind that he thankfully kept to himself.

"So, they're not dead?" Oisin asked. "No offense, Perdi, but who the hell keeps a Soul-Eater alive? Let alone a gnome with the ear of the Dark Courts and the only other Soul-Eater?"

"To bait me," I answered.

"Why would they think that would work?" he asked. "Who walks willingly into a trap?"

Faolan smiled. "Because it will work. Won't it, Perdi?"

"Yes. It will. Once I find out where they are," I replied and released a shaking breath. "They have everyone I love. They have my family. Damn it, I can't think straight."

Oisin held out his hand and blew little snow crystals toward me, putting out the fire in my stomach before it burst over. He winked when I shivered. "Let's not burn the house down, at least not while we're standing in it."

"Thank you." I finally released a hot breath I had been holding. "Any news?"

"We've been everywhere, Perdi," Faolan answered. "We've been from one end of Elphame to the other. There are no signs of Zephyr or Nix, and I will assume no Solas now. There's not a whisper of hate against you, Perdi. Solas, on the other hand? He has earned the reputation they speak of. He's feared and not liked, as you are loved. No one has muttered a single slight against Nix. He, like you, is well liked. As for Zephyr, no one would even talk about him. He's a Soul-Eater. People won't even say his name out loud for fear of calling him or his shadows to their doors."

"No one is this brave," Oisin added. "We're a cocky lot of men and woman, us Fae, born with a sword in our hands. But there's bravery, and there's stupidity. Not many fit the bill of blatant insanity when it comes to poking at the Dark Courts."

I grinned and looked at Faolan. "Oh, I can think of a few people who have thought about it."

Faolan blushed. "In my defense, I was dropped on my head as a baby."

"How many times?" Oisin laughed, decreasing the awkwardness in the room. "What's next, Perdi? There isn't a stone we haven't turned over in Elphame."

"Zephyr said..." I paused and rolled his words over in my mind. "He said I'd search all of Elphame and wouldn't find him. But I also checked the mortal world, and he isn't there. If me and the shadows, along with Solas before he was taken, the Guardians, Seers, Aos Si and you guys, couldn't find them here, they aren't here."

"I don't know where else to look," Faolan said.

"Is there a place here that isn't Elphame? Is Blood and Bones considered Elphame? Because I'm fine with flipping that place upside down. If I must, I'll open the walls and bring that place to the ground."

"Blood and Bones *is* Elphame. It is the original Elphame," Faolan answered. "Solas said he had already been there and found nothing. If Solas has said that they aren't there, blowing up Blood and Bones isn't going to do much more than cost lives and anger people you don't want a war with tonight."

"The shadows told me it was a kingdom they didn't know. The place they're being held is familiar…but not. It looks like everywhere else they've been, but they've never stepped foot there. It smells like Elphame and salt water and moss and fish. It feels like Elphame, but also not. Does that make sense?" I asked.

"Should we head to the north?" Oisin asked. "It sounds like Perdi is describing the north."

"The Golden Court? They wouldn't dare try this," I countered. "They're senseless in their pursuit for power, but they wouldn't try to take it from Solas and definitely not Zephyr. Nix, perhaps, but they'd know I'd come asking questions. And who do you think I'd bring along on my walk to the Golden Courts if I came? The very monster I released from their dungeons."

"Not the Golden Court. I was already there, and you're right. They wouldn't dare and didn't," Faolan explained. "They're hiding something, as usual, but Zephyr and Nix are not part of it."

"Then where are you suggesting?" I asked Oisin.

The shadows curled out from under the table. "The rest of Elphame that isn't Elphame, Perdi. If Zephyr said you would check all of Elphame and wouldn't find him, we need to look outside Elphame. The islands off the northern coast. It is Elphame, but not."

I frowned. "What islands? I've seen the maps. There are no islands."

"No islands we've ever stepped foot on," Oisin replied. "We don't go there."

"Who lives there?" I asked.

"We don't know. We don't go there," Faolan answered. "We know they're populated. By what? I've no idea."

"Literally, no one has ever gone there, and no one has ever come from there," Oisin said. "They've been there for as long as any text has ever been written. I figured that anyone who wants to be hidden from Fae and has worked that hard to remain as such doesn't need me poking around. They've never caused a problem and stay out of our business."

Faolan stood. "I'll grab the texts, and we can meet back here in the next couple of hours."

"I don't know if they'll take you next for helping me," I replied. "You could be at risk, Faolan. You need to know that."

Faolan smiled. "That's sweet, but I doubt I'm at risk. There's nothing to gain from it. They're taking who is important to you, and I am not one of those people." When I went to open my mouth, he lifted his hand. "I know where I stand, and I put myself there. It's okay. You don't need to make any more excuses for me."

"I'll remain here with you, Perdi," Oisin said. "I can help you with your guard and fill your house to the rafters with protection. War and protection are what I do and where I can be of service to you."

Faolan left as the Aos Si arrived. I heard the screech of Sluagh as they landed in our yard. Once, that sound would have scared me. It had happened many times. But tonight, I felt safer for it. As I relaxed to the calls the

Dark Court carried over the wind, I watched Oisin tense.

"I wouldn't want to be out there," Oisin muttered.

"They're not that bad when they're on your side." I smiled but understood his discomfort.

Oisin laughed. "I've never stood on this side of the Sluagh but I'm bloody thankful that's where I am this time. Out of everyone I've ever feared on the battlefield, they were the only ones I've only ever run from."

A shiver snaked down my spine as the Aos Si entered the house and moved throughout the rooms. I could feel their rage pouring off of them like fire I couldn't hide from. It was a familiar feeling. They moved like a force I didn't want to stand in front of. I watched as Oisin stepped closer to me. He wasn't a fool. He knew there would be no safer place to be than by my side in a house filled with men who'd kill him without a second thought. When they moved through the dining room, they didn't stop and demand I act. They already knew I would. It seemed they thought I had a plan, which I didn't.

I motioned to the shadows. "Go find Orrian and her people. Tell her what's happened and ask her to come. Tell her I need her help. If you snatch her, she'll find a way to kill you again."

I'd feel safer with her here. I felt a pang of guilt for calling her back. She had been rebuilding her small court on a chunk of land given to her by Solas and me — a gift for her sacrifice and loyalty. A place that would be hers, and she could war to protect. I hadn't been there yet and wasn't invited until her lands were ready. Only a few had been allowed to cross her tiny borders to help with the building. No one dared, once they found out the Fairy Queen had returned. She would be hosting a party once her court was complete. I made a note to send her a fruit tree from the island, maybe two.

"My Queen, I am Aeden." An Aos Si soldier stepped forward and bowed his head. "The lands are protected. Zeno has pulled every Aos Si into the territory. Everyone has returned safely from outside the Dark Courts. How may we serve you?"

"I'm not your queen," I replied.

"Respectfully, my lady, you are the oathed partner of our king. That makes you our queen—and, in his absence, ruler of the Dark Courts."

My breath caught in my throat, and I turned to Oisin. "Queen?"

"Don't ask me. I don't know, Perdi. The Dark Courts have never had a queen in all of their history. Solas' mother remained in Blood and Bones, and his father never took another oathed partner. Solas has never had a partner until you, oathed or not. You would be the first one."

"I don't know how to be a queen," I muttered to Oisin.

He shrugged and shook his head. "I don't know what your customs are here. If it's like any other court, it's a title of respect. It doesn't come with duties aside from planning parties. So, your guess is as good as mine."

Aeden cleared his throat. He looked insulted for me. From behind him, several Aos Si men snuffed their laughter. Aeden looked around me to Oisin, and it wasn't a nice look. "If I may be permitted to say, only the weakest lead from behind—and our queen is not weak. She is the pulse of our lands, the power that draws our blades. Kingdoms who shelter their queens are weak and will always fall to the feet of ours."

I smiled. "Please, do continue."

He stood, towering over me by two feet and over two hundred pounds of pure muscle, his eyes cutting through the air to meet Oisin. "We are like no other court, Commander Oisin. It is why so many others flock in hordes to the dark lands, tired of the stagnant ways of the old courts. Our queen has the same power and authority as the king. When you speak to her, you speak to the throne of the entire kingdom. And in the absence of our Commander, it is she who leads us to battle. She commands all of the Dark Court and Aos Si, and we will follow her into the pits of hell, to our very deaths, if that is the sacrifice for her victory. We would remove our skin to shield her from the very sun, should it bother her delicate flesh. We march to the beat of her heart, and we will cut yours out if the rhythm troubles her ears. For lack of a better term, she is the very reason you and many others still breathe. And without Zephyr here to calm her fires, we will help her light them and watch you all burn. Unlike our Commander, we will lock you inside a building to burn, just to hear you scream."

"Yeah, that sounds like the Dark Courts," Oisin replied. "How very uncomfortable."

"We are Aos Si. We are not the Dark Court, Commander. We are much worse than that." Aeden flashed a smile that backed up his claim. "Perdita Darkmore has been written into our laws since the oath of their partnership was confirmed. When Solas is not here, she is the very soul of our lands."

"And what about when Solas is home?" I asked, curious.

"The king is absolute law in the Dark Courts, but we must consider all you say. In the end, Zephyr will decide who we follow. It is the law of Aos Si. But no matter who we follow, Zephyr and Solas have decreed that no one, including themselves, may harm you. It is a death sentence to act in harm against you. We are all oathed to this law, regardless of rank."

"You'd kill your own king?" Oisin blurted out with a surprised and nervous laugh.

"If he were to harm our queen, why should he not die like any other who would dare? Why should any man wish to hurt his mate? He is oathed to protect her. If it is not my sword, the wild hunt will take his life just the same. Although I'd pray I got to him before the hunt. It is...how do mortals say" — Aeden waved his hand in search of the word — "fucking horrendous to harm those we have sworn we would protect." Aeden straightened his back. "Men like that, crown or not, do not deserve life and should see death swiftly. And those who stand at his side and watch face the same punishment. It is rather simple."

"Okay, I'm sorry I asked," Oisin replied. I cringed at his mocking tone.

"The law was written by Solas and Zephyr and witnessed by a Royal, Nix Lubdan, of the Ulster Territory and Lubdan line, after Solene tried to take her from us. It cannot be undone," he explained and saw the look on my face. I wanted them to drop the subject, not keep needling each other. I looked back to Oisin. "I am simply making this strong point because I greatly dislike when I've given a warning, only for men to beg for their lives for failing to heed that warning. Zephyr has made it clear. We are to give others a chance to make the right decision. Unless I provide the information for others to make the right choice, I cannot kill you for making the wrong one."

"I'm with you on this." Oisin stepped forward.

"I hope so. My queen appears to like you, and I feel she would hurt to find you missing your heart and your hands. I do not believe there is a hole deep enough for me to hide your body from her."

The shadows twisted around my ankles. "We could help you find a place to hide the Commander. Zephyr has many spots he favors." The men in the room tried to eat their laughter, but we all laughed, including Oisin.

"My Queen, we await your orders." Aeden looked at me as if I had an answer.

"Don't call me that. My first name is fine," I scolded him, uncomfortable with titles. "Go tell the others the same thing." As he stepped away, I grabbed his arm, and he froze. "Have you eaten dinner yet? You've been here all day."

"No, my…no, we have not," he answered and bit his tongue, trying not to address me formally. "It is not a bother. Do not worry for us."

"It is a bother, and I do worry. Go eat and rest. I have a feeling it's going to be a long night and a longer tomorrow."

"As you wish. When you retire for the night, we will guard your door. If you need anything, just call."

"Thank you, Aeden. And when you return, please make sure all the trainees return with you. I'd prefer them to remain closer to me."

"Are you certain you do not mean the Aos Si? The full-ranking members?"

"I'm certain of what I've said. Bring all the trainees back with you, please," I answered, and he nodded, looking slightly confused. I waved him off. When I turned, Oisin was bowing with a smirk on his face.

"My fair queen," he teased.

"Don't start, and keep this to yourself, would you?"

"The Aos Si are pretty damn intense." Oisin scrunched his face into a worried look.

"This is nothing, Oisin," I countered. "The older they get, the less likely you'll have a conversation with one without your head coming off in the process. It's true, though. They will warn you. Whether you still live is a different matter."

"I got that, loud and clear," he answered. "Perdi, I'm glad you sent for us, that you're letting us help. I feel like I owe you not only my life but for my people."

"Why do you think Faolan is willing to help me?" I asked. "I know why you're here, and it has nothing to do with Faolan ordering you to come. You're here because you care. But I don't know why he's here, not really. I read his soul, but much of it is clouded with doubt and shame."

"I think he's scared—in part because the Dark Court is more powerful now than ever before...and also because he feels guilty. Whether you want to see it or not, he feels a lot of shame for all he's done, and he's working to fix it. If given a chance, I think you'd see what I see in him. He's had to travel a long, broken road to get here."

"I can appreciate that. I know what guilt feels like and the wish to do anything in my power to set things right," I answered. If amends were what Faolan needed to heal, I could give him that chance. I knew the drive to repair and not being allowed to do it. "Why is the Dark Court more powerful now than before? Is it because of Blood and Bones?"

"No, guess again." Oisin grinned. "It's because you're here."

"Why does that matter? Is it because of what Zeph and I are?"

"No. We all have monsters in our courts." He winked. "It's because no one is more powerful or fearsome than a man with something to lose, something to protect. Both Solas and Zephyr are a force on their own. Add you, and they'd burn it all if you were cold. Add the power of the wee folk, Nix and Orrian, and holy hell, it's terrifying to border with your land — not to mention the Aos Si. They follow Zephyr, but after tonight's show, they'd follow you into hell just as quickly," he answered, then pointed to the Aos Si, who tried to blend in, but were lurking and watching, even as they spoke among themselves. It was idle chitchat, nothing more. All of their attention was on me. "You've placed yourself between the most powerful of Elphame. But they are only the most powerful because of you. And I think, Perdi, that is why they are gone, and you're still here. It's why Zephyr has told you not to come. And it would be why Solas would tell you not to come if he could. They'd risk themselves to save you."

I laughed. "No, Oisin, Solas wouldn't tell me to stay away. Zephyr and Nix would. But not him. He wouldn't waste his breath like that."

"He'd ask you to come? Even if it means you're at risk?"

"He wouldn't ask, but he wouldn't have to ask. He would just know and is probably digging a hole to shelter himself from my rage as we speak. He knows me well enough to know that asking me to stay away would be a waste of energy. We will always help each other and will always come for the other, no matter the risk," I answered. "Whoever has them is already dead.

They just don't know it yet. But Solas knows, and he's waiting for it."

"Or *you're* walking to your death, and *you* just don't know it yet," he countered.

"Perhaps, but the world will tremble at my passing. And those who survive it will remember my name," I replied. "Go eat, Oisin, before you regret not having a last meal."

After pacing my legs into exhaustion, I dropped myself in front of the fireplace in a small room off the dining room. I curled up and stared into nothingness. I felt nothing and everything. I watched another guard, Finn, take his post not ten feet from me. I didn't know him well, but I remembered him to be mouthy as hell. I felt closer to Zephyr, having a member of the Aos Si near me. But Solas felt a world away. It didn't feel like home without him. Nix, I feared for the most. Although he was strong of heart, he was small and easily injured compared to the battle-worn men he was with. Gnomes were fierce and brutal without hesitation, but they didn't do so well in torturous captivity.

"The day you stepped foot on Elphame soil, the world quaked. I was there. I felt it in my bones." Finn spoke without turning to face me. He was busy searching for the next threat. "And the world hasn't been the same since."

"For worse?" I asked.

"It depends on whose side you stand on," he answered.

"What about for you, Finn?" I asked.

"I enjoy the rumble, my lady." I watched a grin pull at the sides of his mouth. "Rest, before you regret not having your last nap."

"Wake me if anything happens," I called back to him.

"There are other people to drag our enemies' bodies to the fires," he replied. "There's no reason to wake you to clean up after us."

I smiled. "You all are a cocky bunch. You, especially."

"It's not ego, although I have an enormous one, Zephyr has informed me. It's simply the truth. You don't remain the strongest army in all of Elphame by waiting on everyone else to clean up after you."

I nodded in understanding. "You're much politer today than when we first met. What's the catch?"

"Zephyr and Solas are the catch," he replied, his voice tired. I didn't know if he was sleepy or just sick of getting run over by court wheels. "Titles strangle us all."

"Some more than others," I replied, just as tired as him.

"Are you ready for what you will face to get your family back?" Finn asked.

"I'm not scared of who took them. I pity them," I replied.

"You've spent too much time with Solas if you don't fear what can take the Finis, a gnome and the King of Darkness." Finn shook his head. "I'm not talking about who you'll need to face to get them back. I'm talking about Zephyr. If he's hidden himself from you and the rest of us, are you ready to face what else he may do to keep protecting you?"

"The truth is, I don't know. I didn't think Zephyr would do what he's already doing, but here we are," I answered. "What more can he do? He's already captive."

"I don't think I want to find out, either. This is a first for us all, but here we are, and we're ready to find out, but I worry," Finn replied.

"About what?" I asked.

"You're bringing his very tools with you. Are you so foolish not to think he'll use us once he has the chance?"

"No, but I'll have found him. I don't care about the rest," I replied.

"You should care. The unknown will always be what bites you in the ass. It'll be what causes you the most pain," he replied. I knew he was right. But my need to find them overrode my need to keep Zephyr happy. "Get some sleep, little...birdy."

I stared up at him quizzically. "Little birdy?"

"It rhymes with your name. I know how much it would hurt to be called a little Crow right now. And from what I've been told, 'queen' is not an option."

"Birdy." I smiled and let the softness of his comment send me to sleep.

Chapter Nine

Sleep came and went in the blink of an eye. Every noise and whisper pulled me from my attempts to rest. As I kicked off a blanket that had been placed on me while I slept, Aeden was placing soup and tea beside me. He didn't need to say the words for me to know I had to eat or I'd run out of energy. I was empty, completely drained, as if the Gods had reached down and wrung out everything good like a dish rag.

I glanced around the room. "Where did Finn go?"

"He's patrolling. I could call him back if you'd prefer?"

"No. I just didn't hear him leave. You guys move like the wind."

"We're not nearly that loud." Aeden smiled. He pushed the bowl of soup on the table beside me a little closer as a hint to eat it. "It is chicken. It has noodles made by Nix. They were in your private kitchen. He gave me a package a couple weeks ago. I traded him pears."

"It sounds like Nix is quite the bootlegger around here." I laughed, thinking of Nix smuggling goods across borders for jams and cakes. "Thank you, Aeden. Did you eat?"

"I did. Not any of your soup, though. I do not eat meat."

"How are you built like a mountain and don't eat meat?" I asked. "I think you're the first Fae I've met who doesn't eat meat."

"Most Aos Si do not consume animals. We eat products of animals but not the creatures themselves," he answered. "When your very existence brings death to your door at a constant, you stop doing a lot of things that result in death, such as killing for food."

"Makes sense why Zephyr has such an enormous garden," I answered. I leaned back and glanced into the dining room. "What would you do, Aeden?"

"I would need you to be specific. There are many things you could be referring to."

"Would you trust Faolan and Oisin?" I asked.

"I don't think it's a matter of trust, my lady. You must ask yourself, how useful are they to you? Can you ensure they will remain useful? And lastly, what are you willing to do should they no longer be useful to you?"

"This would be a hell of a lot easier if Zeph or Solas were here. Solas can do this in his sleep."

"Why?" he asked. "Faolan and Oisin's use doesn't grow or diminish depending on who else is in the room making the decision. And I truly do think they fear you above everyone else."

"Because they would know what to do, and I don't," I answered.

"I believe you know what to do. You're merely struggling with the tough decisions. Are you seeking Zephyr and Solas because you'd rather they make the choices for you? Or are you seeking someone to still love you after you've made the call?"

"Good point," I replied. "It's always easier when someone else makes the tough decisions and even better when you don't feel like a monster afterward."

"Rest easy. Both will still love you, even if you slaughter your way through the courts to get to them. Don't forget, my lady, you are the Queen of the Dark. Everyone expects you to kill your way to your people. Solas is likely laughing in the face of his captors for what hell they've unleashed by taking him from you."

"I don't want to have to do that," I answered.

"But you will if you have to, and we all know it," he replied. "Use the tools you have or leave bodies in your wake. Both will get you there, but one will hurt more than the other. Be ready to pay the cost for either. You're the only one who will pay for it. The rest of us? We're used to marching through blood."

I drank the cardboard-tasting liquid and carried my tea to the dining room. There, Faolan stood with Oisin. The Aos Si guards moved to the room's perimeter once I stepped in. While I'd slept, they'd kept an uncomfortable eye on my guests. The moment I stepped into the room, I watched both Faolan and Oisin relax.

"Faolan, I'd like a treaty between my court and yours," I told him. "I'm not exactly sure how to do this, so bear with me."

"Your court?" He smiled. "So, it's true. Queen Perdita. It has a nice ring to it."

"Don't start," I replied, then smiled softly. It did have a mighty good ring to it.

"And the first thing you're going to do under your reign is to align yourself with the man who almost killed you on more than one occasion?" he asked. "I can think of several others who would be a better choice."

"First, several others aren't here. You are. Everyone knows my people are missing, and not one of them has come to offer aid. Second, let's be real here. Every other court would likely kill me faster than you ever would. Out of all my available options, I trust you the most, and I'm willing to give you a chance. I'm risking a lot accepting your help. But I need it and feel it is worth the risk," I answered. "I want my people back. I can't do it alone, and I'd like to have those at my back who I know won't sell me down the river. I don't think you'll be the one to stab me in the back, and if you do, we both know you'll die before I do."

Oisin cleared his throat. "I'm not a Royal, but I don't think this is how treaties go. This sounds like more like threats, Perdi."

"It's my first day. Give me a break." I shrugged. "Faolan, I'd like a truce between us, however we do that. I will protect you and your people, and in turn, you protect me and mine until I find Solas. After that, I am willing to come back to the table and discuss further agreements."

"I think I'm getting the better deal. I do not have the power or men that you have."

"No, but you're much better at lying than I am." I smiled. It was one of the first friendly smiles I had given him in a long time. "And you're willing to die for your people, as I am for mine."

"Truce between us, Perdi," Faolan finally said. He walked to the table, holding rolls of paper, with Oisin behind him.

I barely had to raise my hand before Aeden stood at my side. "Was this a stupid move, aligning myself with him?"

"If he trips again, rest assured, we will be there to catch him. No problem is too great for us to correct. No dog is too big to be put down." Aeden threatened Faolan without needing to say the words.

"Good to know." I smiled and left Aeden grinning.

Faolan spread a map over the table, and Orrian fluttered down from the window. She had returned while I was asleep. I'd woken to her shrills and cursing when she was told to be quiet because I was sleeping.

Orrian walked the map. She wore a small belt around her waist with tiny bags dangling, but that was all. Orrian didn't go anywhere without her herbs, especially near me. I was always in need of her salves and medicines. My knuckles and knees had been rescued by her more times than I could count.

"It's good to see you, Orrian. I'm sorry it's for this reason," I said and felt a little smaller for having pulled her back into another war. Her smile, as uncomfortable as ever, told me she'd have come no matter what. "Have you ever been up there, to the northern islands?"

She shook her head.

"Do you know what's up there?"

She shrugged and fluttered to land on Oisin's shoulder, who translated for her. "She says she's heard rumors. When Blood and Bones closed, many decided to split into the courts we see now, but one group of people left for that island and never returned. They've never been seen since. She doesn't know who or what they are, only that they simply *are*."

"Ma'am." Aeden, who hadn't left my side, stepped forward.

"Just wait, please." I waved him off. "Orrian, continue."

Orrian leaned around Oisin's neck and pointed to the guard. I sighed and turned to face him.

"Do you have something to add?" I asked.

"Yes, Ma'am," he answered. It was a step up from being called a queen, but not by much.

"Ma'am? I'm not that old. Perdi... Please, just call me Perdi," I said as I motioned for him to speak. "What do you need? If you tell me someone else is missing, I'm going to burn this house to the damn ground with you inside."

"I may be of some help in this area, Ma'...Perdi." He corrected my name. "I am not as old as Zephyr, but I know what happened when the courts divided."

"Do you have something to add or...?" I asked and motioned for him to continue. "Don't beat around the bush. Just say the words. I'm sorry, Aeden, but I'm all out of patience."

"Very well. Those whom you seek, they are the Satyr," he answered. "They are who occupy that island."

"Myth," Oisin interrupted. "They are stories we tell children to scare them into bed."

I huffed a laugh. "Yeah, and the Fae were stories told to mortals to make us behave."

"I see your point. But Fae stood in your living rooms, wandered your streets and *did* scare your children. We weren't a myth. We were a nightmare you could see and touch. Regrettably, for your people, Perdi." Oisin

156

winced when he realized that although I was mostly Fae now, I had been mortal once and had been hunted like the rest. "No one has ever seen a Satyr, *ever*. Wouldn't it make more sense that they are simply a story?"

"And until the Gate came down, there weren't many outside Whitwick who had seen Fae either," I countered. "Aeden, continue, please."

"Your comment regarding no one seeing a Satyr, respectfully, Commander, is incorrect. All the older Aos Si and some Seers have seen them. They once lived below Blood and Bones. The Satyr are half man and half beast. They were the original halflings of Elphame. Not half mortal and half Fae, they were simply half of us and half magick twisted wrong. When the war broke out, they left and were never seen again. They never fought for a side. They left completely and never came back. They've never reached out to anyone since they left."

"And you just let them set up on some random island?" I asked. "With no one checking on them?"

"Why would we check on them? They are deserving of their lives and freedoms, as any other." He stared at me like what I had asked was ridiculous.

"If they have those I love, they have forfeited both," I answered.

He dipped his head but kept his eyes on me. It wasn't a friendly look. It reminded me of how a wild animal stared you down before it jumped you. "I would gladly hold them down for you."

"Is there anything else that left Blood and Bones and hasn't been seen since that I should know about?"

"A great many things, but I fear we do not have the time for me to list them, nor us to track them down and shake the truth from their bones. Most, if it helps, are here in the Dark Courts, mainly the Court of Less. Solas would be the one to answer that question with the most up-to-date information," Aeden answered.

"Good to know. I won't be taking many strolls out there alone anymore," I replied.

"I believe they fear you more than you should fear them," Aeden added.

"We'll focus on one group at a time, and the Satyr are on the top of that list. How do we get in there?"

"In the words of Zephyr, we can't just kick down the door and walk in," Aeden replied, a smile filling his face.

Behind that smile was a world of pain I couldn't begin to describe. Lost in my own anguish, I felt the pain that Aeden felt, adding another layer to my own. His love for Zephyr ate the air around him and made it harder to breathe.

I smiled softly. "Yeah, that's something he'd say. But I say we can…and we will."

The shadows swirled at my feet. "We can help."

"How?"

"We can bring you there, Perdi. Across the water," they answered.

"How many of us can you bring over?" I asked.

"As many as needed. We'll need to collect energy if the group is large. We cannot risk running out and needing to find more while moving you all."

"Eat the other shadows in the back," I answered. "It's not like they're of any other use. Spit them back out when you've eaten their energy."

The shadows rippled through the room and poured out of the windows.

"You'll go, knowing they are expecting you?" Aeden asked.

"To get my people back, I will."

"We will not be able to go with force. They'll see us coming," he countered.

"I'm open to suggestions," I answered. "But to be honest, they'll know I'm coming, regardless of who I show up with."

Faolan called from the table. "Send a small group first. See what happens. Test the waters."

My mouth dropped, and I turned to face him. "You want me to *what?*"

"Sacrifice the one for the many. It is what Zephyr would do." Faolan stepped to my side.

I shook my head, and both Aeden and I said in unison, "No, he wouldn't."

"Yes, Perdi, he would. If you were on that island, he would sacrifice us all." Faolan lifted his hands and backed up. "I'm not saying he'd indiscriminately offer up his people, but for you, he would — and so would Solas. We can argue about the morality of it, or we can skip to the end where we agree that Zephyr, Solas and Nix would hand any one of us over in exchange for you."

"I'm not going to do that," I replied.

Faolan nodded. He knew I wouldn't do it, even if everyone had agreed to be a sacrificial lamb. He thought for a moment before he said his next words, knowing what I would and wouldn't agree with. "If they couldn't win that way, they would test the waters before jumping in. I do not know Zephyr or Solas nearly as well as their furthest stranger, but I do know that they both know war better than the rest of us, collectively. They wouldn't walk in blindly. Both would have several backup plans before the first plan was even off the ground. Solas wins wars, Perdi, for a reason, most of which he could do without stepping foot on the battlefield. And Zephyr would only jump headfirst if he knew how deep the water was, what was down there, how to kill it, how to get back out and who else he needed to kill if that wasn't an option. And all the while, Solas would be stone-faced because he and Zephyr would have it planned out to the last detail. Never, in all my years, have I seen either of them flinch, for a reason. It is uncomfortable how prepared they are."

I nodded. "*That* is Zephyr. And that is very much Solas."

Aeden cleared his throat. "I know Zephyr, of course, not as well as you, Ma'...Perdi. I have followed him into every battle I've ever fought. I have learned a great deal from him. I believe he would send a small group in before sending those he couldn't risk losing. He wouldn't sacrifice me, but I wouldn't be a loss for his army. I am no one to his army. Send me first. I am willing to go. And I will report back if I can. If I can't, I'll die trying to get my Commander back. It's an honorable death."

"You're not no one to Zephyr. You matter to him, or you wouldn't be here," I countered. "And he calls *me* a bleeding heart. His heart bleeds for Elphame and his people much more freely than mine does."

"Perdi, I am of the lowest rank in his army," Aeden countered. "It's why I'm here with you. Respectfully, it is an honor, but it's because the strongest are out patrolling. Nothing will get to you with them out there. And if they do get past, I am the sacrifice to give you time to escape. Dozens of us can be risked without his army feeling the blow. If I were to die, it wouldn't impact the others in any noticeable way. I wouldn't diminish their ranks."

"They're foolish to think being near me is the safest place to be," I muttered. "Aeden, you're staying with me, and no one is sacrificing themselves. We all go together. We won't walk in blind, but I'm not sentencing anyone to certain death. It's already a risk just coming with me."

"I do not understand. Why?" he asked, genuinely not understanding why I wouldn't risk him if I didn't absolutely have to.

"Because I don't let people die if I have a choice. We're going together," I answered. "You are coming with me, and the others will either follow you or they can stay home."

Aeden leaned in for only me to hear. "With all due respect, there are others who are more powerful, even from the lowest of ranks. I would urge you to select them for this."

I smiled as his energy rolled around me. I could feel everything Zephyr had seen in him. He was all the things you looked for in a friend, in someone who had your back. He felt like an anchor in a storm, a hand that reached for you in the dark.

"I'm sure there are, Aeden. But you will die for Zephyr out of love, not just duty. You serve Solas because you genuinely want him to live. You love your land and your people. Lives are saved because of love, not duty. And fierce loyalty cannot be found in duty. It's the same reason I am driven to find them, out of love, not duty. I can't explain it any better, but when I was speaking with Lily, the Seer, she told me to surround myself with trainees, that you would help me best."

"Lily told you this? She said to bring us trainees?" Aeden asked, and I nodded. "Personal Royal Guard, it is what you'll need to call me, or I can't do it. Unless a Royal commands, I can't step outside my rank."

I pulled back and nodded. "As my personal Royal Guard, you will come with me."

Aeden beamed, then looked sad again. He was only here because his Commander, his king and his friend Nix were all about to die. It was a sobering feeling to celebrate anything at all. "It would be an honor."

"Allow me to escort you?" Oisin stepped forward.

Faolan stepped forward and groaned. "This is going to hurt so bad."

Orrian squealed her approval, that yes, this would hurt, but unlike everyone else, she was absolutely delighted at the prospect. She was building a court for the sole purpose of waging small wars to protect it. I could see why she and Solas had grown to be such good friends. They were similar in their thirsts.

I searched for words, something Zephyr would say before heading into war. But came back empty-handed. Instead, I tried to speak honestly. I spoke from the fire within. "Solas and Zephyr have tried to teach me the art of not causing a war. We will send scouts ahead to bargain for safe passage through the territories. I do not want to enter unless we can get in *and* out without having to slaughter our way through, but I will if I have no other choice," I said. "Aeden, all of your men, call them now and bring the Sluagh. Divide them up. We won't leave these lands alone, but we also won't leave Unseelie territories at risk. The trainees must come with me. The others will remain behind. They will protect all the Unseelie courts, ours and Faolan's. Make it perfectly clear what I mean by that. *All* the Unseelie lands are to be protected at all costs, and that includes Faolan's lands."

Faolan tipped his head. "Thank you, Perdi."

"We have a treaty, Faolan. If I'm taking their king and probably killing him in the process, I should damn well have a plan B to protect them." I turned to Aeden. "I want these lands locked down. No one gets in or out unless this is their home. Every member of the Unseelie court must come home now. We leave at dawn, and be ready to die for your king, Commander and Nix."

"Yes, Ma'...damn it...Perdi." He flushed red, and I smiled as he struggled with his well-trained manners. But I was beyond court protocol.

"Faolan, Oisin, we need safe passage through the Seelie courts. And we won't be marching alone." I groaned. "God, I hate that place."

"How many do you intend to bring through?" Faolan asked.

"Whoever we don't leave here," I answered.

His eyes widened. "I don't know if Morrow or Theo will allow an army to cross their lands, especially not one from the Dark Courts. Killian may raise a stink, but we won't be going anywhere near the Spring Court, so we can pretty much ignore any protest he makes."

"I don't care what it takes. Do you understand what I mean? Bribe them, pay them, burn their crops and land, kill them. I don't care which route you take. Whichever one gets us through, I'm fine with it." My little speech reminded me of every time I'd overheard Zephyr and Solas speak of war. "Today looks like a fine day for two wars, if need be. They either allow it graciously, with my word we will not bring harm to anyone who intends us no harm, or I unleash all of hell to clear my path. It's their choice how they want their day to end and how many holes they want to dig."

"You sound like Solas," Faolan said.

"Thank you." I smiled and knew the look on my face wouldn't look friendly. I wasn't feeling pleasant in the least. "The difference between him and me is that Solas will try not to kill anyone unless he has no choice. I will simply do it to prove my point. I don't have time to go back and forth bargaining. You all can talk for hours about nothing and have no resolution in the end. It's my way or no way. Anything else is just wasting time my people don't have. Make my point clear, so they may make the right choice."

"That sounds very much like Zephyr." Aeden grinned.

"I'll find a way to scrub off the pointy parts of your message." Oisin smiled and clapped Faolan on the back. "To war, we go. I knew the moment I met her she'd make life interesting."

"No, you didn't," Faolan corrected him as they walked out. "You told me she'd be trouble."

"And you know how much I love trouble. This is like caving with the boogeyman, only roomier." Oisin's laughter filled the halls as they walked out.

I left Orrian at the table with Aeden. She was asking him to remove trees, and he was giving her solutions she didn't like. She, like me, was more inclined to remove obstacles, not work around them.

Zeno stepped into the room with his usual stone face but softened once he caught my eye. "Aeden's ego just exploded all over the lawn."

"I'm sorry, Zeno. I need you to stay here."

"Aeden has filled me in. If Lily believes you should bring them, we'll protect the Unseelie courts until you return," he replied. "Before I head out, do you need anything?"

"Do you have any updates on our missing people?" I asked.

"No. It's like they were plucked from the heavens."

I frowned and fought to ask him why he was standing around rather than looking for them. Instead, I swallowed my need to vent at the first unfortunate person in my vicinity and let it go. I knew the comment wouldn't have helped him. The Aos Si were tough but would be insulted had I questioned their ability to carry out their duties.

"Have you ever been to the northern islands? Or seen a Satyr before?" I asked.

"I've never been to the islands. The Satyr haven't been seen since the first war. From what I understand, they were soldiers once but left for peace."

"It looks like their peace has come to an end," I countered.

He squeezed my shoulder. "I don't know if I should wish you luck or wish pity on them."

"Both," I replied. "Keep my people safe."

"With my life, little Crow," he replied. Hearing the term of endearment hurt. He took his leave without commenting on the fresh tears in my eyes.

I took that moment to wash up, change into clean clothes and pack for my trek into enemy lands. I wondered what to pack for war and laughed at the thought. I filled my bag and paced. I wrung my hands together until my knuckles cracked. I braided and rebraided my hair until I started losing strands. The last time I had stepped foot into enemy territory alone, I had just been birthed into the world as a Crow. My brain understood that I wasn't alone, but my heart felt utterly and completely alone.

"What do you worry about? It is more than your worry for your family." The shadows slinked around my legs.

"That I'll waste time going to that island. That I'll come away empty-handed and will have wasted precious moments that we needed elsewhere."

"Why not go see if there are signs of them before marching across Elphame?"

"Wouldn't entering Seelie territory cause a war? I'd rather have our army at my back if that's what I'm about to do."

"Do you even care if you cause a war?" Their laughter raised goosebumps up my arms.

"No, not on this matter. Although, I'd rather not be away when war comes to the Dark Courts. If I'm going to cause one, I should stay to help, no?"

"No, that is why you have an army. But we understand your hesitation," they answered. "Zephyr didn't start wars. He ended them. He has been in every court thousands of times and never has a war come of it. It isn't just the fear of him that staves off war. It's that he can be hidden in plain sight. No one can see him standing there or sense him. We can hide you perfectly. We just can't hide you and your army."

I walked from the bedroom and found Finn. "The shadows are going to take me to the tip of the Golden Court. I want to check it out before we march there."

"Do you need me to come, or are you letting me know the last place you were seen alive?" he asked and gave me a friendly wink. Finn had a spirit within him that made me want to both stand closer to his warmth and step back from a threat that said his warmth was, in fact, a blazing fire rolling through a packed schoolhouse.

I smiled. "My last known whereabouts."

"Safe journey," he replied. He didn't bother to talk me out of it. He had seen me argue with Zephyr and Solas, only to do what I wanted anyway. "I know it's not my place…" He hesitated and thought carefully of his words as if he didn't know what he could say to a queen. "If something goes wrong, I know Zephyr tells you to run, and I should echo his words. He's never been wrong. But don't run."

"Why not?"

"If you run, you'll bring them to your people, or someone else's, who aren't as strong as we are. Whoever can take the greatest powers of Elphame, do not lead them to your home."

"What the hell do I do, then? Let them take me, too?"

"God, no. You make them suffer for trying to take you. No one takes a little Crow without burning for it. Kill them all. Not a single life can be spared. We'll see the smoke from your fire. We'll come and bring the war to them."

"Is that what Zephyr would do?"

"Yes and no. He'd never lead his enemy to his home. But you are a different matter. He asks you to run, not because you cannot protect yourself, but because he doesn't want you to be forced to do what it'll take to survive," he replied and smiled an uncomfortable grin. "But Solas wouldn't tell you to run. He and Zephyr argue over this often. Zephyr wants to save you. Solas knows you don't need to be saved. You need training and someone to reset your bones when they're broken.

He's been trading Orrian jars of her salve in exchange for permission to clear-cut his forest."

"Why did you feel the need to tell me this?" I asked.

He shrugged. "Call it friendly advice. You can't run forever. If that's all you know, you'll never learn to protect yourself and get those you love killed in the process. There is no place in Elphame for waiting to be given what you need. You must always be ready to fight for it against all who stand in your way."

"When I first met you, you were mouthy as hell. This is an odd change of pace," I replied. "You all talked to me then. But now, none of you talk to me without me talking to you all first, and it's never beyond what I've asked."

"Respectfully, you were just a Crow, then. Now, you are a queen. It's not our place. You don't have to like it, but that is the way of this world. This evening, I feel the need to help you ground yourself. I tell you to kill everyone, and your only question is if Zephyr or Solas would do the same thing. If you're always wondering what they would do, you'll never do what you were meant to do. Take your power and stop living off theirs. They can't save you any more today than they could the day you dragged three Aos Si out of Blood and Bones with a knife wound in your gut. They can't make your decisions and won't live with the consequences. I tell you because if you don't do what's needed, you will fail. Courage can be hard to find in the face of your worst nightmare, but you'll find it. But you can only find it within yourself, not in others. Knowing what Zephyr or Solas would do is an asset, but don't base your decisions on the actions of two men who aren't here to carry them out. You will live and die by your decisions — and so will they."

"Thank you, Finn. That was oddly motivating." I huffed a laugh.

"I've spent decades in your shoes, with Zephyr towering over me with his speeches. His lessons were hard for me to learn." He laughed softly.

"Something tells me you've been on the receiving end of his talks more often than the others."

"That, little queen, is why Zephyr has kept me far from you. If Zephyr is the nightmare of Elphame, I am who gives nightmares a reason to look over his shoulder. Without him present, I won't stop you. I won't even think to. I won't just help you light the fires. I'll show you the best places to burn. Unlike the others, it won't bother me to hear the screaming. I've heard worse things than people burning."

"That's an uncomfortable thought." I winced.

"Hence, all the talks." He laughed. "Enjoy your stroll."

The shadows twisted around me, and we were gone from the manor. Moving through Elphame wasn't as uncomfortable as it was when the shadows had first come to me, but it was still unnerving. They rolled and twisted at speeds my stomach could barely handle. When my feet touched down on the sand, it took everything I had not to vomit. The shadows remained around me but opened up just enough for me to feel magick prickling the air.

"It feels...familiar," I whispered.

"Like in your dream. It feels like the power they used to keep us out," they replied.

I glanced across the empty water. Where there should have been land, there was nothing but water and mist. "It takes a lot of power to hide something as big as an island. That's a lot of life to hide away. How do you hide an entire kingdom, ecosystem and souls?"

"We cannot feel our people. We can't feel anything beyond the wards."

"Neither can I. But the wards are the same here as in my dream. We may not be able to feel our people, but my soul tells me this is where they are. The thought of leaving twists my gut."

"Trust your gut, Perdi. Zephyr's was never wrong."

I motioned for the shadows. I didn't need to say the words out loud. My feet touched down in the grass, the last place Nix and Zephyr had been. If I could find a hint of Zephyr or Nix, it could lead me to Solas. I hadn't allowed my mind to stray too far into my dark thoughts about Solas and the possibility of life without him. We had been to hell and back several times over. I couldn't lose him now. I wasn't ready to face this world without him. I doubted I'd ever be.

I searched again for any clue. A smell, a dent in the earth, anything that would point me in the direction of who I would be facing—but nothing. I felt no presence that shouldn't be near or sensation I shouldn't have. I closed my eyes and felt beyond my Finis abilities. I was born a witch. I opened the door to my Malice and let her slink along the ground. She tasted each blade of grass and dug under each rock. She brought nothing back that shouldn't be there.

The shadows carried me to the courtless lands, to the last place Solas was seen. We searched every inch and came back with nothing. The trees crawled with shadows, guards and Sluagh. I wasn't alone in my search, and I wasn't alone in my grief. I could feel hundreds of eyes watching me, and for the first time, I felt at ease with the creatures that haunted our forests.

Their pain prickled my skin, and I was more motivated to bring their people home alive, just to rid them of their anguish.

"I understand how Zeph and Nix could be taken in the Wildelands, but who would be so brave as to come into the Court of Less and take Solas? The Dark Courts are the most feared, and he isn't an easy target," I asked the shadows.

"We don't know." They slinked across the ground like spilled ink, feeling, tasting and pushing rocks and sticks from their path. "This would be the first time."

"To your knowledge, has Solas ever been taken?" I asked. "He's never mentioned it before, but he also doesn't like to talk about the more painful parts of his life."

"Never. Zephyr was taken once but had allowed it to happen, to be there for when you became a Crow. And Nix, we've never heard of a gnome taken, ever. They're quick and ferocious. To take one is to call every wee folk to arms, regardless of their court. There's a reason they are the most feared Fae in all of Elphame. There wouldn't be a war or warning. They'd simply slaughter everyone before the sun rose again."

"Sounds about right." I grinned at the thought of Nix being one of the more vicious of my men.

Aeden's voice carried over the breeze. "Perdi," he called my name again as he stepped closer.

"How did you find me?" I turned to face him.

"It is my duty to find you," he answered. "But I knew you'd come here to check again. Love makes us double back, just to be sure. Finn mentioned you went to the northern coast? Did you find anything?"

"Aside from a ward hiding the island, no."

"Neither did we," he replied.

I frowned. "Why didn't you tell me you had already been there?"

"Because you wouldn't have gone yourself. And you can sense things that we cannot," Aeden answered. "We've been from one end of Elphame to the other. There is no place we've not been. We haven't sensed even the faintest hint of our people anywhere."

"My gut tells me they're on that island. Are the men ready?" I asked.

"We are always ready. Are you?"

I nodded. "To war, we go."

Together, we made our way back to the manor. Aeden filled me in on what was happening throughout the Dark Courts and the search for our missing people. His update on what was happening in the mortal realm didn't surprise me. It felt like something was always happening there. Lily had sent word from the Gate about possible threats beginning in Whitwick, talk of a protest and invasion of Elphame. All I could do was shake my head. There'd be no invasion, only the death of mortals. I'd send a message to Lily to do what she could to keep the peace. I was tired of fighting for peace when I was the only one who gave a damn about it. Fae weren't the only ones born for war. Mortals craved the same fight, and I was caught in the middle.

Chapter Ten

"What do you mean, Theo said no?" I asked Faolan minutes after he returned from Seelie territory. "What is his reason?"

"He doesn't trust you," Oisin replied. "You've decimated his people on a few occasions, is his reason."

"He left me no choice," I replied and felt defensive.

"I didn't say he was right. I'm telling you what he's said. He's scared." Oisin lifted his hands to show he wasn't attacking me. "I'd be scared, too. Let's be honest, Perdi. War usually follows you wherever you go. Whenever you pop out of Solas' territory, it's either because you're running toward death or from it. Either way, wherever you land is where the next heap of bodies can be found."

"I'll do more than decimate his people if he doesn't let me through."

Faolan sighed a puff of white winter's breath that cooled the fire in my stomach. I knew he was pushing his calm into the room. I wanted to be irritated by it but appreciated it more. "And that's exactly what we told him. But he didn't budge. He's willing to meet with you, though, to discuss it."

"Did you try bribing him? Setting fires?" I asked. "How much of his land did you burn to the ground before he agreed to meet with me?"

"I didn't think you were serious," Faolan sputtered.

"She was dead serious, or she wouldn't have said it," Finn answered from the edge of the room.

"I told you she was serious." Oisin spoke with a smile. "I was more than prepared to burn all of his lands and everyone who stood between me and the flames. But Faolan did not believe you'd want that."

"I did," I pointed out, and Faolan's eyes grew a little wider. "And Morrow? Will I be setting fire to his home on my way to speak to Theo?"

"He's agreed but would like you to stop and confirm to him that you're not going to bring harm to his people as we cross."

"Smart man," Aeden spoke up. "His land is vast, but he knows he cannot protect himself from my lady and her army. We'd find him no matter where he tried to hide."

I nodded. "What will happen if I enter Theo's land against his will? War?"

"Likely," Aeden replied. "But not on any grand scale. In the last year, the Dark Courts have eaten away at the armies of surrounding territories. There'd be no need to even set up camp or scout their lands ahead of time. The war would be fought and won on our way through."

"How many men would we lose?" I asked.

"That would depend on how many warnings you make us give them," Aeden answered. "If we go as you say and storm their lands, I doubt many of us would get dirty, let alone be injured — and certainly none of us would die."

"All right then. We go to the Seelie territory," I finally said. "There will be one warning, as is custom...but only one. We don't have time for second chances."

Aeden smiled. "Worry not. It'll be over quickly, and we will lunch on the island."

I stared into Faolan's eyes from across the room while the guards prepared to leave. He, like me, didn't want to kill. In the pit of my stomach, I felt the first seed of regret knotting and taking root. If I waged war on the Seelie, I would water that seed with the blood of my enemies. It would grow into something I'd suffer for. I'd deal with the pain later, when I had to deal with everything else I knew I'd do between now and then.

Faolan moved through the room as if he was gliding on ice to stand at my side. He was graceful where I was clumsy. "There are no easy choices here, Perdi. This is the burden of your reign. What will you do to protect your people? What pain and shame are you willing to carry?"

I paused before I spoke and wondered how many times he'd stood with little choice. "I understand, Faolan, why you did it. I knew before, but today, I feel it — why you sacrificed me for your people, why you made the choices you made. I would do the same. Even knowing how much it will hurt, how much dishonor I'll carry, how many will look at me differently later for it, I'm still willing to do it."

"Yet, it still hurts to make the decision, doesn't it?" he asked. "Knowing what you must sacrifice to protect those you love, it still burns like a thousand suns, and it never goes away completely. Even as you rationalize it, knowing your choices were few and you picked the one you could live with best, later, you will feel like you could have done something different, something less horrible."

"My heart and soul will hurt, and I know the pain of it will eat me up. But I'll have my family back, and they can help put me back together," I answered.

"It'll be worse — so much worse than you think — when this is done, once all the decisions are made and you have to face the person you didn't want to become. Are you ready to carry that in your soul? Trust me, it's a goddamn heavy curse to carry."

"Yes," I replied. "I fear I'll make worse decisions before my reign is over. When I look in the mirror, I won't see the person I didn't want to become. I'll see the monster I willingly allowed."

"It won't just be you, Perdi. We all make the decisions willingly with you. Share the weight, or you'll burn in your guilt."

"You have enough guilt of your own, Fao. You don't need mine," I answered.

He smiled. "Fao."

"Go halfers on a war with me?" I smiled back.

"To war, we go. Again." He laughed. "Anytime we come together, a war follows."

I laughed. "I'm glad there's a long road between us, then."

"When Solas sent word, warning me to protect my people, I knew that road got a little shorter than it was a year ago. Thank you for warning me."

"I don't feel like I've done you any favors. If anything, I'm going to owe your people a king."

"If I'm killed, make sure Oisin takes the throne. I have no heir. He's the only one who will do what is right for my people and not just for himself," Faolan said as if he hadn't just spoken about his death.

"You have my word. I'll do everything I can," I replied.

He smiled. "That's more than I could ask for. Thank you."

"Let's go start a war," I said as the shadows wrapped the room in darkness and brought us to the Seelie court.

The moment the shadows pulled back, I gagged at the sudden and gut-churning assault of flowers. The smell hit me quicker than I had planned. I leaned forward and vomited on the lush green grass. No one said a word about it, even though I knew they could feel my instant fear of being back in Seelie territory. I squeezed my eyes closed and breathed in until the smell coated my tongue, and I was used to it. Although my nose was used to it, my soul still heaved. I stood and took a jug of water from Aeden and cleaned out my mouth.

"I hate the smell of this place," I finally said.

"We all do," he answered. "It smells like they're trying to cover the smell of rot with flowers. It's like a fresh graveyard or decomposing bodies left above the earth for too long. It makes the stench harder to stomach."

"I've described it the same way," I answered.

Aeden motioned his head to the front. "Morrow is here."

"Did he bring an army?" I asked.

"No, just him."

"Do I have any puke on my face or hair?" I asked, and Aeden tried not to laugh. He shook his head. "How tough would I look if I had puke on myself?"

"You could vomit on his chest, and he'd still fear you. The fact you came at all, knowing what we all know about your time in the Golden Court, is terrifying. It is telling of what you'll endure to win."

I took a deep breath and focused on silencing my fear. I was safe. I was in control. I was brave. They wouldn't Take me again and survive. I could do this. I finished my internal pep talk and turned to face the bad places, the places in my memory I hated. The Aos Si stepped to the side in perfect unison, and two stomps echoed around me. Aeden, Faolan and Oisin followed behind me. The shadows swirled around me as they once had for Zephyr. I could only imagine how frightening it was to see us all standing on his land.

"Perdi." Morrow's eyes widened, and for a moment, I saw him regret not bringing his army with him. "Welcome to the Summer Court."

"How is your lovely partner, Morrow?" I asked and pulled the shadows into the edges of my body. I couldn't hide them like Zephyr could, but I could lessen their threat. I went for kindness with him. He was, after all, letting me cross with an army big enough to swallow his entire territory in one fell swoop. "I heard she has had the opportunity to reconnect with her family in Whitwick?"

He smiled the first genuine smile I'd ever seen him make. "She is well. She just returned from Whitwick, visiting her greats and their children. I've not seen her so happy. She has many stories, and I am grateful for her pleasure. I am glad she has been given a chance to know them. Each time she returns, it is with a new tale, photographs and pieces of artwork made by her greatest of grandchildren. To see her happiness is a blessing, and I'm grateful."

"I'm pleased to hear that." I smiled in return. There were many once-upon-a-time mortals who had been able to return to a land they never thought they'd see again. I knew that joy and had only been cut off for a short time compared to the others.

"What brings you to my territory, neighbor?" he asked, and I went for truth rather than a threat. The threats could always come later, if need be.

In the pit of my stomach, my Malice had a chokehold on my fear and radiated courage. I didn't want war. I didn't want any more death to follow me. I prayed Morrow felt the same. "As Faolan and Oisin have told you, I am searching for my people. Solas, Zephyr, and Nix are missing. I believe they are being held on the upper islands off the northern coast." I motioned to his land we'd need to cross. "I would ask you to permit me and my people to cross your lands. I wish I had more time to speak on this matter, but time is something I have very little of."

"Do you come for war?" he asked a direct question and would get the truth in return.

"Not with you or your people," I answered. "But whoever was stupid enough to take my family, or help in their capture, will die at my hands."

"You have safe passage if you give your word that you mean my people and me no harm," he answered.

I nodded. That was a fair enough request. "If you do not bring harm against me or mine, I will do the same. You have my word."

"This is good enough for me," he replied. "I wish you much success, Perdi. But I fear you will not find the same well wishes from Theofanis. As a friendly warning, from neighbor to neighbor, he has already sent word to my court, requesting I bar you from entering my lands to get to his."

"Thank you for the warning."

"Do you care for food or drink before you leave?" he asked.

"Thank you, but no, we haven't much time," I replied and was thankful for his offer. "Morrow, I won't forget this."

"I surely hope you do not," he answered, and in a hot wind of flowers, he was gone.

We moved quickly through Morrow's land. Between the shadows and the Aos Si, we stood before Alfheim, the Golden Court, within minutes. This time, I didn't get sick. My anger curled around my fear and whispered sweet nothings until it died under the pressure of my Malice. The smell was more pungent than I remembered, and I had to blink the strong perfume from my burning eyes. But we all did. Not one of us could ignore it. At the border, we met Theo and his entire army. It struck me as odd. Morrow had come alone, because he, unlike Theo, had nothing to hide.

"A rather large greeting party, no?" I asked Oisin.

"They don't look very welcoming," he replied and smiled. I watched his jaw clench, waiting for a reason to lash out. He leaned into my ear and whispered, bits of frost landing on my shoulder. "Just like the last time, Perdi, they have more to fear than you do."

I stepped forward, Oisin still at my side. "King Theo, I've come to meet as requested. Why have you declined my request to cross your land?"

"You are not bringing your army across my territory. I cannot risk the Dark Court and her enemies," he replied.

"We have no enemies that I know of," I answered. "Please reconsider."

"You may bring a few men to assist you. That is it. And that is a generous offer, given our history."

"*Our* history?" I laughed. I dug my nails into the palms of my hands to keep myself from slapping him. We didn't have history. I was held in his court and killed his father for freedom. The last time he and I were this close, he would have killed me if he could have, to earn favor with Solene. That wasn't history. That was a reason for war. "No. I'm sorry, Theo. That doesn't work for me."

"Whether it does or not is not my problem," he replied.

I felt the decisions weigh in my mind like a scale. If I stepped forward, it would be war. If I didn't, it would be the death of those I loved more than peace.

Oisin leaned into my ear. "Did you come here to turn around? Unleash hell, or you'll never get anywhere in this world. If you can't make them love you, make them fear you. Burn it down, Perdi. He does not deserve mercy. No one who stands against you deserves a second thought, not today."

Theo grinned from ten feet away. Only an invisible line kept him safe. "What will it be, Perdi?"

Aeden stepped to my side. Static of immeasurable power poured from his body. It made me wish he wasn't standing so close. "You will address my lady by her title or lose your tongue. Remember, Little King, you have no oaths with our court, and it would give me pleasure to kill you where you stand. If anything, your blood will dampen the stench of flowers."

Theo's amusement rose. He didn't fear Aeden as he should. "Ah, then it is true. Queen Perdita. What will it be? You may come with a few, or you may leave with them all. I do not plan to stand here all day for you to—"

"This is *your* problem, not mine," I interrupted him. "You either step aside and let us pass, or I'll burn your entire kingdom to the fucking ground. You have five minutes. And count those minutes as kindness, since you were so kind as to meet with me. But my kindness is not endless."

I turned my back on him, and he sputtered, but I didn't turn back around.

"Ma'am." Aeden leaned in. "Would you care for me to ready your men?"

"In four minutes, Aeden, everyone in Theo's territory dies," I answered loud enough for Theo to hear me. I didn't know if I was bluffing, but I'd soon find out.

"All?" Aeden asked.

"For now, just him and his entire army," I answered. "You will hunt his lands, and every soldier dies. Every. Last. One. Then there will be no one left to stop me from crossing."

"You can't just expect me to surrender my lands because your king is missing. It will be war, and many will die," Theo called from the land I needed to enter.

I turned. "We've all got to die someday, Theo. Do you want today to be your day? The clock is ticking, and each minute that passes brings your people closer to death. It will not be me or my people who fall. You hold the fate of your land in your hands. Choose wisely.

I can't bring them back once you sentence them to death."

Theo pointed his finger at Faolan. "Are you just going to stand there and watch? We have a treaty, Faolan."

Faolan shrugged. "It's not my lands she has asked to cross. And I also have a treaty with Queen Perdita and the Dark Courts, which my lands touch. You are the one who is being foolish, and I won't have my people die for it."

"This, coming from you, the man who betrayed her countless times?" Theo laughed.

I joined his laugh. "You've never seen a breakup before?"

"That was not a breakup," Theo replied. "That was war."

I smiled. "You've seen how I treat people I've loved. Can you imagine what I would do to someone I don't like, in a land I enjoy even less? It would give me more pleasure than you can possibly imagine to burn it all. I'd sooner smell charred flesh than those goddamn flowers."

"I have already given my answer. Leave now, and I'll forget all about this." Theo lifted his head as if I was beneath him. He reminded me so much of his father. Smug right up until the bloody and horrible end.

"Two minutes," I said and turned my back to him. "Aeden, begin preparations. I want to be across within the hour and do not want to step through fresh blood to get there." It was all bluster. I was scared, but in the face of fear, my anger always surfaced.

"We will drag them off the path before we kill them," he answered, and I knew he was telling me the truth. There was no bravado in him. I didn't know

Aeden, but I saw anticipation in his eyes. Months of no war must drive a soldier to boredom. No wonder Zephyr had made me train with the Aos Si. It was the only excitement they had seen since the last time I popped out of Solas' territory.

"Wait! Let's be reasonable here. How many men would you like to bring across?" Theo asked.

"The exact number I have come with. If I wanted to invade, we wouldn't be talking, and I wouldn't have asked. I would have simply taken your lives and your land. Instead, I've come asking for permission. What about that says I had planned to do you harm? If you make no move to hurt me or mine, I do not see you as a threat. But you decided to grandstand," I answered. "One minute. Theo, I am not bluffing. My people are on the other side of your land. If you disagree, I will come anyway. You can either grant me permission and live, or I will come without it, and you will die. I don't care which one you choose. I'll still get what I want in the end, and your death is one of the things I'd like very much."

Aeden stepped forward. "I'll take my leave, my lady."

"Go, Aeden." I sighed. "You won't need many. We've already killed most of his people twice over."

"I'm calling your bluff," Theo yelled.

"I see that," I replied and stepped forward, placing my feet over that line. "And like everyone else who has, you'll taste death. I gave you more than one chance to save yourself and your people. You chose this…not me."

Aeden didn't leave, so much as step back ten paces and motion with his head. The shadows rolled across the ground as I had seen when Solas and Zephyr stood toe to toe against an enemy. Behind them, the land crawled with beasts of every size. The entire Aos Si army, both in training and combat-ready, appeared. The sky darkened with the Sluagh, who screamed for blood. It looked like every nightmare anyone had ever had was being spat up onto the border. Any other time, I'd have run or died of fear. I could hear them slither and snap teeth. Today, I smiled and knew my face would become someone's new nightmare.

Aeden stepped forward, and I moved to the side. "Clear this from my path. We're burning daylight."

"My lady," Aeden replied and rushed to the front of Theo before he finished his sentence. He grabbed Theo by his neck, holding him high. In his other hand, he had a knife to Theo's neck. Within minutes, the entire Golden Court army was held on the ground with swords to their necks.

"Wait!" Theo screamed.

Aeden paused. "My lady?"

I stepped forward. "Yes?"

"You'd kill a king for this?" Theo asked.

I tried not to laugh. It wasn't a friendly feeling I had inside. It was rage, and it bubbled out of my throat. "Your father didn't think I'd kill him, either, but you still buried him. Do you want to test that theory with your life as well? You mean nothing to me. You're an irritation I'd like to remove from this realm. The only reason I haven't come into your room as you sleep is because I've been busy. But since I'm already here, today looks like a good day to take the life of a Little King."

"Okay, you can cross!" Theo yelled.

I turned from him with a smile. "Thank you, King Theo. I graciously accept your offer to allow me safe passage through your territory."

Aeden dropped Theo to the ground and moved back to my side. The Dark Court pulled back and left us in the sun, with the stench and the Golden Court. We stepped over Theo and his people and left them on the ground. I didn't look back. I didn't care that they would follow us as we marched, any more than I gave a damn where he chose to die. I was content in letting him pick his burial grounds.

"Would you have killed him, all of them?" Aeden asked.

"Yes, she would have," Faolan answered. "Not only because she hates Theo, but for her people. I would warn you not to get in the middle of her and Solas or Zephyr. And lord have mercy on your soul if you go near Nix. There will never be a warning when it comes to Nix."

"I'd never hurt our gnome," Aeden whispered, almost insulted. I smiled at him, referring to Nix as *our* gnome. "We should have killed Theofanis. He is a bleed on his people, a sickness."

"You're probably right," I answered and regretted, for a moment, that he didn't refuse me.

Theo moved to my side, still angry but trying hard not to show it. "You can't have all the glory, and I have little trust in you now. I will escort you through my territory."

"You can have it all, Theo. I didn't come for glory," I replied. "And I don't need your trust."

"You sound like Solas."

"No, Little King," Aeden interrupted, "she is the war that flows in the veins of my king. And I caution you to remember that the next time or you'll be considered our enemy. That is not a good place to be."

Theo leaned away from Aeden. He looked nervous. "I thought the Dark Court had no enemies?"

"We don't," I answered and walked past him. "They're either already dead or currently being hunted. Which one are you?"

"Not your enemy," he replied.

"The day is young, and you've not shut your mouth. I wouldn't be so certain of that, Theo," Faolan added and moved to my side, leaving Theo to walk behind us. I didn't fear a knife in my back. The Aos Si would kill him before he could get his blade out.

Chapter Eleven

I was thankful for the cleansing smell of the ocean and the gradual respite it provided from the smells of a land I'd never stopped wishing would burn. We marched to where the water met the land and washed away the scent of flowers and the Golden Court. I stood at the edge of dry land, the tips of my boots getting wet, and breathed until I couldn't taste lilies and lilacs on my tongue. Once you'd chewed a bouquet of flowers for hours, any other smell was a treasure. I'd enjoy every second I was spared the aggravation of tearing eyes and a near-bleeding nose. I could hear those I'd brought with me doing the same — breathing in the calmness of the ocean and missing the very air at home. It was the small things in life, the ones you don't miss until they're gone, like air that didn't make you gag.

Oisin pulled a small leather bag from his pocket and pushed it to his nose. One long breath later, he noticeably relaxed. He motioned with his bag and tossed it to me. I could smell it before I even lifted it to my face, and I smiled. Peppermint and pine and the coolness of snow. *Christmas in a bag. Winter Court.* I noticed many of the others were doing the same. I lobbed the bag back and watched him place it in his chest pocket, over his heart.

"Home," Faolan said quietly as he approached me. "Most men bring tokens from home to remind them that only half of their battle is won until they return. And if they don't return, they are home when they fall."

"I'd say that was poetic, but it's rather morose," I replied. "What did you bring?"

He smiled. "Nothing. For me, all of Elphame is my home. In my heart, there are no lines in the earth, no borders. If I fall in the north, I'm still home. What about you? What did you bring that reminds you of why you're here, what you're fighting for?"

"The knife I used to kill Aelfdene with," I answered and flipped it end over end. "It's my lucky knife. I don't leave home without it."

"Now that, Perdi, is morose." He laughed, and I joined him. It wasn't the most comfortable token, but it gave me a sense of bravery.

"If you think that's gloomy, I should ask you for tea in my back garden," I replied. "It's filled with souls and poisonous plants."

"I look forward to living long enough to be made uncomfortable again." He smiled softly. "You know, the Last War, Solas carried a small spray of poisonous flowers in his chest pocket. I thought it was very much him, to go into battle with poison over his heart. Now, it makes sense. He carried you with him."

I sighed and felt my lips curl into a smile at the mention of Solas' name. "I've been on the other side of his war. It's terrifying with or without seeing him decorating himself with poison."

"It very much is that—and more."

"I've never seen Zephyr with a piece of home. Is he like you? Everywhere is home?" I asked.

"Every battlefield I've seen Zephyr, for decades, he's always had a small wooden bird in his hand. I thought nothing of it, until you released him, and I realized he wasn't holding just any bird. It was a little Crow." He didn't look scared, as most did when talking about Zephyr. "The world didn't tremble upon his release. But he shook the very ground looking for you. And now, I believe, Perdi, it will be you who shakes the world in your hunt for him. Are you ready?"

I dipped my head. "As ready as I'll ever be. I'm nervous, while the rest of you look like it's just another day in Elphame."

"It *is* just another day for the rest of us. None of us want war, but we'd never have made it beyond childhood if we weren't always ready for it. Well, aside from the war machines trained by Zephyr, most of us do not look forward to war. The Aos Si are eager to honor your trust in them and hungry as hell to eat the fools who chained their family in a dungeon. They hold utter disgust and contempt for what has been done to their friend, Nix. I could almost pity those who have him. Almost," he replied, and I nodded in agreement. He tilted his head toward the water. "Do you feel that? The magick? I can hear it telling me to turn around."

"It's a curse or spell, depending on who created it and why. It's meant to keep us out. I came earlier, in the shadows, to make sure we wouldn't be wasting our time," I answered and closed my eyes to the hum of magick. I'd felt it the moment we stepped foot on the sand. Now, concentrating, it licked against my soul like a lover's touch. *Familiar.* "It feels like the wards I felt when I dreamed of Zephyr and Nix. I can't feel any of my people through them, but I know they're on that island."

"It feels...scratchy against my mind. It tempts me to look further but also wants me to turn away. I am both acquainted with it and uncertain," Faolan replied.

"That's a good way of putting it. It's familiar in that I've felt it many times before but can't put my finger on it," I said. "But most magick is that way to me. It speaks a language I understand from a place I don't remember."

He motioned behind us. "It's interesting that the Golden Court are the only ones not reacting to the magick. The rest are discussing it, but Theo and his people are pretending it's not even there. Even if he knew of it, he's not mentioning it. You'd think, if he had nothing to hide, he'd have said something about it, even if it was only to win favor."

I nodded. "I think Theo will bring more surprises, and the wards will be the least of our worries."

"I agree," Faolan answered. "The spell, can you break it?"

"I didn't come all this way just to turn around empty-handed," I answered and stepped away from Faolan before flexing my magick. Standing too close to a power as great as Faolan would push against my concentration, and I'd pick up winter, as well as the magick I was focusing on. I motioned for the shadows to investigate the strangeness that closed off the ocean.

The water licked my boots as I closed my eyes and fought the urge to run away and hide. All I could see and feel on the surface was water. But beneath that, where the energy twisted and glided with the currents, I could feel magick. I tested it with my Malice. She slinked out slowly, rolling out over the waves. It felt like the rest of Elphame, no different than the forests, the Gate or the cherry blossoms I enjoyed the smell of. The farther I pushed out from the banks, the stronger the feeling became, and I was reminded of each time I had angered the Gate. Warnings my brain tried to put into words rose from the wards like a hot slap across my face.

You're not welcome here.

"Try to stop me," I whispered back.

You will only find death here.

"I've come with your death on my mind."

Come if you dare.

"Challenge accepted," I answered back.

The shadows curled back around me and drew me from my threats. "It's the same glass wall we found in the dream. It bubbles the island. We cannot pass. We cannot go over or under. It is as if there is no world beyond."

"What is beyond? I've seen the maps of Elphame, and it stops at the water," I asked the shadows.

"More."

"Of what?"

"We don't know. We've never been beyond the water, and we've no desire to see. Nothing good comes from poking around where you don't belong, and we, very much, do not belong here."

"Nothing good comes from not knowing, either. And I don't like not knowing," I replied. But I'd deal with one problem at a time. Eventually, my curiosity would win out, and I'd look beyond. For today, though, I'd focus on what stood hidden before me. "The wall blocking our path, is it a ward or something else?"

"Yes, wards, powerful ones. We sense nothing else but also don't know what's beyond them. We do not know if you can break them and if you do, what will happen."

"Is it more or less than the wards on the dungeon at the Golden Court that held Zephyr?"

"More," they answered.

"More or less than the Gate?"

"Less."

"Then I can break them. Hopefully, it'll hurt less than the Gate."

The shadows flinched against my legs. "Did the Gate not kill you?"

"Yes...hence my comment. If I die now, I'm pretty much screwed." I laughed a little, then hard enough that I could feel the others stare. "Who would have thought my measurement for pain would be whether I died in the end?"

"Perhaps you should not tell them your measurement for hurt?" the shadows suggested.

I looked back at Faolan and swallowed my next laugh. "Good idea. Given the cause of my greatest hurt came with us."

I shook off the nervous giggles and sighed. Once I knew I wouldn't laugh again at something not nearly as funny as I thought, I turned back to my group, who stared at me as if they knew I was losing my mind but were too polite to mention it just yet. On one side of the beach, Theo stood with his people. On the other side, everyone who didn't trust Theo and his people. We had divided away from them from the start. None of us trusted the others. I glanced at Theo as I walked past him. He and his people feared me for many reasons. I could see it on their faces and in their flinches. Today, his brush with death just added to those reasons. Before this ended, I knew they'd give me a list of reasons to kill them, and it would have nothing to do with land and borders.

It irritated me to have him along, but not enough to do anything about it...*yet*. Between his mistrust and fear of me, I knew he was scheming, because I would have been doing the same thing. Either he wanted to find Solas and be owed a favor, or he would kill me in my sleep. Both I'd deal with when the time came. There was no sense worrying about it until I had to kill him for it. I wondered how many times thoughts like that had crossed Solas' mind and if he had come to the same conclusions as I had. Focus on the task at hand and worry about cleaning his knife and hiding bodies later.

"There are wards around the island, and they're pretty damn strong." I stood between Faolan, Oisin and Aeden. The Aos Si stood in a circle around us with the shadows rolling at their backs, blocking out Theo. We made no attempts to befriend them or pretend to. I had no desire to make new friends today, not when I'd probably need to kill them later. "The shadows can't even get past them, and they can worm their way into just about anything. My Malice was hindered as well, and she can go places where shadows cannot."

"Can you break them, witchy woman?" Oisin asked and wiggled his fingers in the air like casting a spell.

I tilted my head and stared at him for a moment. His grin made me smile in return. He had this way of taking the worst of a situation and blunting the edges so they didn't cut as deep. He was the Winter Court's version of Zephyr in how hard he worked to say it would be okay without needing to say the actual words. If ever he ended up on the road, kicking stones, my home would be his for as long as he needed, and I'd be happy for each day he was there.

As my eyes scanned my group. I knew I had brought my own token from home, and it wasn't the knife. It was them. As naturally as the sun rose and set, my family grew in my time of need. It now included soldiers who Zephyr had never given up on, who would down whoever I needed and help me set fires without even asking me why. Beside them, the men from the Winter Court, who were once enemies, caught the watchful eye of Zephyr and earned the start of forgiveness from Solas. Every one of them had a special place in Nix's heart. For that, they weren't my enemies, and they weren't tools, either. With or without the treaty, at this very moment, I'd help the Winter Court, and I'd come to the call of the Aos Si.

"Perdi, are you okay?" Faolan asked.

I nodded and blinked away the beginning of tears. "Yeah, I'm good. I was just in my head a little."

"Do you think you can break the spell?" Faolan repeated Oisin's question.

"It's much stronger than anything I've got in my reserves, but I can do it. To bring the wards down, I'd drain myself. I'd rather not be useless afterward, so I'll need to do a spell," I answered and winced when I thought of the thrice payment. "I don't want Theo near me as I do it. I don't trust him enough to have him watch me tie my shoes, let alone work a spell."

"What is the payment for your spell?" Oisin asked, always curious. But he didn't become a Commander without knowing the inner workings of just about everything and being brave enough to ask about what he didn't know.

"Nothing is free, Oisin. Not even the power you use to wield your magicks is without cost. You take the energy cast off from Elphame. Those more powerful than you can hold more of it. For me, my Malice, the energy it needs is greater than the cast-offs from Elphame. To do something like this, it would need months of energy, all saved up," I answered. "And when I take what I want, more than scraps, I have to pay for it. That payment is usually pain or a bit of my life force. Sometimes, when fate is having a bad day, I suffer the exact opposite of what I used it for. If I used it to keep myself warm, I'd be freezing later. If I used it to keep someone alive, I risk dying in their place."

"And for this?" he asked.

I shrugged. "I don't know. It almost killed me when I used it to free Zephyr in the dungeons. When I used it for the Gate, it did kill me. I try not to twist spells unless I absolutely have to, because payment comes hard and hurts like a bitch. Worse, I don't know when it will come to collect that debt. Sometimes it's instant. Other times it waits it out for days. It's on its own clock and tallies debts in its own way."

"So, breaking this could kill you?" he asked, horrified I would even consider it.

"Getting out of bed in Elphame could kill me," I answered. "This holds the same risk. Yes, fate could decide my beating heart is the only worthy payment, especially because I'm doing this to save people I love. Trade a heart for a heart, seems pretty fair if you think of it. But it could also decide my request was honorable enough that it just shaves a year or two off the end. I won't know until the payment is due."

"I can see why you don't use it idly," he answered.

"I don't think anyone survives long in Elphame if they idly do anything, magick or not."

"I don't like this," Aeden spoke up. "Respectfully, I'd like you not to do this. The risk is too great. You are the only one still sitting on the throne. If something were to happen…"

"I don't plan on going home empty-handed," I replied. "Do you?"

"Take from us. You can take energy from us instead." Aeden motioned around our circle. "Malice comes at too steep a cost, and I doubt very much you'll want to pay it once we cross. We are only as strong as our weakest member. If you fall, we all fall."

"I can't wipe you all out, either," I answered.

"And you won't, not if you take from us all. If it were just me, I'd be useless afterward and would need to return to the Dark Courts. But I'm not suggesting you select one member and drain them dry as a husk. All of us give a little, together. The drain would not be so bad if we shared the burden. It is how you win wars, Perdi, by sharing the cost of success."

"Ask the others individually. Don't put them on the spot in front of each other, and do not demand it. They need to understand that I can't control my Malice in the same ways Zephyr can control himself. I don't know what will happen when we do this. I've never done it before. I could eat you all and not be able to stop myself," I told him before he walked off.

"I don't trust Theo," Oisin whispered as we waited.

"I don't think you trust anyone." I smiled, and he shrugged. "But no, neither do I."

"I don't understand, after you damn near killed him, why he is here? Any sane man would run for the hills and hide, not follow the person who just stormed his territory with death on their mind. It doesn't make sense. My gut is telling me something is amiss."

I groaned because he was right. "I don't know the why of it. Why don't you go ask him yourself? Then maybe we'd all know what the hell he is doing."

"Can't you, you know, get into his head and see what he's hiding?" Oisin asked and raised his eyebrows in some sort of covert hint. I started to laugh until I saw he was serious. "I would be happy to hold him down for you. He isn't that strong. You could probably hold him down yourself."

"And if we're wrong? Sure, I don't trust him, but he hasn't done enough for me to tear his mind apart. Having me in your head while you fight it? Not only is it excruciatingly painful, but I could also kill him or, worse, leave him alive. His mind would break under my touch, then what? Trust me when I tell you, he'd prefer death over how I'd leave him. And that's if things go perfectly. What if his mind is stronger than I give him credit for, and it hurts me as much as it hurts him? It would be a fight to his bloody death, but I wouldn't come out of it unscathed."

"It's not like he wouldn't deserve that fate," Oisin countered. "He's a pest."

"You kill pests, Oisin. You don't break their soul and need to spoon-feed them for the rest of their lives," I answered. "He'd be one more broken king ruling over a kingdom."

"Then it's settled. We kill him. I knew you'd see the simplicity in my way of doing things," he answered, and I rolled my eyes.

Oisin's grin was short-lived when Faolan shook his head. "I think we'll find out sooner or later what he's up to. It could be fear making him stupid, or it could be something more. Until we know, it's best he's with us. Out of sight means out of mind. And I, for one, prefer those I don't trust close enough for me to watch."

"Perdi," Aeden called my attention back.

I left Oisin arguing with Faolan over the merits of killing before asking questions. Oisin had a point, but I also understood Faolan's cautious style. Killing indiscriminately wasn't always the only choice we had. I saw how hard Faolan clung to his humanity and wondered if he'd let it slip to help me.

"I agree with Oisin," Aeden said as I approached him, "on this matter."

"So do I, but I also agree with Faolan. Keep Theo alive until we know why he came. That information could be more valuable than a quick death."

"They all have agreed to feed you energy. They have each been made aware of the dangers and still agree. We have discussed the best way to do this, to minimize risk to us and you." Aeden stood with his men, who were a brick wall between Theo and me. "Rather than you taking from us, we will push our energy toward you. All you have to do is…well, eat it, I suppose. And when you cannot handle more, you let us know, and we will stop…feeding you. I don't know if those are the right terms?"

I laughed. "Yes, that's what I do."

"Ready?" he asked.

"No," I blurted. My stomach clenched. "I've never been fed power like this. I've only ever taken it."

"You have. Each time Solas or Zephyr take away your rage, they're filling you with their power. The times it's been painful, that is when Solas has taken your energy from you. But when it's calm and relaxing, you are being given energy. Both know rage so bitterly well that they know how to calm it." His answer surprised me, but it also didn't. I was more surprised that I hadn't known. "This is much the same, but it will be a great deal more intense. You will need to tell us when to stop. We won't know when you've had enough. I'd hate to give you too much and have you explode into a puff of Crow feathers. I've seen Zephyr take power from the battlefield, and he's always had his shadows with him. They take whatever extras he doesn't need. Perhaps try that, as well?"

"Right, good idea," I replied and swallowed hard. All I could envision was me draining them to bones and flaking skin. The thought of it made my stomach flop. "I'm nervous I'll kill you all."

"I'll stop you," Finn spoke up. "Finis magick doesn't work the same with me. If I see you draining one of us, I'll break the connection. It'll hurt like hell and might toast our brains a bit, but I'll save the others."

"Thank you, Finn," I replied. Knowing there was a backup plan settled the horror of what we were about to attempt.

"Thank me when there's smoke coming out of your ears," he replied.

"Okay, I'm ready, I think. Yes, ready," I answered. The shadows slinked around me. They would hold whatever I couldn't. It sounded easy enough, but all I could picture was them filling me until I popped like a bloody balloon and splattered them all with our good intentions and guts.

Their power was calm at first, like a light breeze carrying the smells of home, the Dark Courts, the manor and the forest behind. It felt like Zephyr when he landed beside me on a calm afternoon. I could feel each energy, as if I could pick them out, one by one. It reminded me of when Nix said he could feel every single person on the battlefield and know precisely who they were. Soon, it grew and pushed against my body. Now, it felt like Zephyr coming when he was angry, a fiery blast of a man who all feared. The energy was almost tangible, like the wind could be on a stormy day, and it blew against me from every direction. I slid across the ground until I hit Faolan's chest. He held me in place while I drank down the power. I filled myself up until I was dizzy and thought my skin would slough off. The shadows ate what they could until I raised a shaking hand.

"Enough," I muttered through clenched teeth and gripped Faolan's arm. If it weren't for him, I'd have bounced into the ocean like a ragdoll and drowned under the weight of power.

"I forgot, you are smaller than Zephyr." Aeden grinned. "A fraction of his weight."

I nodded but couldn't find the words to thank him. "Wards."

Faolan helped me turn and stagger to the bank. Every inch of me burned yet froze. Static lifted my stray hairs into the air and prickled along my skin. I dropped to my knees and placed my hands into the cool liquid up to my elbows. I pushed all the power that threatened to burst within me into the spell that hid the island from us. I unleashed it on the heels of my Malice.

The spell, a mix of webs and lies, was wrapped around that which wished not to be seen. It was not nearly as intricate as the one that had held Zephyr in his dungeon but powerful enough that the strings would not fall like a spider web to a flame. They were too new to simply give up. I dug at them until it felt like I had ripped off my nails in the fight. Seconds felt like they had stretched into hours. But when the spell broke, it burst through the air and pushed me from the water. I skipped over the bank like a flat rock, coming to a dead stop against the feet of the Aos Si as my Malice slammed back into me.

My heart pounded with fear and relief. Every inch of my body trembled. I struggled to form a sentence but mumbled one word instead. "Done."

The shadows rolled around me before anyone else could touch me. "You're not well."

"Just give me a minute." I groaned. My head pounded, a mixture of too much power, the spell falling and being thrown across the beach. "That was one hell of a rough landing."

Faolan towered over me. "You have an odd measurement of rough. I can smell the hair you burned off in the air."

"I cooked off almost all my body hair when I closed the Gate. My right leg still doesn't grow any," I replied. "Maybe my legs are even now."

Once my heart slowed and my limbs no longer felt like jelly, I rolled onto my back and stared at the sky. I let Aeden help me to my feet. He met my eyes with a questioning look. With one nod from me, he didn't ask if I needed more time or if I was okay. He trusted I'd have said something.

"Let's not do that again," I said as I stretched my arms and legs, trying to get the pins and needles to leave. "I feel like I've been chewing on coffee beans for the last week, and I'm finally coming down from a caffeine high."

Aeden leaned in. "You took as much as Zephyr can. I was surprised."

"Perhaps a little too much," I replied.

"Or perhaps it is like a muscle you must work out for it to grow."

"You're probably right, Aeden, but I don't think I want that much power coursing through my veins without Zephyr or Solas guiding me," I answered and shivered at the memory of it. It felt both good and bad. "For a split second, just a tiny one, I could imagine how quickly I could burn you all with it."

"But you didn't." He smiled. "And that, Perdi, is why you are loved. You try for the right path, rather than the easy one, before you set your fires."

"Honorable... That's just a fancy way of saying I like to suffer," I countered.

"No, not exactly. But you're willing to endure what you must."

I shook out my limbs and turned to face the water. In the distance a swimmer could make, lay an island that had been hidden from sight. It was both beautiful and frightening. It mirrored the banks we stood on — lush forest beyond a sandy beach. Rocks jutted up from the edges as if the island had been placed gently on the stones.

I glanced back to Theo's men, who didn't look surprised. Sure, many knew these islands were here, but why hadn't they mentioned them during our walk here. They played as if they had no clue where we were going, yet we walked on a fairly beaten-down path to get here. I didn't say it out loud, but they tickled that part of my brain that said they were up to no good, and once I found out, it would be worse than I thought.

"A dozen thoughts just passed over your face." Oisin stood at my side, his eyes roaming the tree line we had walked through, but I knew he was watching Theo. He was less obvious than I was. But I also didn't care if Theo knew I had him in my suspicious sights.

"The wards were new. I could feel how fresh the magick was when I touched them. I don't think the Satyr had them created when they came here all those years ago. They didn't feel old enough for that," I said.

"Can you tell who made them?"

"No. Unless it was Darkmore blood used, I wouldn't know exactly who cast the spell. I can tell if it was a witch, but that's about it. These wards? All I can say is that no witch made them, but something that feels similar to one, only not as powerful."

"How do you know they're not as powerful?"

I smiled. Oisin craved knowledge. It was what kept him and his people alive. At one time, I would have held back. Keeping my own secrets was what kept me alive for so long. But Oisin was now in my book of people I trusted and people I'd protect. He, like Zephyr, didn't care if he asked a question no one wanted to answer or spoke a truth no one wanted to hear. He didn't care about the discomfort of others if that information helped him do his duty or protect those he cared about.

"Because, Oisin, I'm up and about and not fighting to live. Spells, even from the weakest of witches, are difficult to break. I'd have had to bleed for it. Even with the energy fed to me by the others, it wouldn't have been enough. I'd have had to use witch blood to break witch magick. That I broke it with Elphame magick tells me it's not a witch. It's something else that feels similar but weaker."

"You're the only witch in Elphame, Perdi. If it wasn't you, it was a Mage—similar to witches, but weaker. There are Mages in Elphame, but I'm not sure who would do this. Standing against the Dark Court is a death sentence."

"Does the Golden Court have a Mage?"

"I don't know. We rarely pay attention to powers as weak as a Mage. Unlike you, a born witch, a Mage is but a drop of power in a big world of monsters."

"Just the same, keep a watchful eye. It makes me a little more uncomfortable to have Theo and his people this close."

"I still vote we kill them and get it over with. I don't like dragging our trash around."

"You sound like me," I replied and walked back to the group, all our eyes on the garbage we'd be hauling around like dead weight.

Chapter Twelve

When it came to evoking feelings of dread, the Northern Island conjured a myriad of anxious thoughts deep in my soul. I knew I wasn't welcome the moment we stepped ashore. It wasn't just in the spiteful energy that lingered in the air like an obnoxious stench of rotting fruit. Although it coated my skin, it was not the cause of my dread. The very island felt inhospitable, from the sharp rocks to the branches that tugged at my hair as I walked past, as if they could reach out and pull me back to where I had come from. Every natural shadow, broad and disproportionate, was cold to the touch as if under its bloated night, it had never tasted life. The hostile reception we received, down to the roots of this hidden world, poked and prodded my gut. The wards may have been down, but my wish to hide or run hadn't gone away.

My overly active imagination was heightened with stress that squeezed my heart and made each breath feel clunky. Every noise sounded like fireworks and jerked my attention in every direction. The ground crunched under my boots and echoed uncomfortably loudly. Although the island was plush with growth, it did nothing to hinder or eat the sounds around us. Although my nervousness had sharpened each noise, it still felt like we were louder than a marching band, signaling our location to whatever monsters lurked in the shadows.

"Should we split up?" Theo asked from the rear.

"No," I answered without even looking back.

"We would cover more ground quicker," he replied.

"What part of *no* is difficult to understand?" I asked, still pressing ahead. "We are on an island that didn't want to be found, where they're holding three of my people—two of whom can kill all of us in the blink of an eye and are being held by someone or something more powerful than them. Do you really think splitting up, dividing our resources, is safer for the group?"

"But is it safer for us all to be in one place?" Theo countered.

"You have a good point, Theo." I finally turned to face him. "Normally, we'd split up to cover more ground. But I plan to use you and your people as bait, should the need arise. And before you complain about it, you didn't have to come. You forced your way along."

"B-b-bait?" he sputtered the word.

"You can bet your roses on that. And now that we're not in your territory, I'll do what I damn well please, even if what I please is to string you up, wound you and wait to see what monsters crawl out of the shadows to eat you." Theo glared, but I still smiled. I gave him my back and picked up my pace. I glanced at Oisin, who was amused. "If he breaks his leg, we're leaving him to die here."

"Would you like me to break his leg now?" It was less of a joke and more of a question as to when I'd like it done.

I laughed with him. It was nervous laughter. "Tempting."

"I do not feel Zephyr here," Aeden spoke up. "I don't feel anything or anyone. Nothing."

"Nor do I," I answered. "I don't even feel the life of the island. No hum or flow of energy. I know we're here, but I can't feel it. I don't feel the usual currents, under the breeze, of power or energy. It's like this place is dead, yet the ghosts are missing, the impressions left behind by life."

"It will be difficult to navigate this world within a world if we cannot see or feel anything around us," Aeden replied.

I closed my eyes and saw with senses that no one was powerful enough to block out. To find my family, I'd follow the guidance from a Zephyr I had only just met, in a dream I shouldn't have stepped through, in a time I wasn't alive for. If I couldn't count on my magick or Malice to lead the way, I would use the part of me that was wholly mine...my soul.

"Aeden, close your eyes," I whispered. "Pay attention, but not with your eyes. Breathe the island in, and let your soul hear and feel. Listen with that part of you that cannot be touched by the magick of others. Use the parts that know when a loved one is sad or upset, that sense we all have deep inside us that can't be silenced. Ground yourself in this moment."

I breathed in the air, stale and lifeless, and willed myself to relax. Little by little, under the webs of magick and protection, I could hear a faint bird, the water lapping against the shores, insects scurrying away from our steps. I could see webs around us, floating in the air, bits of magick to quell any hint of life. I tracked the webs until I found the spell that silenced the world. I plucked the strings and felt them fall away. The noise crashed down on us as soon as the last string hit the ground. The stillness popped, and I staggered at the suddenness of it.

"I didn't mind the silence. It's so rare not to be bombarded with noise," Aeden smiled. "But this is better for tracking."

The smell of the island, carried on the breeze, was the first thing to hit me. It smelled of death and rotting meat. I covered my nose and breathed through my mouth, but it was still enough to gag me. I coughed until my stomach could take no more, and I vomited. I could taste the dread on my tongue. I almost missed the flowers over this smell. My mind twisted with horrible thoughts of what could smell this hideous. Under the scent, waves of familiarity wafted. I had smelled it before.

"What the hell is that?" I whispered. "Death?"

"Something worse than death," Aeden replied. He didn't look as bothered by the smell as I was.

"What's worse than death?" I asked.

"Being the only one to survive in a field of the fallen," Oisin replied, and I couldn't really argue that fact, although that wasn't what I had meant.

"It smells of bodies rotting in the sun," Faolan answered.

"I don't even want to ask you how you know that." I groaned.

"I've seen many wars, Perdi. The worst ones happen in the Summer Courts, where the bodies rot in the sun. Why do you think we always meet on our side of the river?" he answered anyway. "I hate to say this, but you'll get used to the smell."

"I don't know about that, Fao. This is awful," I mumbled.

I wanted to maintain that I'd never get used to it, but even as I finished my sentence, my nose grew dull to the overwhelmingness of the sharp stench. It was still pungent, but it didn't make my stomach crawl up my throat. I cleaned the vomit from my mouth, and we began our search for our people. I sent a prayer up to any God or Goddess listening that those smells weren't from the rotting bodies of those I loved. I could handle just about anything except that.

The farther into the island we ventured, the more familiar it felt. I turned to Aeden and paused. "I've never been here, but it feels like I have. It feels like home, but it's not."

"It is not the location that gives you that feeling. It's who is here," Aeden replied. "We all feel it. Dark Court. It's the smell and emotions in the air."

"Is it Solas?" I asked, my hopes rising.

"Yes and no. Solas is here. I can feel his rage. It's not an emotion one soon forgets. But it is more than that. I don't think our family was the first to go missing and land here, Perdi," he replied.

"How the hell do our people go missing, and no one knows about it?" I asked.

"I didn't hear about it until Zephyr mentioned it, and Solas followed up with us. But, Perdi, people go missing every day. We can't track everyone. They either turn up in someone else's court or dead along their border."

"Why does no one report this?" I asked.

"To who? This literally happens daily all over Elphame. People make deals they can't cover, oath themselves and break their word, borrow or steal from the wrong family, are jailed and tortured, sold or are simply in the wrong place at the wrong time."

"If any of our people go missing again, for any reason, I want to be told immediately. I don't care if we need to knock on everyone's door at the end of every day. I want to know everyone made it home safely," I replied. I cringed at the thought of our people being held in some dungeon. I had been on the receiving end of a prison sentence in Elphame, and I'd do anything to keep that fate from one of our people. "How many of our people are jailed elsewhere?"

Oisin laughed from behind us. "None. Who would be so stupid as to jail one of Solas' people?"

I motioned to where we stood. "Obviously a few, or we wouldn't be here."

"Currently none. We never leave our people behind," Aeden said. "After every war, Zephyr sends the Aos Si to find our people and bring them or their bodies home. When we do know someone is missing, we look for them. But we need to hear about it to do anything."

"Do you know how many of our people have been found so far?" I asked.

"I'll send word to Zeno and ask how many have turned up. It'll give us an idea of how many we're looking for and how many need to be packed off the island."

"If our people are here, they are our first priority," I replied and felt my heart sink at the prospect of choosing between our people and my family. "We find them and get them home before we burn the place down for my family."

"Our people before the throne, at all costs," Aeden answered. It sounded like he was echoing something hammered into their heads by Zephyr.

I followed the feeling of home. We cleared half of the island before we took our first break. I knew we'd have to search several times over, and the first time was more for scouting than anything else. But I still held out foolish hope we'd stumble upon them by accident. I knew better, but hope didn't care about the truth. Each time Aeden offered to rest, I shook my head. I didn't want to stop, not even when he finally forced me. I needed food and water...and rest. I knew this, but it still bothered me that my body wasn't built for war.

"Wars aren't won in one day," Aeden said.

"What rock have you been living under?" I asked and politely disagreed with his assessment. "Wars were fought and won in minutes. Those fighting on the field just don't know it yet."

I finally relented when he refused to budge. He reminded me that it wasn't just me who needed the break. All of us did. I could have argued longer, but it was easier to take the break. I moved away from the group and paced while they ate their meal. I glanced back every few minutes, hoping they'd be done and we could go. But they lounged, they whispered to each other, laughed and smiled. All the parts that made them a unit, they shared with each other. I watched some trade fruits while others traded entire meals. They weren't just a group of soldiers. They were brothers. I stopped begging them to hurry with my eyes and took a seat, enjoying the view of their shared experiences. I knew, even in war, even in struggle, sometimes you found the very reason for why you were there.

"You need to eat." Aeden sat beside me and passed a small white sack over, and I smiled.

"When Solas led me from the Gate to the Golden Court, we stopped for a break. He gave me my lunch in a bag just like this." I opened it up and pulled out some fruit to pick at. "It looked worn, patched and repatched."

"Grandmother Elda makes these for us all. It was probably his bag that you were using," he answered. "When I asked why she made them, she said, no matter where we are or what we're doing, it'll always feel like we're eating at home. And it does feel that way, no matter where we are or what we're doing."

"She's pretty terrifying for a little old lady. At least, for me, anyway. She scared the hell out of me the first time I met her."

He nodded. "All of us see Elda — the Aos Si, I mean. Both Zephyr and Solas make us go."

"Why?"

"At first, I thought it was to see if they were wasting their time on us. Why train us if we'll be no good, you know? But after a few minutes with her, I realized it was to welcome us into their family." His answer came with a smile I could feel in my heart. "She didn't talk about my future or my fate. She simply made me tea and talked to me like I was real, like I mattered, like someone actually cared that I was scared to death of what was yet to come. She didn't pry the questions from me. She already knew what they'd be. She answered honestly and put my worries about my future to rest. At the end, after hours with her, I left my fears behind. And each time I've seen her since, she cups my face in her hands and reminds me of every reason I wake each day. She gave me hope when no one else could. Even with those hard truths, I left with hope."

"Sounds like we had different experiences." I laughed softly. "The only answers I've ever gotten from Elda have scrubbed off parts of my soul."

"Only because that's how you chose to hear them. She gave you hope, or you'd still be in her caves, demanding answers. You're just that stubborn." He motioned to the group. "Look around, Perdi. Every Aos Si here is fated to die, as are you. We all are. They before you, and they know it. They've been told early on that they will die earlier than most and later than some. It doesn't make death any less scary, but it does help you look into its eyes and dare it to take its best shot. Because fate or not, we will never simply go willingly without a fight. We'll make death work damn hard to take us."

"It still makes hearing it sting, doesn't it?" I asked.

"No. Not really. We are born with a single end purpose, which is to die. That is the fate of us all, no matter who you are or what you do. You are dying the moment you're born. It's up to you to decide what you do with the days in between. You can give the world a reason to remember you, or you can fade out, and history will not remember your name."

"You've spent too much time with Zephyr." I rolled my eyes. "You sound just like him and his little pep talks."

"Although you mean that as an insult, I take great pride in that statement," he replied, and his back was a little straighter after the comment. "What about you? You saw Elda when you first came here, and I know she would have told you that you'd die when you closed the Gate. Yet, you still went and made death fight tooth and nail for you."

"I don't remember it that way." I huffed a laugh.

"If you didn't fight death into submission, you simply would have died, and we'd not be having this conversation." He pointed out the obvious, as Zephyr would have. "You saw Elda after Zephyr and Nix were taken. She would have offered you a warning. Zephyr and Nix would not tell you where they were, for fear you'd die. Yet, here you are, on the island they didn't want you to come to, having this conversation with me. You don't fear death any more than I do. You won't call it into your welcoming arms, but the fear that once lived in your soul is gone. Because some things, some people, are worth breaking yourself in two and not making it out alive."

"For a trainee, Aeden, you certainly are a brilliant man."

He cleared his throat. "Ma'am, I'm the personal Royal Guard to the Queen of Darkness."

Before I could correct my statement, the shadows slinked down from the tree beside me. "Perdi, we've checked on the Gate."

"When?" I asked.

"We have been checking periodically since we last left there," they answered and swirled to my front. "We were wrong to assume you'd wish to do as Zephyr would? This is how he keeps tabs, as you'd say, on many things at once. We are the tool he selects most often. We have been checking on the Gate and our people."

"No, you're not wrong. I was just surprised. I don't think of you as a tool. You're a lot of persons in one."

"That is kind of you to say," they replied. "We have never been gone long, never completely, in case the wards returned and you needed us. Half of us go, and half of us remain with you. It is what Zephyr would do."

"Is there an issue at the Gate?" I asked, cringing at the thought of needing to go.

"There is, as usual," they replied. "This is about our missing people. Zeno has informed us that a few dozen are still missing. Aside from this island, all of Elphame and Whitwick have been searched, and they're nowhere to be found. Our people don't vanish without a trace. They are here."

"I agree." I nodded and turned to Aeden. "They're either alive somewhere here on the island or were killed when the Satyr realized it wasn't enough to get my attention."

"They're likely alive and what we've been sensing," he replied. "If I were the Satyr, I'd have kept them alive to use as a bargaining chip."

"And if you didn't want to negotiate?" I asked.

"I wouldn't have taken a soul to begin with. I'd have simply killed them where I found them," he replied. "They want something, or everyone would be dead."

"Here's to hoping they want something," I answered.

"They do... You," the shadows replied.

Chapter Thirteen

I had tasted blood by the time we set up camp. I wanted to scream at the very thought of stopping our search and had chewed on my curses and cries, gnashing my cheeks in the process. Aeden was right about our need to rest. I felt it in my exhaustion and jellied legs. But it didn't make it any easier to stop. I stood in the circle of men and panted, sweat dripping into my eyes and burning them with salt and dust. Leaning forward with my hands on my knees, temples throbbing, stomach knotted, I listened to them discuss the options for sleep. *Sleep.* I had my doubts I'd be able to close my eyes long enough for it to count as sleep.

Now able to breathe without wheezing, I stood with fire in my belly, ready to rally them once again. But the eyes that stared back were as weary as my own. They would continue if I ordered them, but at what cost? They, like me, were on the very dregs of energy. Night had set in hours ago and robbed us of the few senses we still had. I finally gave in and nodded, then scowled at the mouth of the cave I was led to. The others would sleep outside and would take turns guarding. They all would take turns—everyone but me. I tried to be insulted but was too wasted to argue about it. Logic won out. I knew I was safer inside the cave than out. But the petty voice inside told me I was as tough as they were, and they'd think less of me if I didn't sleep on the dirt or watch for whatever went bump in the night.

I protested, even though I knew it would get me nowhere. "This is ridiculous, Aeden, to stuff me in a cave. I'm no safer in here than out there."

"Although your shadows can protect you in here and out there, I wouldn't feel right if you slept outside in the open. None of us would get any sleep at all." Aeden countered my objections.

"I'm not a delicate flower," I replied. "I can suffer with the rest, like a big girl."

"Let's just get this over and done with right now."

"What?"

"Your insecurities. Don't project them on me or any of the other men," he said and folded his arms. "You seem to think you have something to prove. You don't. And the more you push, the more uncomfortable the rest of us feel."

"I don't want to be treated as if I'm vulnerable or too delicate," I answered.

"That is not what I said. And delicate is not how I'd describe you, nor would anyone else who's had the pleasure of meeting you. Perdi, we were all raised by mothers and sisters long before the harsh hand of war. Being Aos Si doesn't mean we don't believe in properly treating ladies. If someone made my sister sleep outside, or my mother, I would be insulted they thought so low of them, to have them sleep like dogs.

And if they dared have her sleep within a group of men, I'd kill them for it. That is not how you treat a lady of any standing, queen or not. It has nothing to do with who *you* are and everything to do with who *we* are," he explained, then sighed.

"Perdi, if you sleep outside, we will worry. Not only of you sleeping on the ground and the disrespect we would feel we treated you with, but of being fully unprotected. We are the wall between you and whoever comes. We can give warning to your shadows, who can take you away if we fail. Please don't make us worry. If we do, we do not sleep. Without sleep, we are useless. We are here to help you. Do not make us a burden because you wish to suffer with the rest of us. Why suffer when you do not have to? The suffering will come, it always does, but why call it into your waiting arms so soon?"

I finally raised my hands in surrender. "You're right. I'm sorry. I'm picking a fight because I don't want to stop looking. Sleeping arrangements were just an easy target."

"I get that. We all do. None of us want to stop. We just know we must. But if you're tired tomorrow, you won't pay as close attention as you would want to. What if we miss something because we are dragging our feet? What if they're moved while we have to take another rest because no one slept? If it makes you feel any better, Zephyr also had us on a clock."

"What do you mean?" I asked.

"Have you ever seen the entire Aos Si in a battle at once? No, because it's never happened. He rotates us. Whoever isn't fighting is resting. Nothing is won through exhausting yourself. The rare occasion we are all out together is usually at the very start, as a show, and at the end, when there's nothing but cleanup to do. But never does he wear us all out at the same time. Solas is the same. The Sluagh... Do you think they're all out patrolling together? Have you ever seen them all together? Never, in all my years, have I seen them as one unit. There are thousands of them, and you only see a few dozen at once. Solas shifts them out to make his threat last as long as he needs it. And don't even get me started on the wee folk. Nix has taught Solas how to perfect the art of war. Lest you forget, Nix kept you alive for days, while the entirety of Elphame hunted you. But at least then, you actually asked him to rest."

"How do you know?"

He smiled. "Everyone knows the story of how a wee gnome and a fairy kept a little Crow alive."

I smiled and remembered back to Nix and how massive his ego had gotten after learning our tales had reached every corner of Elphame. "Thank you, Aeden. And I'm sorry."

"Don't be sorry. Learn." He winked. "It always sounds better when Zephyr says it."

"No, he sounds like an asshole when he's saying it, too." I winked back.

I dragged my gear inside and thanked Oisin, who brought wood to the mouth of the cave, along with flint. I'd add that to the list of items to pack for war. I could light a fire with stones, but tonight, flint was the pinnacle of luxury as my fire came to life. The moment the heat touched my body, every pain and sluggish muscle came to life. On legs that grew in weight, in a matter of minutes, I unrolled my bedding and poured myself a cup of tea from a bag that appeared beside my fire. I could hear the men talking about strategy, the island and what they'd do when they got home. None spoke of *if* they didn't go home. I didn't get a sense of cockiness from them. They just didn't talk about death as if they had some fooled grip on it. They couldn't keep it from coming, so they talked about what they could control — life after war, moving trees for Orrian, helping their loved ones with gardens and roofing and repairing fences. It was calming to hear them talk about something other than death, to know they were here with me, so I'd have a life after war, so I'd have my people back and wouldn't need to plan one.

On my back, with my eyes closed, I whispered to the shadows, who were half with me and half scouring the island for any signs of life. They reported nothing of interest, besides the fact that there were no signs of the Satyr, either. They flickered from place to place and told me what they saw, which was the same wherever they landed. The only difference was in the vegetation that grew, but it was no different than any other island they had visited. They, like me, could feel the familiarity of home in the air. It was more than my family. They could sense souls from the Dark Court but couldn't track them.

They checked on the Gate before finally coming back for the night. Things had settled in Whitwick, but they didn't feel that had anything to do with us leaving, rather everything to do with it being night and people being too tired to care about invasions. If they decided to come here, they'd see that Fae were ready to war in the middle of the night. Fae didn't care where the sun stood in the sky. They would fight in the dark.

"My gut tells me it's more than that," I whispered to the shadows. "I don't have a good feeling about this."

"Nor do we, but nothing looks or feels any different than the last time you were there. Even as mortals slumber, the air still holds a tincture of hate and wishes for death." I felt them sigh. It rolled over my skin like a hot breeze. "They fear us. Even we fear our own kind. We were not surprised to feel those emotions when we crossed over. But we agree, we do not have a good feeling of how they will be driven by that fear or where they found insurmountable courage to stand against those who haunt their dreams."

"Fear breeds creativity. As someone who's needed to be damn creative in this world, I'm afraid of the imaginations of those who feel they've nothing to lose." I groaned with frustration that had only worsened with each passing day. "I'll worry about tomorrow, tomorrow."

"Fear and rage do not allow the holder to sleep, Perdi. We think they've already decided on what their next move will be, and it will not be against all of Elphame."

"It'll be directed at me." I groaned. They didn't have to answer for me to already know. "How do you know for certain?"

"Because no one ever looks too closely at shadows. We hear that which was not meant for us. Each time we've gone to Whitwick, their hate is directed at only you. Even you have felt it. They fear Fae, but they blame you. They forget their history and have built up a lie in their minds that the Darkmore witches are to blame for everything. They think it is Darkmore blood that has kept the Gate open all these years. And because of that, they've suffered for you, not with you." Their truth felt like ice in my veins. They blamed me for it all. But I had held out for the day that they'd remember I once was like them, mortal and every bit as scared of Fae. Instead, my return gave them darker ideas.

"Great," I muttered. "The Darkmore line was hunted to damn near extinction after the Gate opened. Mortals always found a reason to hate us, to burn us. And now, if they still think Darkmore blood is why they've suffered, they will hunt me until the end of time."

"You're the last Darkmore, Perdi. We don't think they'll ever stop hunting you." They replied and twisted around me a little tighter. "We feel we should tell you that your father is packing his belongings. He plans to come to Elphame."

"Things must be bad if he'd rather be with the Fae," I answered.

"He sees their blame and fears for your safety. He'd rather be with you than out there with those calling for his child's head," they replied and answered the question on the tip of my tongue. "Lily is aware your father is coming and has informed the others that he is not to be harmed. He will be aided."

"Thank you. Can you tell Lily that my dad may need help with Fae sickness?"

"We already did. She is aware and has called on the Winter Court healers for help."

"Why the Winter Court? Don't we have healers?"

"The Dark Court has one, but we doubted very much that your father would like to wake up in the caves of the Sluagh with Elda. It is not a pleasant place to open your eyes," they replied. "Healing Fae sickness is not a common skill the Unseelie courts have since it is forbidden in both courts to Take a mortal. Seelie court healers are all trained, as those are the only courts that enjoy that type of entertainment. For us, Elda is the only healer in our territory, trained. Faolan's court has only one who was specially trained in Fae sickness."

"I didn't know it was a specialized skill."

"It's only specialized in your courts because Solas and Faolan don't allow mortals to be Taken. Elsewhere, it's a skill like any other. Both Faolan and Solas have kept one for the day you came."

"Keep me informed on my father. If he gets worse or something happens, let me know."

"You must rest, Perdi. We feel your exhaustion, both of body and mind." They pulled back a little and rested calmly around me, allowing me to feel the world around me, but softening the harshness of its edges.

I blinked away the start of tears. "I miss home. I feel empty and not just of energy. I feel like half of myself is missing."

"And home misses you," they replied. "Rest, so you may continue your search tomorrow and find your other half."

I turned to face the fire, then away from the reminder of what would happen to the island if I failed. Staring at the rock reminded me of the dungeon, being on the run and my once certain death. I rolled onto my back and tried to close my eyes, but it felt like the ceiling was pushing down against me. Nothing calmed me. My bones were exhausted, and I wouldn't be of any use in the forest tonight, but it still felt like I was giving up. I couldn't stop my mind from filling with thoughts I didn't want—of death and burying my people, of having to move forward without Solas. I felt the first tear roll from the corner of my eye and drip into my ear. I knew the reason I didn't want to be in the cave, and it had nothing to do with what I could accomplish in the middle of the night and everything to do with hating being in a place that reminded me of days I thought I'd die, days I'd begged death to come. Even after I had made peace with being in Elphame, I still struggled with the hate I had for this land. Whenever I was backed into a corner or smelled something that reminded me of being forced into this life, I fought to remain calm and grounded. Tonight, I felt trapped and alone and homesick and scared.

"Perdi?" Aeden knocked on the entrance to the cave.

"Yes?" I called out and sat up. I casually wiped the tears from my cheek as if they hadn't been there. "Come in."

Aeden walked to the back of the cave, where I sat with the shadows dancing against the rock behind me. "I'll never get used to using your first name. It feels very personal. I've never even referred to my mother or sisters by their first names. Ma'am and Miss, to this day. To tell you the truth, I don't even know the first names of those my brothers oathed themselves to."

"And you're standing in a cave with me as we hunt for those I love. I'd say we're long past formalities," I answered. "Is that why you're here, to talk about calling me by my first name? Or is break time over, and we're packing up?"

"No, to both. Forgive me, but I can feel your fear and sadness. It's rolling out of the cave on the heat of your fire. All of us can feel it. I came to check on you."

"Sorry for disturbing you all. I'll lock it down," I replied and sighed. My words sounded sharp and rude. "I'm feeling a little on edge, and I'm sorry if I'm cutting you all up with my thoughts. My mind won't stop spinning. I can't control it."

"Don't be sorry. Your fear feels familiar to me, like a memory I don't want of a place I like even less. We're sorry that this, the cave, was the only place we found to keep you safe. We can tell you don't like being in this cave any more than we would have liked to be stuck in here." He shuddered. "Becoming Aos Si used to be very difficult at first. And caves are not a favored place to sleep."

"Dungeon, torture, wishing for death? That is the Elphame way." I motioned for him to sit with me. I was thankful not to be alone in my head.

He kept a respectful distance but took a seat close to the fire. "Similar, but yes, especially the death part. We're trained to see beyond death. We learn that death is not the worst thing to happen to you. But those moments, before we learn, are a damn hard place to be. What I feel tonight reminds me of times the world hurt too much, and I wasn't strong enough to take it. It reminds me of every time I was weaker than those around me. And you know, as well as the rest of us, how terrifying it is to be lower than everyone else. People get mighty creative when you're weaker than they are."

"Why the hell would anyone want to become Aos Si if that's what it's like?" I asked.

"Why would anyone remain in Elphame if they knew freedom was just a breath away?" he countered. "I mean no disrespect, of course."

"Aeden, please don't tiptoe around when you're with me. If you insult me, it's probably because what you said was too close to a truth I'm unwilling to see. I see your point, though. All that suffering and fighting just to stay in the end. But I couldn't leave. This is my home. Solas is my home."

"And I endured for the same reason. Elphame is my home. Zephyr and Solas are my home. And you, Perdi, are my home. I stayed for the same reasons as you, to protect those I care for. But it comes at a cost." His voice held a touch of hurt. A quiet pain. "You didn't see me the day you closed the Gate, but we all saw you. We all knew your cost, and not one of us doubted you'd pay it willingly. We watched you die, and most of us stepped forward to give our power, our life force, to Zephyr, to save you. No one should pay that dearly alone."

"Thank you. I didn't know that."

"That is when I noticed Nix. For the first time, I really saw him. We saw him, his bravery, love and loyalty to you. Perdi, it was glorious, like reaching for a star and touching it. We watched him climb atop the biggest Sluagh in the army and demand the beast take him into the Gate." He smiled yet shivered at the memory. "I remember his little voice, ripping through the air and slapping us all with his sheer love for you. The fury that rolled off of him, I can still remember it like yesterday, and damn it, if it didn't shame me. I had forgotten the gnomes and how utterly fearless they are, how bold and honest their souls are. And it was beautiful." His voice shook just enough for me to notice his eyes sparkled a little more than before. The passion and pain in his voice moved me to silent tears. "He rode on the backs of hell, him and a fairy bearing her blood-crusted teeth, and made us all feel tiny. I remember thinking, how could a gnome, who could fit in my boot, have more courage than I do? How could he be so brave as to touch the Sluagh, a beast not even I would dare go near, let alone convince it to die for his cause. And when he dragged you out, begging the Gods to take him instead of you, he became my home, as well.

"We are not just here for Solas and Zephyr. We are here for our brother, Nix. He is our friend, as much as you are. More than that, he'd have come here for you or me or one of the others. He would give away all his favors, beg and borrow, to save any one of us. We're all scared for Zephyr and Solas, but fear isn't what I feel when I think of where Nix is. We feel pity for those who took him."

I didn't bother hiding my tears. "Nix would be proud to hear his name spoken like that. He'd probably write it all down and remind me of it every chance he got."

"He does have a fairly large ego for such a wee man." Aeden grinned. "I understand why Zephyr is so protective of him."

"You must miss him, Zephyr, a lot. You haven't had him back for long, and because of me, again, he is gone."

"Not *because* of you, *for* you. There is a difference," he corrected me. "When you say it the other way, it takes away his choice. The Dark Court cannot be forced any more than the Aos Si."

"That doesn't help settle my guilt, unfortunately. They're still gone, and I still feel responsible."

"It is the curse of love, isn't it? To always suffer, to always fear. It wouldn't be valuable, otherwise," he said, and turned to face me. "It's why we've chosen to follow you." His smile softened, making him look much younger and less terrifying. "When the Last War came, we refused to go into battle. No rank would wage war because you were on the other side of the field, and you had chosen to be there. It's what took so long for the war to begin. We wouldn't answer the call."

"I bet that thrilled Zephyr," I joked.

"He didn't answer the call, either. He forbade us from going when Solas called. But none of us would have, regardless. We, like Zephyr, gave our allegiance to the Crow." He smiled. With his hands on his hips, he mimicked Zephyr's voice, "*Foolish little Crow is going to be the death of me. Now I must fight every king in this godforsaken land because Solas and Perdi have decided to save the fucking world again. I swear to all the Gods and all the Goddesses, if they don't fix this shit, I will strangle them both. Finis are supposed to outlive the very Gods, and at this rate, I won't see tomorrow.*"

My laughter echoed in the cave. "That was perfect."

"When he finally said it was time for war, we stood at Zephyr's back and waited for the call of a Crow."

"Thank you." I touched his hand, and he froze. He looked like he was going to climb out of his skin. "It's okay, Aeden. It's okay to accept kindness and love from another. It doesn't mean you're crossing a line or doing something wrong."

"If Solas or Zephyr smell your scent on another, they'll cut the smell off of us. Zephyr said as much."

"I'll protect you." I smiled.

His head dropped, and his shoulders heaved. "Forgive me."

"For what?" I asked.

"I actually believe you." He lifted his face and blinked until the threat of tears was gone. It bothered me more to see him fight against his tears than it would have to see him cry. "I shouldn't be relieved that you'd protect me. It should be *me* telling you that I'll protect *you*. I think I'm just exhausted."

"You're not weak to feel relief in someone's protection. This world is too bloody cruel to do it alone. A family protects each other. It will always go both ways, all of us protecting each other, or this isn't the family I want. We're either in this together, or I'm on my own with a bunch of bodies around me, waiting to die," I answered.

He took a few minutes to calm himself, and I appreciated the silent company. I was comfortable with silence. It was better than being alone with my thoughts. "Perdi, can I tell you something without you charging outside to interrogate everyone?"

"I can't promise that. But I can promise I'll wait it out until my head cools."

"I don't trust the Seelie court," he replied.

I smiled. "That's not the first time you've said that, and others have said it, too. Neither do I."

"No, I can feel it in my gut. It's not a fleeting dislike for them. I don't like or dislike them. Something is off, and I've noticed it all day. They aren't surprised to be here. They weren't surprised about the wards or the stench we found when we arrived. They have gone from currying for your favor to whispering behind your back. I've asked several men to remain with them. I simply do not trust them near you. Something is telling me they are here to help, but you are not who they would help. It is part of the reason we put you in the cave, to ensure we stood between you and Theo. And before you comment on how you can protect yourself, it will only take one blow to your still very mortal skull for you to die."

"I agree. Whether I can defend myself means nothing if they find luck under a rock and brain me with it," I replied. "If you don't trust them, Aeden, do what you must. Keep a close watch and do what you need to keep us moving forward, whatever the cost."

He nodded. "Thank you for your confidence."

"If you were not trustworthy, you'd already be dead. That you are in Zephyr's army, whatever your rank, tells me I can trust you with my life and those I love. That Solas would allow you to step foot near me tells me he trusts you as well."

"You're a lot like him, you know." He smiled.

"Zephyr or Solas?" I laughed.

"I'd say Zephyr more, but more and more, you remind me of standing too close to Solas when he's angry. And you're every bit as brutal as Nix. The gnomes aren't known for their diplomacy," he answered. "But the part of you that reminds me of Zephyr is calming to talk to. You're rough around the edges, but it reminds me of how Zephyr will cut through the crap with his honesty."

"If I remind you of Zeph, why don't the others, the Aos Si, talk to me? Finn has said a few things at the manor but nothing since we left," I asked. "They don't even look me in the eyes. Did I do something wrong? Have I said something that makes them think I don't want to talk to them?"

"They, too, have stood too close to Solas when he's been angry." His laughter echoed in the cave. "Finn talks a lot when he shouldn't, but he did it privately. Once we left your home, we left the familiarities behind. You're the queen, Perdi. And we aren't even ranking members of the Aos Si. You've taken us into battle, so to speak, and we have much to prove, whether you like it or not. One slip-up, one word, one wrong look could cost them everything they've worked so hard for. Their entire lives and dreams could be dashed in one moment they can't take back. That is a pretty big thing to ask of them. They will give you their lives without a second thought, but they would think twice about dishonoring their families, their brothers, their Commander or the very king of the most powerful court in Elphame. Their families depend on them. Their families are protected because of their position within the Aos Si. If they make one wrong move, all of this was for nothing."

"What about you? You're in here. You talk to me."

"I'm your personal guard. It's expected of me to converse with you, check on you and be as we are right now. *You* are my duty. I am here to protect you against all and would give my life for you, but my main duty is to offer you counsel. I can cross lines the others cannot, and I won't suffer as the others will. It is expected of me."

"It makes me uncomfortable, like I'm not a real person. I understand that I'm a queen and there are rules, but it feels like I'm removed, above them, and I don't like how it feels. I don't like being more or less than anyone, Aos Si or not."

"I understand. If this isn't what you want, may I suggest you're honest with the others, then? Giving them your truths makes it easier to trust you with their own. How can they treat you as Perdi, when you are nothing more than the queen to them? That you're asking me and not them doesn't say a lot about your cause. Talk to them as you talk to me. Talk to them as Perdi and not as the queen. Some might never come around, but a few just may. And if the others see that relationship and that trust, it might help."

I nodded. I hadn't thought of it.

"But know this. You may not see yourself as above them, but our Commander does, as does our king. Nothing you say or do will change that. So, if you ask this of them, you must be willing to stand between them and those who see you as the sun and moon. Are you willing to protect their futures because your crown feels uncomfortable?"

"I'm a dirty fighter. I think I could get Solas to hold Zephyr down for me until he saw reason. Nix would help me." I laughed softly until it hitched in my throat.

"I feel your sadness. I'm sorry your journey through Elphame has been a fight for each day."

"Nothing is free in Elphame, not even love."

"Room for one more?" Oisin dragged his bed to the rear of the cave.

"Are you okay, Perdi?" Faolan came behind with his gear. "We thought you'd want some company. Memories have a way of beating us up long after we think we're healed."

"I am now, thank you," I answered.

I curled back into my bed, pulling my blankets up to my chin, and listened to Faolan and Oisin ridicule each other. Away from the eyes of others, they were family and needled each other as brothers would. Aeden finally brought his bed into the cave, and the three of them whispered about days so long ago they weren't written about, stories of fantastic beasts they battled for land and small critters who had chased them without a single sword lifted. I drifted to sleep, wrapped in shadows, looking for Solas once more.

* * * *

My heart skipped in my chest the moment I saw Solas. To see him alive softened the spark stone of pain that had taken root in my throat. To see his chest rise and fall gave me hope. It settled my fear and spurred my want to wake everyone to keep looking.

"Hello, little Crow." Solas glanced up from the wall, chained beside Zephyr, who held Nix. Solas breathed me in and smiled. I knew he wouldn't fight me if I came to his dream. "As you can see, I found Nix and Zephyr before you did. I'm taking that as a win. I found them first."

I couldn't help but laugh. "I see that. Your rescue attempt has gone off smashingly. Now that you've found them, what are your big plans to get back out, oh great king of mine?"

"You, of course," he answered and grinned. "You're close. I can feel you like an itch I can't reach."

"I am, and you'd get a real kick out of my rescue party," I replied.

"I can only imagine. I don't feel the Sluagh. But I can hear the banter caused by booze and smell the campfire. Why are you in a cave? Are you on the run again, little Crow?" he asked.

"No, and I left the Sluagh at home. None of them would let me put them on leashes. No leash, no glory." I laughed. "I left the Unseelie courts guarded to the teeth while the rest of us came to save you from your obvious failed rescue attempt."

"We haven't much time." Solas breathed me in again, and a small groan slipped from his lips. He tried to hide it with another smile but was in a world of pain. Even from here, I could smell the cold iron they'd used to hold him with and the blisters they brought to the surface. "I smell Faolan, Oisin, and...who the hell is that? Aeden?" He breathed in and held it for a moment, rolling the smells around in his mouth as I had seen him do before. "Do you have Zephyr's trainees with you?"

"Yes," I answered.

"Well, I, for one, am excited to see just how smashingly your little rescue goes. If you end up on this wall beside me, you don't get to count that as a win." He huffed a laugh. "You make friends everywhere you go."

"I'm trying, but they don't want to braid each other's hair anytime soon," I replied.

"They're not your pets, either. Treat them as people, not tools, and you'll make it here a lot quicker."

"You're not going to try to send me away, like Zephyr?" I asked.

"I tried that once. Remember how that turned out? And I'm not foolish enough to think you'd listen. Zephyr, though, thought he could save you from this, from having to taint your soul for him. I think you can save yourself and will do whatever the hell you want with your soul. You weren't meant for crystal towers and planning parties. And we can cobble your soul back together later," he added. "But those who took us are counting on your arrival, Perdi. They know you're here. They know you are coming. They have purposely cleared the island, leading you right to us." He shuddered with another painful sigh. "You must get word to the Dark Courts, to the Sluagh. There are mortals and Mages in Elphame. They are who built the wards. They ran from the island when they realized how deep of a grave they had dug for themselves. I don't know if they're kept by any court or if they came here with your death on their minds. Either way, they're still here. They wouldn't have made it back to Whitwick with Seers at the Gate. But the Sluagh will find wherever they're hiding. I'm sorry, Perdi, but they cannot be allowed to live. They'll only keep hunting you if you allow it, and eventually, they'll succeed. I know they're your people, but they'll do more damage if left alive. We can't risk you or our people any more than we already have."

"The mortals are not my people, not anymore, Solas. I knew, eventually, Whitwick would find a way to come for me. I'll have the shadows tell Lily." I groaned. I didn't like the idea of hunting mortals, but leaving them alive wasn't an option. "The Dark Courts are my people, and the Satyr have taken our people. I can feel them stronger now, through you."

"I can feel them here, too, but they're not locked away with us," he replied.

"Are they still alive, or am I wasting my time looking for them?" I asked. "I'm sorry to ask this, but do I give up the search and return for their bodies, or do I keep looking? I could feel them the moment I stepped foot on the island, but I can't sense them as I do you."

"Keep searching. Most are still alive," Solas replied. "Find them before you come for us, or they're as good as dead. Our people before us, always. We protect our court before our throne. I'm sorry, Perdi, but you cannot come for us first. Our oath puts what we want last when we sit on our throne. Promise you'll go for them first."

"I promise. I'll find our people," I replied. "Do you know where you are?"

He shook his head. "Not the slightest idea, aside from being on this island. I don't know if I'm underground or above. We're heavily guarded. If I had to guess, I'd say a small army has us, maybe two or three hundred. It's doable, but it'll hurt, little Crow. I won't lie to you. Your soul will bleed heavily for this and what you'll have to do to get us all home."

"Is there ever a time this shit doesn't hurt?" I asked.

"Not from where I'm sitting." He grinned and jiggled his chains.

"Solas, would it be considered an act of war if I held Theo down and drained his mind? I don't know what part he played in this, but I have a feeling he is involved. My gut is telling me he's hiding something, and it will bite us in the ass if it already hasn't."

"Yes, it would be an act of war." He laughed. "But so will what I do to him when I get out of here. Eat his fucking soul for the information. It'll save me from pulling it out of him through his asshole later."

"You're so sexy when you swear."

"Oh, I've got moves you haven't seen before."

I laughed. "You're chained to a wall. What moves do you currently have?"

"Final moves, little Crow. They're coming back to discuss our surrender. I'd wish very much for you not to see our refusal."

"Don't be a hero, Solas. I can't lose you." My heart sank. "I love you."

"I love you, too. It's time to wake up, little Crow. You have a hunt to prepare for," he whispered and nudged me from the dream.

"Wait," I replied. "Let me feel them. If I can feel them, I can find you."

"You won't like what you'll see," he replied.

"I already don't," I answered.

"Little Crow, I warned you." Zephyr groaned and opened his eyes. "Why did you not listen to me?"

"Zeph, I'm close. I'm so close."

"I told you not to come, and now it's time to go home," Zephyr replied.

The shadows rolled up the glass ward between me and my men. "Perdi, someone is pushing against your dream. We won't be able to keep them out."

"What? Who?" I asked. "The Satyr?"

"It's Finn," they replied. "Zephyr is pulling his pearl into your dream."

"Please, don't make me do this," Finn whispered, moving into the dream to stand at my side. I glanced at Finn and back to Zephyr. Before I could ask any questions, Finn answered them all with his next words. "The moment we use this magick, Sir, the wards will return, and we won't be able to come back for you."

"You know who to take. Take him and go." Zephyr closed his eyes.

"No!" Solas yelled, cluing in to what was about to unfold. "Take our people! Not me. Save our people first."

"Do it, Finn," Zephyr commanded. "Leave us and take our king. Our people need their king."

"No!" I screamed, but it was too late. Finn's hand was on my arm, and the fight was gone in a flash.

"I'm sorry, Perdi." Finn pulled me into his chest. "Please don't fight me. I don't want to hurt you."

My will to pull away from him was gone. My desire to struggle left in the same instance. His magick felt like coming to terms with drowning. I was calm, almost sleepy. My limbs were as heavy as my eyelids. My mouth and tongue didn't want to work for anything more than a groan. My Malice heard my call and roared to the surface, giving me a chance to focus. "Finn, no. Please don't do this."

"I have no choice. I owe Zephyr an oath, and he's cashing it in. It is me or one of the other men who will be forced," Finn replied and whispered into my ear. "I have the same choice as you in this matter, absolutely none. Command half of the shadows to remain on the island."

"Why?" I asked, my brain a jumble of thoughts and confusion.

"Because this ends with us taking Solas and leaving Zephyr and Nix behind," he replied. "Do it, Perdi. Before you give up the only card you have left to play." Finn's magick coursed through every muscle and settled into my bones. "Tell half of the shadows to hide and not follow us back out. Now, Perdi, before you spend the only chance you have left at saving them."

"Half of you will remain on the island with Zephyr. You will not follow us when we leave," I whispered to the shadows before realizing I was saying the words. I felt the sudden weight change in my soul as half of the shadows fled for cover.

Finn's grip relaxed a little, and I struggled against him. "Now call Solas home. He gave his entire soul to you for the taking. There is no power stronger than you, who can command his soul. Call him back to the mainland while the wards are down. Bring your Malice to the surface and pull Solas home."

"I can't," I replied. "I promised Solas that I'd save our people before him."

"We can't take them all. I have given you the only chance I can afford without breaking my oath. Do it. Please don't make me force you."

"I won't leave my people behind," I replied. "They're counting on us to bring them home. We never leave our people behind."

"But we both know, without you having to say the words, who you would choose if forced to," he replied. It was true. I wanted to grab Solas and run, but I couldn't bring myself to do it. I couldn't stomach the thought of being the one to sentence the rest of my family and my people to save him. "Let me make the choice for you. You won't hate yourself tomorrow if you let me do this for you."

"I choose my people." I shook my head and closed my eyes. I fought tooth and nail against the sudden desire to do as he'd commanded. My Malice slinked along the surface of my soul, drinking down his power, doing all she could to help me.

"I'm sorry, Perdi," Zephyr commanded. "Now, Finn."

Finn groaned and pushed against my fight. Although I resisted, it was no use. His power was too great, and my Malice was too weak against him. I now knew why Finn had been sent in first against the Caller of Crows, why Nix had said he was the most powerful of the Aos Si. The calm waves of energy rolling off him were but a drop in the bucket. Had he pushed a little more, I'd have had no choice.

Finn hugged me tighter. "You can't fight it. Use your Malice, bring Solas home or this was for naught. I'm sorry, but we leave everyone else behind."

"You knew this would happen," I muttered.

He nodded. "Yes, I did, and I warned you about bringing Zephyr's tools with you. You weren't so foolish as to think he wouldn't use us, were you?"

"I will eat your fucking soul for this."

"I'd have it no other way," he replied, and the full force of his magick rolled over me. "I'm sorry."

"Perdi, look at me." Solas' voice was far away. "Perdi!"

I glanced at Solas, my eyelids feeling heavier by the second. "Solas, help me. I can't fight it."

"You're stronger than him." Solas' voice dragged along my mind like razor blades. "Focus. You are a Darkmore. Remember who you are. You're Finis. No one commands you. Our people need you to focus. Do not pull me back. Whoever we leave behind will die if you allow Finn to control you. This is the curse of ruling. You must choose them and be willing to die for them."

"They'll kill you," I whispered.

"No, little Crow. I can take more than they could ever give." He grinned. "When you return, burn it down. You know how much I love a good fire."

"Fuck," Finn groaned as he felt my awareness return with more force than before. "Perdi, take him."

"Fuck you, Finn," I replied.

"If you fight me, Perdi, we leave empty-handed," Finn whispered. "Choose wisely. One way or another, you leave this island tonight. Perdi, that is my oath. I must take you from this island."

"Save our people." Solas' voice was a slap of awareness.

I dug my nails into the palms of my hands, allowing dribbles of blood to break free. I mumbled to my Darkmore line, begging for aid. My Malice roared to the surface, thirsting for vengeance, as Finn whispered in my ear, holding me against his chest. His magick felt like bleeding from my eyes and ears and soul. It was cold and hot and sharp. I closed *my eyes and screamed as the world tilted and my legs gave out under me.*

"I choose my people," I screamed in Finn's ear. "We leave with my people, or we all die here right now. You will die with us, Finn. I swear to you, you'll taste death before me. It's your turn to choose. You let me take my people, or you die with the rest of us. Your oath will be fulfilled. I will let you take me off the island, but I won't leave without my people."

"Do it." Zephyr finally told Finn.

I reached through Finn's power and squeezed his soul in my hand, flexing the only muscle I had. Power. If I died, I'd take him with me. If my people died, he'd be next. It felt like holding on to a bolt of lightning while being held under freezing water. My vision sparkled, and in a flash of searing pain, the dream smashed, and we were blasted from the dream with enough force to skip my body across the water like a stone.

Chapter Fourteen

As the air slowly returned to my lungs, I stared up at the stars and wondered, for the briefest of moments, where I was. From the beach across from the island, all of us, save Solas, Zephyr and Nix, found ourselves lying in piles. I could smell burned hair and tasted vomit. The men around me groaned. Each had been woken to being thrown from the island. I rolled my head from side to side and fought the rage that boiled in my stomach as soon as my eyes landed on two dozen broken and battered bodies, but no Solas, no Zephyr and no Nix.

My arms were numb and tingling, as if I had slept on them for days. I pushed myself to my knees and crawled to those we had rescued. I silently prayed they were still alive. One glance at their bruised and battered bodies told me they were close to death and wouldn't have lasted much longer. I could smell the burns from iron and infection that had set in. My throat convulsed as I tried not to be sick.

The shadows twisted over the bodies of our people. "They're not here."

I shook my head. It took me several tries to speak. "They're still on the island."

"We'll come back for them," they replied.

"Take them to Elda. Tell her what's happened," I motioned to the shadows.

"We'll come back for you," they answered and started wrapping around groups of the broken. It would take them a few trips.

I turned my attention back to where we had come from. I closed my eyes and felt for the wards. I pulled back and shook out my hands. They were stronger than before and felt like fire on my fingertips. It would be near impossible to get back without killing myself in the process. My hope leaked from my soul like a draining sink—and I blamed Finn.

I stood and scanned the beach for Finn, finding him already on his knees and waiting for my wrath. The rest of the Aos Si stood in a half circle around him. Each of them looked from me to him with pity in their eyes. I didn't know who they felt worse for, me or Finn, but no one got in my way. Aeden motioned for the others to take a step back. He was smart enough to know what I was about to unleash—rage.

"Run," I said to Finn through clenched teeth.

Finn shook his head. "I'm fine where I am, thank you."

I launched myself at him. Wordless screams filled the night air. My Malice coated his body, and together, we burned. I pushed him onto his back and let my anger and hurt pour from my soul, praying he'd burn the worst, hoping he'd feel the edge of my hate for him. I gripped his throat and begged for the strength to strangle his very life from his body. The more I tried and failed, the angrier I became. I'd never be strong enough to kill him with my bare hands, but my bottomless pit of rage could burn him.

"You left them there!" I screamed in his face and shook him by his collar. "You left my family behind."

"I know," he replied.

"You left Solas and Nix." I choked on his name as if it were a rock in my throat. "Zephyr... You left your Commander, my family, behind."

"I did," he answered. "I tried to give you a choice."

"Why?" I asked. "Why would you do this?"

"Unlike you, I had no choice," he replied.

I pulled his face to mine and screamed until my voice cracked under the pressure. "I'll never be able to get back without killing myself to drop those wards. You've sentenced them to die. I will kill you for this!"

"There is no rage that you could touch me with that I haven't endured before," he replied, pulling me down to hear his whisper. "I'm the only one here who can take the anger of a Soul-Eater. It is why Zephyr chose me."

"I hate you," I replied. "I'll never be done with you. There will never be a day I don't hunt you."

"You'll never hate me as much as I hate myself," he answered.

I wormed my Malice through his mind, doors slamming shut as she dragged her claws through the corridors of his thoughts. But even with his strength, I could taste his tears on the back of my tongue as if they were my own. Sadness and regret had a flavor one never forgets, and he was coated in it. I gagged on the putrid flavor of it, but I'd willingly drown in his guilt before letting him go.

"We will never know who did this, who built the wards to lure me. Because of you, I'll always need to look over my shoulder."

"You've had to do that since the day you were born. Rest assured, little Crow, your enemies will keep coming, whether you're on that island or not."

"But you left behind those who will help keep me alive."

Finn pulled me into his chest, his eyes focused solely on mine. "Don't ever put your life in anyone else's hands. You give them the power to decide when it's over."

"You've put your life in mine," I yelled again, unable to control my anger.

He let me go. "You'll never be able to stomach what it will take to end my life. Because you, Perdi, are the only one here who still listens to their bloody soul. That is your curse."

"Perdi!" Faolan's voice cut through my rage. His cool touch reached through my flames, and his hand sizzled when he gripped my shoulders. With force, he pulled me off of Finn. "Not like this. We will regroup and return. I give you my word."

I pushed Faolan from me and turned back to Finn. The urge to attack him and allow my fear to pour from my fists was a force I hadn't felt in a long time. "You are not welcome in the Dark Courts, Finn. If I find you, if I so much as see you, I will end you. Do you understand? I will take everything you love and burn it to the ground. Trust me when I say, you will regret this day for as long as I allow you to live."

"I expect nothing less from you," Finn replied and pushed himself to his feet.

The shadows returned and wrapped around me. "Your people need you."

I looked at the other Aos Si. "He does not step foot in any territory that is mine or Zephyr's. One hair over, and whoever allows it will suffer the same fate. Do I make myself clear?"

"Yes, Perdi, crystal clear." Aeden sighed.

I glanced once at Faolan. "If I catch him in yours, I'll burn your glittering city to ash."

Faolan nodded his head. "An enemy of the Dark Courts is an enemy of mine."

Oisin shook his head, but I didn't expect him to blindly follow, not even under threat of death. He had made that mistake once, and his people had almost died because of his blind following of Faolan. "I won't kill him for you, Perdi. I know you're angry, and so am I. But I won't take his life because he's pissed you off. I'll send him packing, but you can't ask me to do anything more than that."

"I don't need you to do my dirty work," I replied.

"Perdi." Lily stepped through the trees, and I felt her words at the Gate hit me like a ton of bricks. "Did you forget so soon what I told you? These are Zephyr's men, not yours."

"Trust Zephyr's men, but remember, they are his men and not yours... The Aos Si will follow you, but they are utterly loyal to Zephyr, his calling, training and his word. They will not go against him and survive twice. They got one free pass for helping you in Blood and Bones, but Zephyr will not allow them to have two. Do not get them killed because you pushed them to abandon their duty."

"You're the one who told me to bring them with me, Lily. You told me they would help me," I replied. "Did you know this would happen?"

"No, but you'd have to be a fool to think Zephyr wouldn't find a way to save you and use the very tools you brought to him. Had you brought someone else, he'd have found a way to use them as well. With the Aos Si, at least you had a chance in hell to save your people," she replied. "This isn't Finn's fault. Had he broken his oath, he'd have paid with his life."

I smiled and felt the emotion drain from my face. "He should have. He's dead either way. My hand or the wild hunt, I'm not that picky."

"We made sure you'd get there. You'd feel who built the wards and know who your true enemies are. Now you know how to protect your people, who is coming for you and who you need to protect yourself against. It wasn't for nothing, Perdi." Finn spoke up. "I resisted Zephyr's pull for as long as I could. We all did. We walked the line between duty and death to ensure you'd know who was hunting you and your people. This isn't just about Zephyr or Nix…or even Solas. It is about keeping you alive. That is what we are oathed to do. Each and every one of us is sworn to follow Zephyr, and that's what we did. I'm sorry, Perdi. But we are bound in ways you couldn't possibly imagine."

"Screw your oath, Finn. Come sunup, your name is on my list," I replied. "You have hours until I hunt you to the ends of this realm. I suggest you start looking for a place to hide."

"I'm on everyone's list for worse reasons than pissing off a little Crow," he answered.

"You've pissed off a Soul-Eater," I corrected him. I stepped forward, and Faolan touched my shoulder in a warning. "I'm *not* your little Crow. Don't you ever call me that again, Finn."

Lily stepped in front of Finn in an attempt to block my path should I lose my temper again. "You're angry. I understand that emotion better than most. Go be with your people. Standing here isn't going to help them or your men still on the island."

I glanced back toward where we had come from. The wards clouded the water and hid my men from sight. The urge to try again rattled around in my soul. I was torn and struggled with making the decision. The shadows returned and wormed around my ankles. Feeling their touch reminded me of Zephyr.

"I can't leave them behind," I whispered, more to my own soul than anyone else.

"You didn't, and you're not. I will call on the Seers, we will remain here and I'll grab you the moment anything changes," Lily replied. She helped Finn to his feet, who whispered for only Lily to hear. "You left half of the shadows on the island?"

I glanced at the shadows twisting around my legs. "Did you all get pushed out?"

"No. There's only half of us here. The rest are on the island."

"Can you hear them?" Lily asked.

"Faintly, but we can still feel them," they replied. "They're moving through the tunnels, likely looking for our people."

"Perdi, between the shadows and Seers, you have eyes on the island. Go be with those who need to see their leader. Knowing you didn't leave them behind will mean a lot to them. Tomorrow, we can regroup."

I left the man who'd shattered my heart on the beach with his people and landed in the mouth of the Sluagh caves. Elda's home had been turned into a hospital of sorts, with Jare commanding the ranked Aos Si and running the show, as usual. I pushed my way through winged flesh and warriors, to Jare.

"Perdi." Jare smiled. His voice was calming, as usual.

"How are they?" I asked.

"You got them home just in time," he replied. "Another day or two would have been the difference between needing a healer and a burial."

I moved around the room, stopping at each bed. Most were unconscious, but I stopped just the same and asked the Gods to spare them. They had given enough. They shouldn't have to give their lives as well. Those who were awake, I found myself crying with them. It wasn't that long ago that I was locked in a dungeon, thinking I'd die. Once the shadows and I had touched each one of them, feeling for any lingering signs of who else could be behind this, I stood on the edge of the room and watched.

"I'm sorry, Perdi." Zeno leaned against the wall beside me.

"Sorry for what?" I asked and panicked a little, staring out over the room. My eyes jumped from bed to bed. "Did someone die? Was I too late?"

His hand found mine and squeezed it. "That your first noble act as a queen was to choose between your people and your family. It's never an easy choice."

My eyes watered. "I don't know if this makes sense, but I'm thankful I got my people home and I've paid a hefty price, but I'm also angry that I didn't save my family. Is that selfish of me to wish I had picked Solas?"

"It's not selfish to wish Solas was here now," he replied. "You still chose your people. What you wish for doesn't change that you did what only this court will do."

"What's that, leave their family behind?" I asked.

He shook his head. "No. You sacrificed your wants for your people."

"Heavy is the head that wears the crown," I replied.

"Indeed," he answered. "Go home and rest. Tomorrow will come whether you want it to or not, and with it, new problems."

My breath hitched in my throat. "If anything changes, find me."

"You have my word," he replied.

The shadows grabbed me, and, in a blink, I stood at my front door. As much as I didn't want to step inside an empty house, I turned the knob. Solas' smell hit me like a punch, and I finally broke apart. I staggered toward my bedroom, walking past Aos Si and the guards. Each tipped their head, but no one asked me the stupid question of if I was all right. I showered, pulled on my pajamas and crawled into bed. My head hit the pillow, and a draft of Solas filled my lungs, settling my nerves.

The shadows settled over me. "We will go back, Perdi. The Satyr won't kill them, not yet. They'll be hoping you'll come back for them."

"I'm cursed." I groaned the words as though they came straight from my soul. Finn's final words to me echoed in my head. I was the only one here with a heart, and that was my curse.

"That is love. From any throne in Elphame, love is a curse so dark and twisted that many do not risk it," they replied. "To love is to suffer, but there is nothing worth having that isn't worth suffering for."

"I will kill Finn for this," I answered.

"I know," they replied. "We'll hold him down for you."

"I miss Solas," I whispered, my voice cracking. "I was so close."

"Rest, for tomorrow we go to war. Together, we'll bring our people back," the shadows replied.

* * * *

"Little Crow," Solas' voice filled my dream.

"Solas," I whispered. My throat was tight and dry, as if I had been screaming in my sleep. I turned to see him sitting next to Zephyr and Nix. My heart broke to see him there. "We made it home."

He smiled. His jaw was lopsided from injuries I didn't want to imagine. "I heard the good news an hour ago."

"I wish I hadn't left you behind," I replied.

"Neither of us could have lived with any other decision. This, the torment you feel, is what it means to lead and lead well. We protect our people before ourselves."

"I know, but it still hurts," I replied. "I went there to save you and came home without you."

"It wasn't for nothing, little Crow. You did what our crown has sworn to do for those who come to our lands. You protected them over all others," he replied. "I hope you have your boots on. Your fight has only just begun."

"I don't know if I can get back, Solas. The wards are stronger now."

"Finn will find a way. He's the only Aos Si without an oath." Solas grinned. "Use your tools, just as Zephyr would."

"I'll make sure to get that information out of him before I kill him," I replied.

"Good luck trying to torture an Aos Si." He laughed. "I've never seen one break before."

"Speaking of torture, how long do you think we have before they start amping up yours?"

"I've been tortured many times, Perdi, and this isn't torture. This is an uncomfortable vacation without a view. Trust me. I can take this and more, for months on end, without so much as flinching."

"Bragging while chained to a wall, how very Dark Court of you." I smiled. Solas could stand in the middle of the world's end and not flinch.

"I can afford it," he replied. "I have a little Crow coming for me. Fear is not something I feel right now."

"Warmonger," I replied, and Solas' eyes darkened with the same anticipation I'd seen on his face before he stepped onto the battlefield. "What about Nix? How is he holding up?"

"The lazy gnome has been asleep this whole time. He'll outlast both of us," he replied with a small laugh that looked like it hurt. "You need to find one of the Mages. Finn can force them to help you break the wards again."

I nodded. "I love you."

"I love you, too. Stay focused. You are the only person standing between hell and our people. When you find who is responsible, keep one alive. The dead can't be interrogated," he replied. "Once you get to us, the Satyr will no longer have the leverage they need to hold you back. There will be nothing left to stop you from burning this place to the ground."

"I hope the flames find you last." I smiled. I breathed in deeply. Although Solas smelled like blood and torture, he also smelled of home, of hope and of a fucking war we'd bring to that island. I'd burn it to the ground before I allowed them to claim the lives of my family.

"Keep Finn close. Do not allow your anger about what he's done to eat away at his usefulness. He's the only one without an oath," he repeated and turned his attention to the room. "It's time to go, little Crow. I love you." He gently pushed me from his dream as voices filled his prison. Solas' laughter was the last thing I heard before waking up.

I curled on my side, no longer filled with grief. Now, it was vengeance that coursed through my veins. One move at a time, I'd face my enemies, great and small. I didn't care how many fires I had to set. One way or another, I'd smoke them out or bring them to ash where they stood. The Satyr had my family, but now also had the full attention of the Dark Court. The mortal world, which once had my heart, now had the same focus as those who had my family. Being on my mind was not a safe place for anyone, mortal or Fae. I wasn't a Crow to pluck—not now, not ever. I was as much a curse as Solas was a blight. Together, we were a plague unlike anything Elphame had seen before. I would show them all a curse so dark and twisted that they'd remember my name. I would show them a pissed-off Soul-Eater. There would never be anything as dark or as twisted as the Finis. We burned worlds and ate souls, and I was holding a gas can and was starved.

Want to see more from this author? Here's a taster for you to enjoy!

A Cursed Crow: A Reign of Ruin
Lanne Garrett

Excerpt

Time moves differently when you're wounded. Agony has this way of stilling a clock and allowing you to feel every passing minute. Down to the second, I felt the moments limp by like a wounded animal, scared and alone. While the pain of life crawled by unbearably slow, my days bled away like lightning bolts flashing across the sky. That was the ebb and flow of Elphame. If we weren't on the verge of destruction, we weren't living. If we weren't running from the monsters, we *were* the monsters. Although I was born for this, to suffer in Elphame, my feathers plucked and my will drained, each day since leaving the mortal realm I was reminded of how close to my grave I got. But after being cast off the island, leaving my family behind, I looked into that hole in the ground and felt no fear. I was too angry to be scared. It's hard to dread the only thing in this realm that stops the suffering.

Putting one foot in front of the other wasn't as easy as others made it seem. But whether it was easy or not, I pushed forward, each step more deliberate than the last. The very lives of my family depended on my drive and ruthlessness.

Anything that took my attention away from finding my way back onto the island drove my Malice to the surface. My heart was torn in too many directions, and my soul screamed whenever I was pushed to do anything other than find my missing family. My mind may have grown used to war and fighting for every inch, but my heart and soul weren't made for horror. I was homesick for my family, and every hour that passed felt like an eternity in hell. Those who had given everything to ensure my survival were still lost to me, and it ate away at my calm.

It had been days since I had stormed Satyr Island and rescued our people, those taken as a warning I hadn't heard. Given a choice to save Solas or our people, I'd left Solas behind, chained to a wall beside Zephyr and Nix on an island I could no longer reach, and I had tried many times. My guilt for leaving my family behind had tugged on my soul. Although it had been the right decision, there wasn't a moment when I didn't think I could have done something different and saved them all. But I couldn't protect everyone and chose to save those who had depended on the throne to help them. And what a prickly throne it had become. It felt like sitting on shards of glass.

I didn't wear a crown. We didn't own a throne. But damn it, if it didn't feel like both were pressing down on me with the weight of the entire realm. Balancing the safety of the Dark Courts, smoking out traitors and enemies and trying to rescue my family while keeping the mortal realm at bay felt like torture. I finally understood why Elphame had so many mad kings throughout history. Each day felt heavier than the last. But that was the reality of Elphame, and I had not been spared any of those lessons.

Since coming to this vile place, I had learned many brutal truths the hard way while living an existence most would consider cursed. Misery spared no one — and neither did fate. We all suffered, regardless of birthrights, which court we belonged to, what blood pumped our hearts or which God we prayed to. Nothing was free, and no place was safe. It was the way of the world. It didn't matter which side of the Gate you stood. When the suffering came with your name on it, it arrived with more hurt and hate than the soul could handle. It had no mercy or kindness. And we shared that anguish like a drowning man, almost desperate to unload the weight onto someone else. Fae rose and fell on the backs of others. We crawled and limped our way from one day to the next, stepping over each other if needed. Truth be told, the mortal world was no different. No realm was unique in how it tormented its people. We all suffered equally.

But no lesson learned had prepared me for who I would willingly become to survive this realm, to protect what was mine, to keep my head above water. No truths had readied me for the incessant conflict that would become my daily routine. From Crow to crown, I wasn't spared any more than anyone else. But this was the way of Elphame, the very pulse of this realm. And I had learned this brutal reality on my knees, like so many before me.

I shouldn't have been surprised. Before the Gate was cursed to be a one-way ticket, Crows had returned from Elphame with enough horrors to fill dozens of Darkmore journals. Committed to memory, I believed every word of what it meant to become a Crow. It was hell and horror with no room for anything more. There would be no days in Elphame without a fight for another sunrise. That was what it meant to be a Crow, to suffer, to feel life in its rawest and most gutting forms. This was also the path of a Soul-Eater. From birth, I had been cursed to look death in the eyes and dare him to try, and every day, he took his best shot. That was the hardest truth to swallow. This would never end until the day my heart finally stopped beating. I had been warned, and I still picked this path. Even knowing what I knew now, I'd still choose it.

Until me, no Crow who had survived remembered their truths with clarity. But horror has this way of stealing from your mind, clouding your memories and turning them into something grotesque. For the lucky ones, they simply were too damaged to recount what caused their brokenness. Most stories were from fragmented minds and long-shattered resolve, destroyed souls who remembered nothing more than unanswered prayers. But what remained true was that each Crow recalled their first day as if it had only just happened. Every detail was crystal clear. No one ever forgot their Taking. Many couldn't remember the parts in the middle, the parts their minds refused to hold on to. I wasn't that lucky. I hadn't forgotten. Not a single detail was out of place. And it was in those memories where I was tormented, day in and day out. But that was the thing about misery... It would remind you daily of your suffering. It taunted you with promises that would never come true. But it wouldn't be Elphame if it didn't hurt. I wouldn't be Fae if I didn't have to look over my shoulder. And Whitwick reminded me of how very Fae I was each time I stepped through the Gate. That I was dragging around a wounded soul reminded me of how mortal parts of me still were.

My entire existence surrounded the Gate, from birth to my first death, and today was no different. It didn't matter that my world felt like it was burning down around me. The world still turned. Wars were still pending. And I still stood yards from the doorway between realms, willing myself to step forward. But my feet were firmly planted. I didn't want to go into Whitwick to deal with their problems. I had enough of them of my own. Saving those who protested against the presence of Fae was not high on my list of problems to solve. I had tried to convince the Seers to deal with the issues, but mortals were my people, not theirs, I was told. But they weren't. Not really. Not anymore. Mortals stopped being my people when they started seeing me as the enemy.

I stood on the now-trampled grounds of the Court of Less. The creatures and beasts of the Dark Courts had lifted every rock in search of our enemies, taking up chunks of earth in the process. They'd get no complaints from me. I was one more useless comment away from setting a fire and watching it all burn to the ground in hopes of smoking out the conspirators. And if they weren't here, I'd willingly go to Whitwick and start a fire on that side of the Gate. I was on the dregs of my patience and pitied those who called on my attention.

Aeden, my Royal Guard, stood at my side. When I arrived, he kept a noticeable distance between us. He had said he could feel my temper and Malice rolling just under my skin, and it reminded him of standing too close to Solas and Zephyr during war. I took it as a compliment.

"I don't know why Lily couldn't have dealt with this? It's not like I'm not busy." My voice was bitter and heated.

"I'm sorry, Perdi," he replied. He sounded sad for me. "But court matters do not stop because there is a different issue on the table. The wheels don't stop turning, not even when you want them to."

"Are you telling me that even in battle, Solas still deals with this crap?" I asked.

"First, you're not at war. Close, but not quite. But, to answer your question, yes, unfortunately, Solas would still be dealing with this. The only time he was not at work was during his mealtimes with you. His voice in the court literally stopped for you both to have dinner. Zephyr dealt with matters for those few hours Solas was with you. With both of them gone, you're the only one left."

"This never ends," I replied. A groan that sounded more like a growl escaped my lips. Whitwick had turned from a problem into a smoldering fire, and I didn't think I would help the situation.

"It will end, Perdi, if you want it to. You just won't like the choices you'll need to make for that to happen," Aeden replied, and I couldn't argue his point. I put myself in the middle. No one but me had expected me to remain there.

We stepped through the Gate together to find eight Seers standing shoulder to shoulder, blocking the Gate. On the other side, there were arguments, screaming and cursing the Fae. Lily turned to the Gate and opened a pocket for me to step through. Her eyes went back to the crowd. The Seers had been rotating between Whitwick and the island. They didn't trust either place—and neither did I.

"What's going on?" I asked her.

She didn't take her eyes off the few dozen men in front of us. "They say they would like us off their land. We can leave willingly, or we can leave through some force they speak of. I believe they mean to say *they* will force us." She huffed a laugh at the threat. She was amused. I was not.

I stepped forward, Aeden a foot behind me. "What is the meaning of this?"

My father made his way through the crowd. "Perdi, there are some men who wish for the Fae to leave."

I nodded and glanced around. I walked from one end of the group to the other and back to my father. "I see no men here."

"These men." My father motioned to those who stood behind him.

"Again, the only man I see is you," I answered.

Mr. Nicholas, a grocery shop owner, drinker of whatever didn't kill him and smoker of what would soon kill him, stepped forward. The moment he was close enough for me to smell, I knew he'd die of sickness within a couple years, tops. He smelled like death was already writing his name on a list. Both his eyes were bruised, and I fought not to smile.

"I want them gone," he said, while pointing to Lily and her people.

"Mark, it is lovely to see you. However did you get two black eyes?" I asked.

"That is not your concern." He spat his words but glared at Lily. I knew exactly why he wanted Lily gone.

"Where is your lovely wife Helen?" I asked with a smile that was forced and as friendly as I could muster. "It has been a long time since I've paid her my respects. Where can I find her, Mark?"

"At home, where she belongs. This is no place for her."

"Lily, please go and get Mrs. Nicholas for me," I asked without taking my eyes off Mark. Lily was gone with a wind that forced me to step forward from the push of power that bested most Fae. Her unrivaled strength was why she sat at the table of Blood and Bones.

Although Blood and Bones now belonged to Solas, by birthright, he was shaping the court back into what it had once been. It was never meant to be a place of threat or war. They had been forced into that position during a revolt and kept there by Solene. Initially, it had been a place of peace – a place to train their people, give solace to those who needed it and heal those who found life was too much to bear. To return to the ways of peace, Solas needed a Seer to help him, and Lily was a wise choice. In these last months, she had formed a council, a small group of trusted Seers whose primary purpose was to heal Elphame. Lily was fair, reasonable and held no hate for anyone. To see Mark with bruises on his face could only mean one thing. What he had done to earn them would make me want to wring the life from his neck. I did not have the calm resolve of a Seer. I had the temper of a Soul-Eater.

"You have no right to meddle in my business." Mark stepped forward and brought my thoughts back from Elphame and the hope for peace.

Aeden stepped to my side, not to scare Mark. No. He was giving me room for whatever choices I would make, and being behind me would limit my movements. Mark took another step forward. I stretched out my back and neck and let my arms fall to my side. I could feel the tension vibrating off him. If he was going to swing, I'd be ready. "Is there something I can do for you, Mark?" I asked, but he didn't answer. I glanced at the distance he had closed between us. "Is there a reason you've stepped into my personal space?"

His fists clenched and unclenched. I looked back up from his hands and met his eyes. I raised my eyebrows as if to invite him to do what he so desperately wanted to do. I watched him struggle between decisions. Before Mark could do something stupid, Lily returned with Helen. I didn't have to look too closely to know she was covered in bruises, some old and some as fresh as hours before. She couldn't have come, even if she'd wanted to. I looked into her eyes and felt my rage boil. I turned back to Mark and could see him shrink. It's one thing for everyone to know he beat his wife, but another to have it put on display where it couldn't be ignored.

"Here is how this night will go, and this will be your only warning from me since you clearly haven't listened to Lily or her people," I started, but Mark decided to step around me toward his wife. "Whatever it is you plan to do, Mark, I really wouldn't do it. I'm warning you."

"She is *my* wife. You may be the whore of Elphame, but you're not *my* whore, and I don't have to listen to a damn word you—"

The moment he pointed his finger in my face, Aeden was gone from my side. One moment he was there. The next, he'd grabbed Mark and had him pinned on the ground before I could warn the man again. The heat that poured off Aeden was enough for me to step back. My stomach knotted with unease. I didn't know if Mark would die for what he had done, but I wasn't going to protect him from Aeden, either way. Aeden twisted Mark's pointed finger until it crunched under the force, then leaned into his face.

"If you touch her, if you even *think* of touching your wife again, I will return, and I will fucking end you. I will do it for your wife and children and to send a message to the rest of your realm. The weak have the protection of the Fae. I will oath myself to every man, woman and child in this entire goddamn land, just so I know every move you make and every thought you have. Do I make myself clear?"

Mark opened and closed his mouth, finally nodding.

Aeden shook him against the ground. "And it goes without saying but allow me to make it clear as possible. If you want to keep your tongue, you will not speak to my queen in such a way. If you lift another finger to her, you will lose both hands. I believe in warnings, but only one will ever fall from my lips. You are very much beneath my warnings. You will stand, apologize, go home, pack one bag of clothing, leave all valuables behind and wait for your wife to forgive you or call me back to kill you. No oaths between our realms protect you from me, not for this. If you harass her, hunt her, harm her or scare her, you will be found and skinned alive. You best wish it is me who finds you, not the ladies who guard this Gate. They will do things to you that I haven't the stomach to even think of. You may live in the mortal realm, but you best hope they don't drag you back to ours."

Aeden stepped back and lifted Mark to his feet. Mark scurried from Aeden and apologized as he ran from the crowd. I couldn't help but smile. I had been waiting for the day someone would protect the weakest members of Whitwick. I had spent my life watching it happen and not being strong enough to help.

"My lady," Aeden stood back at my side. "I apologize for the interruption. Please, continue."

"As I was saying…" I smiled and readdressed the group. "The only ones I see here are those struggling to live decent lives. You harm yourselves, and your families and are a bleed on Whitwick. You leave chaos and misery in your wake. You drink too much and fall into drunk madness. Rage, I understand. I, too, struggle with mine. But you allow that anger to rule you, and with fists, you take it out on those you love. So, it appears the only ones who want the Fae to leave are those who are scared of the Fae paying them a visit."

"You can't kill all of us." A voice from the crowd.

"Yes, I can," I answered matter-of-factly. "I will. I will do exactly that to protect the peace and your families. Since you won't protect them, I have no problem doing it for you."

"There will be war," he called out again.

I shook my head. "No, you fool, there won't be. War requires two sides to battle each other. There will be nothing more than death between both realms—and death isn't war. A fight between Fae and mankind is nothing more than a well-planned funeral for you all. Do not sentence all of Whitwick to death simply because you can't hit your wives anymore. How many people will charge into Elphame, a certain death for you all, just so you can keep drinking and abusing? From where I'm standing, only a couple of dozen, and I can deal with that without needing anyone to help me."

"Fae doesn't rule here, and neither do you. You are not the law."

"You're wrong!" I screamed. "There are laws here that protect others from partner violence. No one follows them. There are laws that do not allow you to use physical violence to solve your problems. You just don't follow them. Many laws govern Whitwick, but no one cares enough about their neighbor to follow them. If you will not protect your people, I will, and that is final. If that means I have to come back here every bloody day to check on your family, I will. We will go door to door, checking on your wives and children. If it means we patrol your streets, we will. And if it means we have to drag every one of you into the town square and hang you for your crimes, I will weave the rope myself — not because I am now Fae, but because I grew up watching you do it, listening to it, seeing your children at school with scabbed lips. I watched as each of your wives limped home from the grocery store with barely enough strength to keep their hearts pumping but too terrified not to keep moving forward. I was once powerless to stop it, but not anymore. There will *never* be another day where that will be allowed."

My father sighed and turned to the group. "The Guardians will not turn their eyes from this any longer. We have spoken of this many times. Those who disregard the law will be arrested and jailed. We were going to address new laws and enforcements at our next town hall, but now is as good of a time as ever. It is unfortunate it took the Fae to show us that we, too, can be monsters."

I stepped back to Lily and spoke loud enough for the others to hear. "Take Helen home. Make sure Mark doesn't come back. If this happens again, alert the Guardians, but do everything you can to protect them until they arrive."

"And if the Guardians can't or won't stop them?" she asked. She searched for the freedom to act, to defend. Now that the Seers weren't locked away, their very duty was to protect. Without that, she wasn't entirely herself, who she was meant to be — and I could relate.

I swallowed a rock in the back of my throat. "Then you act in any way you must to protect those who are too weak to save themselves. This…" I scrunched my face, fighting between tears and vomit. "This cannot happen again. And if the prisons of Whitwick can't stop them, the prisons of Elphame certainly will. If they survive stepping through the Gate, justice will be swift, but it will come."

The crowd silenced at that threat. It was one I didn't want to make. The Fae had been the nightmare of Whitwick for as long as they could remember. And I used the Fae again to control them. I didn't feel guilty this time. I wouldn't let them beat their wives, and if I had to drag the Sluagh through the Gate to keep the men in line, I would.

"Perdi," Lily leaned into my ear, "things are getting a lot worse here. I fear you'll be returning and soon."

I nodded. "I know. I can feel it. Something has changed."

"We'll do what we can for as long as possible, to buy you the time you need. But I don't think it'll be enough."

"Unfortunately, I agree. Blood will spill, and by then, it will be too late to stop what's coming," I replied. Aeden followed me back to Elphame and waited for me as the wave of nausea subsided.

"I do not like going there," Aeden finally said.

"You have quite the temper, Aeden," I said as we moved through the Court of Less. I rubbed my arms, feeling dirty from my trip through the Gate. The dread I had experienced, hanging in the air in Whitwick, still clung to me like sweat.

"I could say the same about you," he answered without even a hint of judgment. "My father was a strict man, but he had honor. He had one hell of a temper but never once lifted a finger against my mother. Only once did his anger make my mother step back. He begged forgiveness and cowered from his shame, as he should have. He would have killed anyone who touched her. He valued her and her love above all else. It was something he made sure I had learned before I left for the Aos Si. I am made for battle and death and dolling out punishment like candy. But that? Harming your family? It's something I can't stomach and will not tolerate. I could never harm my partner like that. The very thought of someone doing that to those I love...? Rage doesn't describe how that man made me feel."

"Disgust, embarrassed for her, ashamed for him, angry at everyone else for letting it happen, regret that I didn't kill him to prove a point and take her nightmare away. That's what I felt," I told him.

"That sums up what I'm feeling."

"When we go back, Aeden, we have to work to fix the relations and not beat on them all. We can't fix violence with violence."

"Yes, we can," he countered. "But I see your point. If we want peace, we must offer peace...until that is no longer the option."

"Exactly," I replied. "But all peace comes with a price."

"And we'll all pay for it." He sighed and rubbed the creases starting between his eyes. "Do you think there will ever be peace between both realms?"

"I want to say yes, but no. I don't believe so. I think, eventually, it'll come to a head, and many will die before there's silence, not peace. We'll exist together, but I doubt there will be more than that."

"A bleak future," he said.

"Bleaker for those of us who have to live with it for centuries," I replied. "I'll meet you back at the manor later."

Aeden nodded. He would be meeting with the Aos Si for updates on the island and their progress in finding a Mage. "Perdi, remember. If you kill Finn tonight, you won't be able to hunt him tomorrow."

"Good night, Aeden," I replied. I didn't comment on his remark without lying to his face.

I was uncomfortable with the secrecy I was now living, but trust was something I couldn't afford—not when traitors were alive and well and had my name at the top of their lists. I was hunting, but it wasn't Finn who I was tracking. I was pursuing my traitors in secret, and at my side, an unlikely ally, Finn. Together, we followed the trail of those seeking my death, the traitors of the Dark Courts. The roots of hate had spread far and wide, leaving me and Finn no choice but to play dark and dangerous games, unable to trust a soul. When we returned from the island, someone close to the crown began hunting us both. The energy of our dark traitor was the same we had found on the island, in Elphame and even as far as Whitwick. His magick was both familiar and unplaceable. Whoever was following us would be the key to getting my family back.

I had two choices when I had returned from Satyr Island. I could swallow what had happened and work together with Finn or I could die alone, never having saved my family. Teetering between truth and lies, right and wrong, absolution and revenge kept me looking over my shoulder. I spent my days trying to keep Whitwick from boiling over and invading, only to die on Elphame soil and the nights with a mask on and stalking my enemies across the entire realm. I didn't know what was worse, hunting them or living with the horror of the aftermath once I'd finally caught them. But one way or another, vengeance would be swift. Those who did this to my people and my family would pay dearly...because nothing was free in Elphame. I would hunt them to the ends of the earth for what they did. No one takes from a Soul-Eater and survives. I was pretty sure that rule was written somewhere.

About the Author

Lanne Garrett writes books. Considering where you're reading this, it makes perfect sense. She lives in Vancouver, here she spends her days getting lost in the beauty of reading and writing and can be found behind a mountain of books on any given Sunday.

Lanne loves to hear from readers. You can find her contact information, website details and author profile page at https://www.finch-books.com

Sign up for our newsletter and find out about all our romance book releases, eBook sales and promotions, sneak peeks and FREE romance books!